WHITE TRASH GOTHIC

EDWARD LEE

deadite
press

deadite
press

DEADITE PRESS
P.O. BOX 10065
PORTLAND, OR 97296
www.DEADITEPRESS.com

AN ERASERHEAD PRESS COMPANY
www.ERASERHEADPRESS.com

ISBN: 978-1-62105-250-0

Printed in the USA.

ACKNOWLEDGMENTS

Special thanks to Wendy Brewer, every one at Deadite, Keith Giffen and Jessica Chen at DC, Nici Hope, James Daly, Claudia Rossner, Amy Witt, Vivian Lamade, Jonathan Yudkin, Heather Chesna, Bob Taylor and Jaime, Sandy and Tony, Karolina, Pawel, Bartek, Raquel Sleeman; Honza Vojtíšek, Chandler Morrison, Christy Hamby, Matthias Felber, Kevin Hector, Bob Hinton, Roy Klammer, Corey F., Josh Slusser.

AUTHOR'S NOTE:

First, I must express humble apologies to my fans for taking SO FRIGGIN' LONG to finish this book. I'm afraid my only excuse is as simple as encroaching age, a bitch. Nevertheless, here it is, a book I might describe as my pride and joy. In a sense it sequelizes many previous stories and novels. Also, it is the first leg of a series of novels or novellas, a continuing sojourn. I believe (and hope!) that it works fine as a stand-alone novel but it might be better enjoyed if you first read my novels THE BIGHEAD and MINOTAURESS.

Second, I thank you for buying this book. I hope you like reading it as much as I liked writing it.

Best wishes,

Edward Lee

WHITE TRASH GOTHIC

"There was a knock at the door. When Nikoff Raskol opened it, he espied a baleful purview of imprecations, an apophysis of dolorous *spiritum*—perforce: the Nietzschean Abyss. He'd dreamed of utter blackness, of dripping sounds, and screams, and it was all those things that he found himself looking at beyond the transom of his solitary motel room. The blackness that was somehow fulgent, in which traversed the fallow masses with faces like poultices and acuminated grins. His heart beat in mordant rubato when the gracile hand—certainly that of some outerworldly *woman*—reached out from the festering clough and took his own. He thought of light's absence in the flesh, he thought of ataxia undiluted.

He thought of lost worlds.

Surely, this curvaceous silhouette could only be the answer to thirty years of aesthetic query, like Pynchon's cryptic V., like Burroughs' Joan—the target of every writer's most sincere quest: the search for the woman he can never have. *Alas,* he thought. *Here am I, face to face with the Goddess of the New Dark Age,* and what a terrifying and joyous thought it was!

The hand tightened about his. He was beseeched by eyes wide and lambent as diminutive moons, but as bottomless as an ocean trench, and the voice resounded as if from the highest precipice of the earth, to offer, "Come. Come with me...and *see...*"

Nikoff Raskol followed her out of the room into the living dark."

***

Here, then, is my conundrum. The above page, I'm told, was found in an old manual typewriter, in a fleabag motel, in the mid-'90s. Evidently I am the author of the page. I am totally unapprized of the motel's location, nor do I have any idea of what I was doing there.

My name is _____ ___, and I was born on May 25, 19–. This I know only because of my driver's license. Some time ago a doctor told me that I exhibited chronic symptoms of transient global amnesia, dissociative amnesia, and retrograde amnesia, three types of catastrophic memory deficit that rarely occur together. MRIs revealed no trace of prior cerebral accident or disease mechanism, nor any evidence of a good ole konk on the head. It was actually an interesting affliction: I could recall not one single detail of any aspect of my life, yet I remembered all major world events that had occurred in my lifetime, and I remembered all that I had learned. For instance, I knew that I had attended Harvard and Yale, and studied language, art, philosophy, literature and much else. I remembered the exact layout of Harvard Yard, I remembered Kirkland Street, the Ted Williams Tunnel, Memorial Hall, and the school's founding date of 1636. Yet I don't remember being there. I don't remember a single student or professor. I remember that Tycho Ottesen Brahe was a Danish astronomer of monumental import, and that he died from a ruptured bladder and had a silver nose because he'd lost his real one in a sword fight. I remember that Emanuel Swedenborg began to publish the *Daedalus Hyperboreus* in1715, and is asserted to have converted lead into gold in 1770 after proving the absolute unity of a Supreme Entity in essence and being. I remember that in 216 B.C. the Carthagenian Army under Hannibal Barca annihilated the largest Roman army yet amassed on the plain of Cannae, killing 75,000 legionnaires in one afternoon.

Yet I don't remember my parents, friends, nor where I was born.

I don't remember when exactly any semblance of

cognition returned to me. People claiming to be close friends told me I was a speculative novelist of some manner of renown. This undoubtedly was true, for one of them told me I owned a storage locker, the key to which was in my wallet along with my license, credit cards, etc. There was also a small card with the storage facility's address and the number 154. In this locker, I found all my published books, dozens and dozens of them, all with younger author photos of me in the back. Evidently I'd been quite the existential man, no wife, no kids, and no settled abode. The indication is that for years I'd been a denizen of motels, always seeking out new naturalist locations in which to write. I also had a bank account, with money in it, a considerable sum–royalties, apparently, direct-deposited from publishers. I could relate endlessly of my faltering rediscovery of myself, but that would be inconsequential. I felt driven to discover one single thing: my last location before the onset of my amnesia.

This prospect plagued me. I thought perhaps that the secret must lie in one of my books; therefore, I expended no little time in reading every single one...and not one of them kindled a single memory. (And most of them were stodgy, rather pompous, not altogether interesting, nor altogether coherent, in spite of rave endorsements by the likes of the *New York Times Literary Supplement, Chicago Tribune, Atlantic Monthly* and scores more.)

How could I be aware of the celebrity of, for instance, the *New York Times* but not be aware of being reviewed in it, nor of writing the actual book that was reviewed? Mine, truly, was a bizarre malady but also, somehow, an *exhilarating* one.

It seemed I had nothing to live for in the future because I didn't know what I'd been living for up to that point. I didn't know what to do with my life now, after nearly the entirety of it had gone by with my being none the wiser. I thought of Voltaire's *Candide,* reckoning the world as a useless terrain of terror and foolishness and emerging from its churning orifi to find himself reborn in a terrain of truth and actualization. I thought of Roquentin in Sartre's pallid *La Nauseé,* and I thought of the *Pequod's* final voyage.

Nothing mattered, and that realization seemed exciting and scintillant, just as Ahab's quest for the great white whale must've been. A neurologist seemed to take stock in the suspicion that my amnesia must've been caused by a severe psychological traumatic shock, something exceedingly horrific, and he finished his speculation by pointing out, "In all likelihood, this trauma was so potent that your memory loss may actually be a blessing."

A curious deduction, the prospect of which enthused me. Didn't God appear to Moses as a burning bush because the sight of God's visage is so intricate, complex, and unreckonable as to cause instant madness? What, then, did I see that could be so catastrophic that my memory would be wiped clean? Not that I suspect I'd glimpsed the unglimpsable face of God, but what if it were something else more corporeal and rooted in empirical existence?

A murder?

A ghost?

A natural disaster?

To my core I felt it must be beyond things of that ilk, something unmitigated, something too appallingly calamitous to be cogitable. It made sense. Since the resurgence of my self- awareness, my dreams at night were exclusively populated with horrors beyond pondering. They exhibited elements of—

1) The psycho-sexual: twenty-two caliber gun barrel brushes quickly plunged into the urethras of throbbing

penises; comely women hanging naked by their wrists only to have their epidermis expertly pulled inside-out off their bodies like suits of skin; rustic men cutting holes into women's skulls, to effect coitus with their still warm, still living brains; screaming pregnant girls raped *en masse* until the wares of their wombs were perfunctorily ejected, and men, still more rustic men, calmly copulating with curvaceous headless bodies.

2) The allegorical and the patently absurd: A woman with the physique of a Playboy model rampaging through a kindergarten in a wake of shrieks and flying blood, yet this woman possesses the head of a bull; a man on a bus telling other passengers, "It was me and Lou Rawls. They stuck us in that cage and didn't give us nothin' but milk bottles and soup"; a penis and its accommodating scrotum, six-feet tall and stalking through the woods on human legs.

3) The Luciferic: Things arising from smoke. Pug faces on stout, corded necks. Flesh the hue of riverbed clay, pit-nostrils and chisel slits for eyes. There's a black moon in a red sky, a vale, horrid and vast, refulgent with luminous fog, and a lake of steaming excrement. From fissures in the black rock, the pitiable naked horde is expulsed. A great black grackle flies overhead, its black-marble eyes gazing down in reverent delight. The horde is a mass of screaming bodies, terror incarnate, living chaos. And from the steaming lake, the ushers come to bull into the horde amid suboctave chuckles, their fat hands at once twisting arms and legs quickly out of sockets, wrenching heads off flexing necks, yanking whole spinal columns out of stretched open mouths. Fire gushes in the distance, greasy black smoke pours from cracks and rabbets in the vale's stone face. Stout pinkies calmly squash eyeballs in howling faces; ears, noses, lips, and fingers are bitten off and nibbled as tidbits. Talons swipe

to lay open bellies, misshapen fists are thrust into rectums through which innards are extricated like tissue paper from a gift box. The ushers grunt and chuckle, plodding on, popping heads with malformed feet, inhaling blood, holding faces steadfastly down to drown in the tarn of bubbling shit whence they came, all in the name of Satan.

And one more–

4) The monstrous: for no other word can be better suited—yes—a *monster,* in overalls, with bunched muscles, and seeming to be sucking the feces out of the anus of a nude woman with a crushed head. Closer dream-scrutiny suggests that the woman's brains have been eaten out of the cranium, just as her waste was now being eaten out of her bowels. The monster rubs its crotch in some disconnected excitement; the erection which prints though the overalls is as big as a rolling-pin. When the last of its meal has been sucked down, it looks to the sky with a grin, as if giving thanks to some deity for the bounty of food it has just enjoyed.

Its head is the size of a large watermelon, but warped; one eye huge, the other tiny.

Yes, these were the dreams I experienced nightly, these and further images and scenarios much worse. What could have happened to me in the past, or what could I have seen, that would cause such a tableau of atrocities to brew and ferment in my subconscious?

I had nothing else to do than endeavor to find out.

But where to start?

The query took me back to that one sheet of paper found in the typewriter twenty-odd years ago. My inclination was that it was the first page of a novel. I knew now that I was a novelist. Therefore?

I must write the rest of the book.

I sensed with certainty that if I finished the book, my

life's memories would come back to me, and all my questions would be answered. What made me feel this way? I have no conscious clue. Perhaps it was a whisper from the ether, a sign from Dante's Sisters of the Heavenly Spring. Or perhaps it was just bullshit concocted by an insane mind.

Oh, I forgot to mention one thing. That single page in the typewriter? It had a title at the top:

WHITE TRASH GOTHIC

***

These were the words the Writer seemed to hear through some veil of dream—indeed, probably the most bizarre arrangement of words he'd ever heard, and perhaps even the most bizarre sentence ever spoken: "Mom! He's putting a gummy worm in his dick!"

The Writer's eyes shot open, which was understandable, where he found himself, after a moment's recollection, dozing in the high seat of a Greyhound bus. The vehicle was more than half empty—a rare luxury. No other passenger sat in his row, and evidently the bus had been recently cleaned because there was no vestige whatever of that all too familiar "Greyhound odor," an amalgamation of b.o., bum urine, soiled diapers, and dollar store perfume. And as for the mysterious sentence he'd heard, or *thought* he'd heard...there was really no one on board who could've said it. His accompanying riders were all oldsters, broken down alcoholics and addicts, and the like, and all were riding without the company of a companion. The "mom" from the sentence was clearly the mother of the speaker who possessed a voice like that of an enthusiastic young woman. No such couple occupied the bus at this time.

The Writer's presence on the bus can be explained in a very few lines. He was on a journey of "self-discovery." He was following the advice of his doctor, engaging in the same activities he used to before his memory loss had occurred. What he knew of himself at this point in time was what he'd gleaned from people professing to be close associates (yet, all the same, people he did not remember) and book editors he was told he'd worked with but did not remember working with. He was a novelist of some obscure repute, he'd had scores of novels published, all wholly unfamiliar to him. He was a man of some financial means due to revenues from said books he did not remember writing. He's been told further that he was a man very much alone in the world, very happy in that solitude, had no settled abode, and had spent much of the last 30 or so years as a tenant of motels because apparently he never wrote more than one book in the same place. His eerie unfamiliar friends revealed that he was quite a "slice of life" type of writer, and living in *between* those slices was where his creativity was fueled. He did not want to write of folly and fantasies, nor of mainstream bombast nor of optimistic falsehoods simply to fill gaps in a "market." He wanted to write his own interpretations of reality, just as Rembrandt and Munch and Rothko had *painted* theirs, just as J.S. Bach had *played* his, and just as Michelangelo had chiseled the statue of David.

Ah, an aesthetic endeavor, and a noble one! His past life—his *unremembered* life—had been a sojourn following the paths of Ibsen, Kafka, and Dostoevsky, taking real life between his teeth and, unmindful of the often awful taste, chewing it up, swallowing. And in the symbolic sense? What he defecated were his visions. *The true mechanism of any real artist,* he thought.

The bus, roving through winding darkness, with only

two dim headlights for eyes, rocked gently back and forth over roads lined by primeval woods. The effect was lulling, hypnotic, and pleasant. But of that preposterous sentence he seemed to have heard? The conviction now that it had been some vocal spillage of a dream was the only feasible answer. *Aural hallucinosis,* his doctor would dub it, for these things had happened before. But was it hypnopompic or hypnagogic? *Why, I'm not sure,* he admitted to himself, and that surprised him because the Writer typically remembered everything he'd read. Everything. Every book, thesis, article, even every poem. It was only the damnedest thing that he didn't remember *reading* it in the first place. *I'm... fucked up,* came a very rare tincture of profanity to one of his thoughts. But of course, it was true. A recent observation he'd made to his doctor: "I have an eidetic memory with total recall," he said. "I'm an unprecedented *genius.*" "That," the doctor affirmed, with some veiled envy, "is undeniable, unquestioned, and absolutely incontestable." "So how is it, for example, that I can remember that the last line of David Hume's essay from *The Balance of Trade and Power* is 'And the melancholy fate of the Roman emperors, from the same cause, is renewed over and over again, till the final dissolution of the monarchy' but I can't remember my parents, I can't remember a single friend or acquaintance, and I can't remember any single place on earth that I have been?" The doctor, an elegant, raven-haired woman named Offenbach, shrugged and responded, "Such are the entails of memory trauma, Mr. —. The human brain isn't like a knee or an ear or a tonsil. Afflictions to the like are easily understood and rectified, because these things exist in simplicity. The human brain, however, is anything but simple; instead it is probably the most intricate *thing* in existence, more intricate than the sun or the solar system, more intricate than a black hole or a quasar, than any component or physics or math, more intricate even than the most intricate chemical reaction that has ever taken place in the universe. One hundred billion neurons, 10 trillion glial cells, and 100 trillion synaptic connections, all working together every second of one's lifetime. All regulating, manipulating, and overseeing every molecular aspect the host's existence. In fact, some might say that the human brain could not exist without the admixture of the metaphysical," and then she offered a tiny white grin that in a moment of unexpected vertigo seemed... vampiric. It was an interesting moment, and an eerie one. She continued looking at him over her glasses. "It's the old idiom," she went on, "about the machines with the most moving parts, wouldn't you say? One hundred billion neurons, 10 trillion glials, and 100 trillion connections... Drop a monkey wrench into all of that and the result can be, among myriad other things, unpredictable; and with regard to memory anomalies? Anything goes. Even such ultimately rarefied memory deficits as yours."

The Writer, not at all given to much in the way of sexual response, realized that a "raging" erection now occupied his groin. *Of all the preposterous things!* Dr. Offenbach, in spite of being in her sixties, seemed to exude sexuality: the shining black hair; the glimmering eyes of unspecified color; the peerless curvature, and what was evidently a pair of D-cup implants that proved her plastic surgeon was at the top of his field. The white skin of a flawless complexion seemed lumescent; her movements were gracile, swanlike; even her dry lilting voice possessed a cryptic sexual potency. The previously mentioned erection was betraying a copious leakage of pre-ejaculant that the Writer dreaded might be spotting the front of his pants.

He diverted his attention by staring aside as if in deep

thought. "What's your practical advice, Dr. Offenbach?"

"The traditional methods of rekindling memory loss are quite unelaborate. Revisit the locales of your past–not an easy thing, of course, since you are unaware of these locales. Are you just book smart, Mr. —, or are you perceptive as well?"

The Writer thrilled at the challenge of self analysis. "Why, I...don't know!"

Did she sigh just a bit? "Outside parties have proven to you that you're a novelist, correct?"

"Correct. Internationally published, by the way, acclaimed by the most reputable literary journals in the country, and—"

Her frown severed the rest of his bragging rights. "You've read all of your books, and though you don't remember writing any of them, you've been informed by editors, etc., that you wrote each book in a different location, correct?"

"Yes."

After a pause, she rolled her eyes. "What was the last book you had published and what was its setting?"

"The novel was entitled *Look Downward, Angel*, a symbolic tribute to Thomas Wolf. He was a fascinating author—Maxwell Perkins was his editor. Did you know that Wolf, a very tall man, hand-wrote all of his novels on the top of his refrigerator, standing up?"

"Just—please. Answer the question."

"Oh, ah! Of course. The book was set in Ipswich, Massachusetts. No, I haven't gone there yet, and I suppose that would be a practical journey. However, as it's been told to me, the very last book I was working on was called *White Trash Gothic*. The first page of this book was found in a typewriter in a motel somewhere in the underdeveloped south. It was given to me with other effects in a manila envelope sometime during that unclassifiable period when my consciousness and self-awareness returned."

"Who gave you the envelope?"

"My editor in New York, his name is—"

"Who gave *him* the envelope?"

"Police. Some sheriff's department down south, I believe."

She stared him in the eye, asmirk. "*What* sheriff's department? What *county?*"

Feeble gears seemed to spin in the Writer's head. "Why...I have no idea."

Dr. Offenback rubbed her face in what was clearly exasperation. "Please don't take this the wrong way, Mr. —; it's only a clinical observation. But for a man with a genius IQ and eidetic recall, you, I'm afraid, are—"

The Writer gave a sheepish grin. "I know. Dumber than a box of rocks."

"Ask your editor exactly which sheriff's department delivered the envelope to him, and then go to that place."

The task was at hand. Finally some efficacious direction! "Thank you for your insights, Dr. Offenbach. And now, I'm off to. . .wherever it is I'm going!"

"Please keep in touch with my office several times a week. I need to know the extent of your progress, any problems you may encounter, and your overall frame of mind."

"I'll do exactly that, doctor," he replied enthusiastically.

"And prepare yourself for unexpected shocks. It's quite common that once you are in proximity to your target, you'll experience an outpouring of memories, and I suspect some of them may be very traumatic."

"Understood," the Writer said, rather oblivious to the possibility. He stood up, shook the woman's cool smooth hand, said "Have a good day," and made his departure from the office, oblivious, too, to the fact that upon rising, the erection behind his zipper and the now-half-dollar-sized spot of pre-ejaculant was more than visible to the doctor.

***

No significant expenditure of time was needed to follow Dr. Offenbach's instructions. A phone call to his editor revealed the "target" location was in ———— County, West Virginia. Then he'd paid the librarian to go online for him and check his credit card records. He was not lucky enough to find any record of the mysterious motel; however, the last thing he'd paid for via his Mastercard was evidently a bar tab (for $126!) at a tavern in someplace known as Luntville. This tavern was called the Crossroads.

The Crossroads, he thought. Did the name ring a tiny bell? The Writer wasn't sure, but he did like the pleasing, metaphorical feel of the name. At any rate, the next day found him on the Greyhound bus. On his way to Luntville, West Virginia, the journey of which was now taking effect and, if we bring our minds back, we have just found him wakening from a drowse, where he'd heard, or *thought* he'd heard, some ludicrous comment about, of all things, a gummy worm.

Eyeing the amorphous dark beyond the window, just as amorphous thoughts surfaced: of Poe's imp of the perverse, and Lovecraft's "evil genius" in "The Diary of Alonso Typer." Could such an entity be at work here? It did seem strange that Dr. Offenbach's cut and dry instructions hadn't previously occurred to him, a clear engagement of deductive reasoning. Had some spectral "imp" blinded him to these simple solutions? Or might—

His eyes widened on the roving darkness without.

Or might Dr. Offenbach herself be functioning as the "evil genius?"

Food for thought, he thought, and, on the topic of food, so many hours in the bus had left him rather hungry. Now the faintest tint of a smell—a pleasant smell, a *fruity* smell—solicited his senses and a glance two rows down showed him a rather ragtag, whiskered man of indeterminate age eating some sort of fruit-flavored candy, and in the tiny overhead reading light, the Writer was able to discern the actual brand-name nature of that candy—

Of course, the reader will have already guessed just what kind of candy it was: gummy worms.

Coincidence? Or some mode of omen? The Writer peered into the consideration. Certainly, this raddled elder... this, well, *bum* could hardly possess a voice like that of the young woman he'd heard making the outre remark.

Coincidence then, he decided, but the thought was severed of a sudden when the intercom crackled and the driver announced, "Listen up, folks. Just up the road a piece be Crick City where we gotta stop for a time-point. We be there for twenty minutes, so if ya wanna stretch your legs and grab a coffee, make dang sure you're back aboard by leavin' time 'cos I can't come back. Everybody understand?"

The reply came in the way of sleepy nodding heads and murmurs of affirmation.

"Awright, then. And next stop after this is Luntville."

***

The dimmest lights quickly bloomed into a great cone of sodium glare, and there, in the middle of nowhere, materialized the Crick City stop: a desolate roadside outpost which offered a Sinclair gas station (the Writer had always thought the name had been bought out half a century ago), a mercantile establishment called Hull's General Store, and the Greyhound annex, apparently, consisting of a bench next to a metal bus sign on a post. Several riders—the Writer among them—left their seats to file off the coach, the driver leading the way. Once debarked, the Writer noticed that a dark figure had alighted from the bench—a woman, he noticed, in a dark rain jacket and hood, and shiny black boots up to her knees—and made her way toward the driver in a manner of movement that seemed, well, *eerie,* perhaps due to the setting, the hour, and the lighting. Wordlessly, she produced a ticket, the driver punched it, and she boarded the bus in silence. Why the Writer felt distracted by such an insignificant occurrence, he couldn't figure.

From atop the dead Sinclair sign (which sported, of all things, a cartoon dinosaur) some species of night bird cawed loudly enough to be irritating; it seemed even to stare the Writer down.

Quoth the raven, he mused, and entered a stuffy, brightly lit store.

Inside smelled like cinnamon and ginger snaps. Someone with a voice that creaked like wood, greeted, "Hey, Joe. Top'a the evenin' to ya." So the driver's name was Joe, who returned the greeting crudely by squeezing his crotch and saying, "Here be the top'a *your* evenin', Tobias," after which both men laughed. Tobias, clearly the proprietor, was a broomstick of a man likely in his '70s, puffs of gray hair sprouting from either side of this bald spot, and a third such puff on his chin. Here the Writer took a moment to survey the driver for the first time in sufficient light, and found him to be...unusual in appearance. Short blondish hair cropped close defined the very odd hairline on the back of his neck, a hairline several inches higher than a more typical man.

Further, unpleasant creases of flesh crawled up the back of that neck, and when Joe turned with a sardonic smile, the Writer noted still more unpleasantness: a sallow complexion of largely pored skin, very little in the way of chin, and over-large watery eyes that seemed to protrude as if by inner pressure. *Yikes,* thought the Writer. Some regrettable affection of a congenital nature. The Writer had no desire to look at the man further, but one question he needed to ask made another glance unavoidable: "Excuse me, driver, I'm not fully familiar with your company's policies, but I see the beer cooler here and I'm wondering if I might be allowed to imbibe modestly."

"Dun't know what ya be getting at, sir, but if it's a drink yer lookin' for, no booze be allowed on the bus," and at the same moment the man purchased several miniatures of Black Velvet."

"I...see," said the Writer.

"A'course, I ain't got no x-ray vision like Superman, and I can't see through a paper bag, if ya catch my drift."

A convoluted consent! My favorite kind! "Many thanks, sir!" and the Writer proceeded. *All great writers drink,* the strange motto seemed to leak into his head, even though he still didn't remember ever being a writer. But the cooler offered little that would appeal to the inveterate beer snob, or–no! There in the corner, hemmed in by dismal mass market domestics, stood a promising discovery: *Collier's Civil War Lager.* He'd never heard of it, but the 6.8 percent alcohol content made the choice for him (as did the bottle's size: 25 ounces). But just as he would journey to the counter, some very queer sound eddied in through a side window, through which the Writer immediately cast a glance—

What in the name of Cromwell's ghost is GOING ON out there?

24

"Out there" was a flank of the building and two dumpsters, and in the area of space that existed between the dumpsters, a melee of the most barbarous sort was taking effect. "Gonna git my joy juice right *up* in this here tramp's back door," a man grunted amid rapid slapping sounds. "Yes sir! Gonna put it right smack dab in the middle'a her last food-card meal, I am!" "You go, Horace!" another man reveled, and then the Writer's vision focused upon the grisly scene in which a 300-pound man with a buzzcut was sodomizing a 100-pound blond woman whose cut-off shorts had been pulled apart on her buttocks and whose halter top was whisked off and stuffed in her mouth to stave any vocal objections she might have. The Writer, naturally, winced at the scene. It was like watching a mountain gorilla mate with a spider monkey. Retching sounds grated beneath her gag.

The vision dizzied him and then he remembered that another man was out there too, but a quick pan of his gaze showed him his error. It was not another man, but other *men*, three of them, all in the vicinity of 300 pounds, all with identical buzzcuts. *Well, that's a rum thing,* it dawned on the Writer. *They're identical quadruplets!*

It was beyond doubt. Even in the intermittent yellow glare, he could see that all four of these huge, obese thugs looked exactly like each other.

Here the Writer's gaze narrowed, and he saw a fifth man (not related at all to the quadruplets) pinned down to the ground by two of the brothers, while another quadruplet...

My lord, what is he...?

The pinned man's jeans had been pulled down to his knees. He squirmed within his human fetters, whimpering, sobbing beneath the fat hand that sealed his mouth shut, and it appeared that the fourth quadruplet was engaged in some meticulous activity between the victim's legs, "'Fore we get to the real fun, buddy," he said, "I'se gonna kick your day up a notch." The Writer could not see what the huge assailant was doing; whatever it was, however, caused the victim to mewl like a just-gelded pig beneath the hand that sealed his mouth, and flip-flop like a frog in a wok. "One down, and one to go," chuckled Quintuplet Four, then the victim's mewls and thrashes doubled in intensity. The assailant, next, held the offending implement up—

The Writer squinted but could just discern the tool's nature. *A lemon press?*

There was no mistake; likewise, there was no mistake what the handy kitchen device had been used for: to crush the pinned man's testicles.

Without delay, the Writer fumbled with his cell phone, dialed 911, then noticed he had no bars. *Seven hundred dollars and it doesn't work!* he raged to himself. He meant to shout out to the proprietor but the next sight shocked him in place.

Back to the sodomized blond woman: her rapist stood up, fastened his dungarees, and was now liberally drenching the woman's hair with lighter fluid. "Don't worry, sweetie, likely as not this won't kill ya but it'll sure as shit give ya a reminder why's you shouldn't sell drugs in our town—ever mornin' when ya look in the mirror." The woman was rousing in the dirt, rising to hand and knees, croaking, "Please, don't! I'll never come back, I swear! Just let me go!"

"Oh, I'm-a-gonna let ya go right now," promised the mammoth of a man, then he flicked his Bic, and—

Poof!

—the woman's head burst into flame, and in a moment her feet were carrying her across the parking lot before a wake of screams.

Another quadruplet stood aside, slid his thumbs up and

down his suspenders. "Yes, sir! If a dog had nipples, that'd be the cat's meow!" and the four brothers bellowed laughter. The Writer's eyes narrowed. He didn't get it.

"Somebody call the police!" he shouted to the oldster at the counter. "There's a brutal assault taking place in the parking lot! Some ruffians just set a woman's head on fire!"

The bus driver, the oldster, and several customers, all started laughing, which bewildered the Writer.

"Ruffians," one of them chuckled. "That there's a good 'un."

"Did you hear me?" the Writer raised his voice. "They just set a woman's head on fire, and they're torturing a man in the parking lot! You've got to call the police at once!"

Suddenly a woman's voice floated through the air. "Those four men are the Larkins brothers, mister. They'se all quadruplets..."

"I can see that!" the Writer began, turning to face the woman who'd spoken, but what his eyes fell on struck him speechless.

A tall woman in a clerk's smock smiled back at him; evidently she'd just emerged from the back. Her face was less than pretty: it seemed elongated, and her jaw protruded. But what shocked him were her bright pink eyes, crinkly pale white hair, and a smooth, poreless white/pink skin tone. An albino.

"I—," he began.

"The Larkins boys *are* the police, in a manner of speakin'," she said. "Cops round here, the state, the county sheriffs, they'se all on the take."

"Yeah, mister," affirmed the driver. "Down here, we take care of our own. It's the way things is."

The proprietor nodded. "Them two pieces'a trash out there, what the Larkins are takin' care of? They ain't nothin' but a pair of drug dealers from Pulaski. Them types come here all the time tryin' to pollute our fine towns with the drugs, get our kids 'dicted to the stuff. But they never last long afore the Larkins boys git wind of 'em."

"Yeah, Tobias," said the albino, watching out the window. "They'se doin' the job on them two," and this statement seemed to function as invitation, for everyone in the store now eagerly drifted to the side windows.

All the Writer could do was stand dumb, and look back out himself.

The undistinguishable Larkins brothers were now hoisting the shuddering drug dealer to his feet, and in moments had tied him to a lug ring on the dumpster, his pants still down, and the ruptured testicles in his scrotum already swollen to several times' their natural size. "Well, they can't raw-ball the fella, cuz' they done pulped his balls," celebrated Joe the driver, and then he high-fived the proprietor. "Maybe they're fixin' to give him a dick gnarlin'," someone else said. "Could be, could be," said a customer, "But I was kind'a hopin' for a box-job or a good ole fashioned dead-dickin'." "Yeah, man! Been a spell since I seed me a good dead-dickin'."

Suddenly, the albiness was standing right behind the Writer, her hands on his shoulders. "Well lookit that! Sure as shit that's 'zactly what they're fixin' to do!"

The woman's surprise touch made the Writer jolt, and when she whispered right in his ear, "Excitin', ain't it?" her long fingers ever so slightly squeezed his shoulders, and that along with the feel of her warm breath on his neck, and the light fragrance of some fruity shampoo, caused an erection to rouse in his pants as spontaneously as 16-year-old's.

His awareness of the girl half-distracted him from the horrors outside. *Dead-dickin'?* The spectators all pressed their faces close to the window, standing on tip-toes, and now it was getting clearer just what a "dead-dickin'" was. One Larkins brother gagged the victim with the blonde's halter, while another brother tied a shoestring at the base of the dealer's terror-shrunken penis. Then another knot was tied after—of all things—a Sharpie pen was positioned over the first knot.

"You'se obviously from the city, mister, so you wouldn't know what dead-dickin' a fella means," the proprietor said.

"No, but I'm getting the idea rather quickly," the Writer droned.

"See, they put what's called a Turner Kit on his dick—which I reckon was invented by a fella named Turner—then they twist it tight as they can'n tie it off. After five minutes, the dick turns red, and five minutes later, it's blue, the purple, then black. Twennies minutes is all it takes afore his Johnson is dead meat. Once that Green Gang set in, it starts to rot and there ain't no savin' it then."

Turner? thought the Writer. *Kit? They're putting a tourniquet on his penis!*

"Bet he's raped a *lot* of gals," a customer suggested.

Joe the Driver nodded. "And got free ass from all those he 'dicted. Well, that fella? That fella there? Ain't no more hobknobbin' for *him*, no sir! Hope the last nut he busted was a good one, cuz he shore's shit ain't havin' no more."

"Amen to that," someone else said.

"But-but-but," the Writer stammered.

"But-but-but-*what*, mister?" challenged the proprietor.

"Tell me, please. What part of a thousand years of Anglo jurisprudence were you referring to when you decided that somebody else wasn't entitled to the same rights you would demand yourselves? Like the right to due process, a fair trial according to the recognized rules of evidence, to examine accusers, have a jury of your peers, to receive legal representation, to call witnesses on your own behalf, to appeal to a higher court? You're completely disregarding the specific components of law that make this a free country. Those two people out there are innocent until proven guilty. Surely you see that."

The room silenced. The Writer was content with his oratory and believed it to be succinct, intelligent, and effective.

Then, in an instant, the entire room erupted into honking laughter, and even more so when someone yelled, "And who the hail is Shirley?" The laughter, indeed, pushed him toward the front of the store. *I give up,* he thought, paid for his beer, and headed for the door. The bus would be leaving soon, and it could not be soon enough. He only hoped that his final destination wasn't worse than this.

It was the albiness who rushed over, grabbed his arm. "Aw, don't mind them. 'Tis just the way things are here. City folks got their city ways, and hill folk got theirs. Believe me, if'n the Larkins boys say they'se guilty, then they sure is."

Her shampoo scent was rousing him again, printing a more than obvious erection in his pants. *For the love of...*"Oh, I understand. It's like an Ibsen play. I'm the outsider. I'm the stranger in a strange land. All that we are, all that we hold dear, are implements of a specific environment."

The odd-faced woman ignored the observation and looked directly at his crotch. "Wish I could see ya again but I guess you're fixin' to head out on the bus."

"Yes, it's nice to have met you, though," the Writer said, his daze split by the woman's bizarre allure and the hideous acts he'd seen outside. "My name's _____ ___. What's yours?"

Her long face smiled, and the red eyes twinkled. "Snowie, Snowie Howard."

A fitting moniker. With skin as white as new fallen snow...
"Where you headed?" she asked, and she seemed absolutely incapable of taking her gaze off him.
What's the big deal with me? he wondered, amused. *I'm a fat old man, and she's looking at me like I'm Tom Cruise...*"I don't think it can be much farther. A town called Luntville."
"Mercy!" the woman, Snowie, celebrated, "that's where I live! So's I *will* see ya again!"
"That's wonderful," and now the Writer saw some cards falling in his favor. "Perhaps you could help me, as I know nothing about the town. Where might I find a room to rent in Luntville? There's very little info online."
She squeezed his arm again, insistent. "Just you march yourself right across the street from the bus stop and check in to the Due Drop In. There's where I live! Ain't this a coincidence!"
"Indeed it is," the Writer said while still densely distracted by the woman's appearance: the odd, elongated, almost manly face atop a voluptuous physique–a synergistic juxtaposition. "Thanks very much for the information."
"And just you tell the night clerk you's a friend of Snowie Howard, and you'll get a discount. See, the night clerk is my ma!"
"How absolutely delightful, Snowie." Riders were now re-boarding the bus. "I hope you'll allow me the honor of taking you to dinner some night, in exchange for your generous font of assistance."
"You can *bet* I will!" and of a sudden she delivered a big hug and a hot sloppy kiss on the cheek. "I'm in room 4, drop by whenever. See ya soon!" and she was back to work.
The Writer left the store confoundedly numb, altogether a pleasant sensation. *I'm a graduate of Harvard and Yale, and I just got a dinner date with an uneducated, inarticulate hill*

31

woman with a body like Raquel Welsh in Fantastic Voyage and a face like Calvin Coolidge. Still, he'd asked a woman on a date, and he had no idea if he'd ever down that before.

Back aboard, he placed his beer in the seat and retreated to the coffin sized cubby in the back, which sufficed as a lavatory. So intrigued was he–intrigued essentially by himself and his current situation–that he paid no conscious mind to the staggering "bus-bathroom odor." His urine cascaded into the aluminum funnel, his mind brimming with questions. How would his "date" go? What sort of accommodations might the Due Drop In offer? How would he pass his first night in these almost otherworldly environs?

And would his date result in a sexual encounter?

Soon, urinating became more difficult for the effects of more uncharacteristic arousal...

No way to wash his hands nor dry them. *Of all the primitive incompetence!* Some lines of writing caught his eye: the sort of graffiti to be expected in such places. Scrawled phone numbers promising oral prowess, women's names scorned and damned, and men's names scorned all the worse, and the like. But here was one quite interesting and atypical:

IN MayFair HoUSe tHere WaLKS, tHey Say, tHe pregNaNt gHoSt
WHo roiSterS iN HeadLeSS purLieU aNd SigHS
WitH corpSe-piLe breatH.
UNto deatH, taKe Heed, LeSt SHe cHriSteN tHee iN NigHtMareS.

How absolutely uncanny, thought the Writer. The clipped verse was morbid and unpleasant yet somehow so curious he felt mildly enthralled; it reminded him of Shelley or George Gordon Byron.

The bus engine grated, then rumbled to life. Just as the Writer would leave the john, he spied yet another odd graffito. It read as thus:

THe BigHead WiLL get you iF you don't WatcH out.

Back in his seat, he sighed, leaned back, then opened his beer with a Widener Library bottle opener. "All aboard!" Joe the bus driver called out over the engine rumble. The Writer liked the Greyhound; and he was certain he'd liked them many times in the past in spite of his inability to remember a single trip. The vehicle seemed possessed of its own *élan:* the dim lights, the motor rumble, the gentle vibrations. *Yes, this is the perfect frame of mind to ponder a novel. I feel ecstatically creative!* The heavy lager seemed the perfect companion for such reflections.

But here creativity and the muses of eccentric novelists disintegrated, as the bus pulled out of the little outpost. The Writer had just time to spy the Larkins brothers standing raucously before the unfortunate young man locked to the dumpster lug. Though the scene was too far distant for the Writer to discern details, he saw one ruffian shine a flashlight into the victim's groinal area. *I guess,* the Writer thought with a gulp, *I guess they're waiting for the man's penis to begin to rot...*

The bus drove on, leaving the atrocity behind it. *Dead-dicking, obviously a southern invention, and WHAT a contribution to society! Those wacky southerners. Gee, I wonder if William Faulkner ever witnessed a dead-dicking?*

Thank God the horror was behind him...or was it? Now only dark woods lined the road ahead, and deep in those woods he could see the tiny fluttering yellow light, like a distant moving flame. It zigzagged along his line of sight, and he realized the only thing it could be: the woman whose head had been set ablaze.

The Writer sat back with his bottle of beer, eyes straight ahead. *Welcome,* he greeted himself, *to the grand old South...*

***

Further details relating to the Writer's arrival in Luntville need not be expended. It will suffice to say that after fifteen-minutes' journey down the tree-lined road, he arrived and debarked, bags in hand. After stepping out, he turned to the driver and said cheerily, "Thank you for the ride, sir, and have a wonderful night."

In the weak light from his dashboard, the driver's face looked fishlike. He said, "This place ain't for you, mister," and then the door flapped closed and the bus rumbled off, raising a cloud of parking lot dust which glittered in the street lamps.

This place ain't for me? Ballyhoo! The secrets of my entire life are here, awaiting discovery!

It was too dark to observe much of the town: a meager line of shops, all closed at this hour–or, no! A neon OPEN sign buzzed behind dark glass, some sort of massage parlor evidently. More neon blinked at the end of the street, taverns, he guessed. Could one of them be the Crossroads, where he'd paid a hefty bar tab over twenty years ago? Now was not the time to find out.

Brisk strides took him across the gravel-paved road, where, as promised, the Due Drop Inn awaited. It stood before him as a ramshackle three-story pile, probably a plantation house in the Civil War era. Several oldsters sat on the dark front porch, creaking in rocking chairs and sipping beers. The Writer nodded cordially as he stepped up on the porch, knowing that stock was being taken of him. There were no cordial nods in return.

After passing through a fan-lighted front door, rather seedy ill-colored carpet led him to the front desk where—

That's DEFINITELY Snowie's mother!

The clerk stood taller than her offspring but was otherwise a carbon copy, save for a twenty-year age difference. The same pallid crinkly hair, pink eyes, paper-white skin, and the same curvaceous physique and stacked bosom. Likewise, she had the same long, narrow, and vaguely mannish face, not to mention a similar protruding jaw which caused her overall visage to be dominated by chin.

"How do you do, ma'am. I'd like to engage a room for a week a least, And I was informed to tell you that Snowie is a friend of mine."

"That little trashpot daughter of mine?" the woman said, asmirk. "Well, at least you're well-spoken, unlike what she usually cavorts with. I take it you're an educated gentleman?"

The Writer meant no gloating when he answered, "I have multiple degrees from Harvard *and* Yale."

"Oh, never heard'a them. Community colleges from up north, I guess—"

The Writer winced.

"Anyway, I'm Hazel Howard, and welcome to the Due Drop In." She put a key down. "You get Room 6, the best in the house.

"Much obliged, ma'am."

The woman's long over-makeupped face seemed to scrutinize him. "Why, I guess you're the writer I heard was comin' here. Are you a writer?"

Now the Writer scrutinized the bizarre query. "I am

35

indeed a writer, ma'am, but I'm at a total loss as to how you heard I was coming."

She touched her chin in thought. "That shore is funny, 'specially for this town. Tomorrow we'se got a famous TV preacher man checkin' in, and now we got a famous writer."

Dumbfounding. "I'm a speculative novelist, and though it's true I've achieved some critical acclaim in literary avenues, I could hardly describe myself as famous. And I'm frankly baffled. By what means exactly were you informed that a *writer* was coming for a stay?"

The woman's eye turned nebulous as one trying to recollect something but knows that the task is impossible. "It's the dangedest thing. I just *knows* I heard it from someone but fer the life'a me I don't know who..."

"How...peculiar," but then he was forced to think of the "evil genius." Dr. Offenbach? *No, no, she didn't know I was coming to this hotel. I didn't know myself until only a short while ago when I met Snowie. And I'm certain I didn't tell HER I was a writer...*

"No matter," the bosomy woman said, "one'a them weird things. Like the time years ago just after Snowie were born. I worked part-time at the library as janitor, and I'se remember pushing the sweeper in the M section, and then—whap! A book up'n fall off a top shelf and hit me smack dab on the top'a my head."

"I hope it wasn't a Minchner book," the Writer tried to jest.

The comment didn't register. "'Twas just a li'l paper-cover thing, real thin. Didn't hurt none. But the second it hit me in the head, I got this *flash* in my brain, and I knew then'n there my husband Biff had left me. And as it stands, I never saw him again."

The Writer considered something premonitory but

immediately rejected it. *So what?* However, the question he asked was fitting for an English major. "What was the book?"

"The book? Aw, dang, just some thing. Death of a Milkman, Death of an Ice Cream man, Death of—"

The Writer's eyes bugged. "Death of a *Salesman?*"

She snapped her fingers and pointed. "Why, yeah! That's it!"

Perhaps his rejection of a premonition had been made in too much haste. "How uncanny. It's a play by Arthur Miller, one of the most important in the history of U.S. literature. *Abandonment* is the central theme." Then he realized his petty indulgence in the comment. "But I'm very sorry to hear that, ma'am. What a horrible time for a spouse to leave, just after the birth of a child."

The woman *smacked* her hands together and belted out laugh so harsh, so loud and boisterous, that it was almost uncomfortable. "Mister, that limp-dick alkerholik piece'a shit leavin' me were a gift from Above, it were! If ever a man could be more useless than a picnic basket full'a possum shit, it was him! I partied so hard that day, I *still* got a hangover! Shee-it! Only time that man ever got his dick hard enough to actually *stick* in me was the night he put Snowie in my oven...and I didn't even cum!"

Well, that's what I call a superfluity of detail, the Writer thought. Before he could say more, Hazel abruptly raised to her tiptoes, the effect of which produced a startling accentuation of her bosom. It made them stick out like mangos. She looked left and shouted, "Portafoy!"

As if conjured, a thin elderly black man in white cuffs, white bow tie, black slacks and black vest, was beside the Writer.

"Take our gentleman here to Room 6," and she passed

him the key. "Famous writer such as himself deserve the room with the *best* view."

"I'm-I'm...not that famous," the Writer interjected.

"Pish-posh," she said. "Thanks for stayin' with us, and when that trash-mouth haughty daughter'a mine git back from work, I'm tell her you's here."

"Thanks, and it's a pleasure meeting you," said the Writer, after which she winked and smiled in a manner that could be called sleazy.

The stately porter was hoisting the Writer's two heaviest back; surely he was nearing eighty.

"Mr. Portafoy!" the Writer alarmed. "Let me take those."

"I won't hear of it, sir. If you'd be so kind, I've answered a door, waited a table, and carried a bag since Lucky Lindy crossed the Atlantic.

Make that closer to ninety, the Writer realized when he realized the reference to Charles Lindbergh.

"If you'll follow me, sir. Thank you, sir."

The hotel's former poshness could be detected with trained glances. Once quality carpet now threadbare, seedy; wallpaper long ago elegant and byzantine patterned, now bubbled and smoke stained. A troubling deja vu occurred to the Writer, but at once he realized that he quite credibly could have been a guest here in the dim past but did not remember. *I...I hope that's true,* he thought for no reason that seemed logical. He followed the porter up the creaking stairs and, as was his obsessive habit, counted each step, not surprised to find them terminate at thirteen. Why did so many accommodations leave out a thirteenth room or thirteenth floor when most stairs contained thirteen steps? *Up the thirteen steps to the gallows walked the condemned man,* came the vague recital. *Yes, a song by the Guess Who!* Travel of all sorts was lessened on the thirteenth day of the month, especially Fridays. *The Last Supper took place on a Friday, and there were thirteen places set at the table. Hmm.* But why did this listless fear, common as it was, affect rooms and floors but not something as ever present as stairwells? The Writer pondered the question a bit further, then concluded, *Who cares! It's a waste of Dr. Offenbach's essentially infinite cerebral synaptic connections to even think about it!*

"A pleasant journey was had by you, I hope, sir?" Portafoy bid, leading the Writer down a musty, sound dampened corridor. Carriage-style lamps projecting from the walls lit their progress, and none too effectively.

"It was indeed a lovely, meditative, and relaxing trip," he answered, for it truly was when he rejected from inclusion the anal-rape, the setting a woman ablaze, and—last but not least—the *dead-dicking.* He wondered if the victim had yet roused enough to see what had become on his penis...

"So glad to hear that, sir. And I trust the same will go for your stay with us."

"Why, Mr. Portafoy, I have a feeling of undeniable certainty that I will."

It would be stretching things to say that this optimistic assertion was entirely accurate.

***

Room 6 it was. The Writer had no alternative but to reflect, *6, the Biblical IMPERFECT number, and the designation of evil and error...*However, this superstition could be no more well-grounded than his previous observations about the number thirteen, could it not? He paid it no mind.

Along the way down the hall, though, he noticed an array of vaguely interesting paintings—*vaguely,* in most cases, such that most of the paintings were so obscured by murk, mold, dust, and age as to be next to indecipherable. Two, however—one in the staircase and one closer to his room in the hall—bore an identical as well as a far more legible central subject.

A man, from the waist up. Spectacled and short-haired, wearing an old fashioned suit jacket and a slender tie. An expressionless face staring straight ahead. Most notable was the face itself; it was very long and narrow, and he possessed a minor malocclusion of the jaw which resulted in a protruding chin.

Just like Snowie and her mother, the Writer recognized. Obviously the man in the picture was a relative from many years back. The pictures were neither paintings, nor photographs, but articulate drawings or engravings. He looked forward to inquiring their history, and more than that, the Writer could not shake some nagging familiarity with the faces in the portraitures...

Portafoy led him into the room, turned on a light, set down the bags, and announced, "Your room, sir. I hope it's to your liking, sir. It's too bad the sun has set, there's a spectacular view at dusk."

"I look forward to enjoying that view tomorrow, Mr. Portafoy." He gave the porter a $10 bill. "For you, with much thanks."

"You're too generous, sir. I'm at your service, sir."

"And I at yours. Have a good night."

"You as well, sir," and then the elderly valet nodded and left.

What a nice man, concluded the Writer. The room, however, was only a notch above a hovel. *If this is the best room in the house, I'd hate...*

A quick inspection introduced him to a decrepit four-poster bed laced with some cobwebs, a small couch the color of a louring sky, a put-it-together-yourself dresser, and, he was happy to see, a desk of sorts. A quick snap of the bathroom light left him content that no roaches had scattered, though a few dead ones floated in the toilet. In all, he found satisfaction here: *A perfect abode for a novelist of naturalist and existential observation,* which he presumed he was. A not-very-good landscape painting adorned the wall by the bed. It appeared to depict a distant mountain range, and none-too-well; he'd say it was paint-by-numbers but even that wouldn't be this shoddy. Next, he parted the vermiculated drapes which might've once been tablecloths.

Spectacular view?

True, the distant line of mountains promised to be an interesting vision at sun-down, and he suspected it provided the model for the inept artist. But it was just a non-descript jagged bulk in nighttime. More unidentifiable bulk filled the plain beyond the back of the hotel, and what this bulk actually was he discerned after making out a large white metal sign:

COUNTY DUMP
CLOSED

What secrets await in the Wasteland, he thought if overly positive. He thought of the monumental poem by T.S. Eliot.

Next, he turned, almost as if bidden by some unseen influence...

How absolutely peculiar!

Just by the door hung another sketch portrait, of the same narrow-faced man in the other two.

Who IS this man? The Writer knew that an imaginative power of suggestion could well be at play, combined with the exciting distractions of being in a new and alien place.

41

But the notion would not be away from him: *I just KNOW I've seen this person before, and it's not at all relative to the facial similarities between him and Snowie and Mrs. Howard...*

It was sustenance for ponderment, and perhaps grist for the new novel...which he didn't feel like embarking upon just yet. A better embarkation might be...

A drink, to help me think! so after freshening up in the barren bathroom, he left the room, locked it behind him, and indeed, embarked for the tavern called the *Crossroads.*

***

No lightning bolt of buried memories struck him when he entered the Crossroads. *But am I ready for that?* came a strangely hesitant question. He should be, but...*Right now the only thing I'm ready for is a beer.* He pulled up a stool at the long bar, at which only a few patrons sat. But slow nights in bars were the best kind for writers. Loud music, loud talk, and boisterousness in general weren't conducive to creative reflection, though he did recall reading somewhere that John Irving—or was it Tom Robbins?—enjoyed sitting in rowdy low-life bars reading Shakespeare, and when some bullyish "redneck" mocked him, he promptly and efficiently "kicked their ass." *But I'm no tough guy,* the Writer reminded himself, *and if I've ever engaged in fisticuffs with anyone, I suspect I did NOT emerge as victor...*

Arcade machines lined one wall, booths lined another. The establishment's center was occupied by billiards tables and one foosball table, bereft of players. However, the bar's topography was of little importance. Eventually a barkeep approached, but not with the question he wanted to hear...

"What you doin' here, man?" said the keep, tall lanky,

long gray hair and goatee. He wore a sleeveless denim jack and a leather cowboy hat. "You got *balls,* I'll tell ya that. 'Twas a time not long ago, a motherfucker run out on his tab *here,* in *this* bar? No one see him again till he's out of traction."

The Writer's eyes bulged in terror, "Sir, I'm afraid this is a case of mistaken identity. I've only been in town an hour, I just got off the bus from _____."

The barkeep grabbed the Writer's throat, squeezed a little. "Hey, Neenie! Ain't this the same swamp scum pig-butt-licker that walk out on his tab last week? The dude drinking all our best scotch?"

A skinny fiftyish woman cleaning beer pitchers paused, squinted over, and frowned. "Ray, let that man go, you asshole! That ain't him! You forgit'cher glasses again?"

The grip didn't release. "Same long hair, same shit-lookin' beard? You shore?"

"It *ain't him,* ya dickweed! Fella run out on his tab was much younger than that 'un there, and not as fat...no offense, sir."

"None taken," the Writer choked.

The barkeep released him. "Sorry, friend. It's just..." More peering scrutiny. "I just could'a sworn..."

"He do look a bit like him, but was at least twenty years younger," the woman snapped. "Sir, you gotta forgive that over-the-hill badass shit for brains creeker."

Southern hospitality has come a long way since Gone With The Wind. The Writer rubbed his throat, could feel his reddened face regaining its normal hue. *Am I that fat?* he wondered and after a glance to his mid-section, he stifled an answer. "It's quite all right. A simple misunderstanding, and it can be said that misunderstandings prove the most apparent element of human existence. If interested, investigate the philosophies of the superlative French mathematician Rene Descartes."

Both attendants stared at him. "He's from the city, Ray, that's all," ventured the woman.

"Uh, yeah," replied "Ray" the barkeep. "What'll it be stranger? First one's a tin roof on account of the roughin' up."

"A tin roof?" the Writer asked.

Ray rolled his eyes. "It's on the house."

Dismal possibilities looked back at him from the beer taps, but upon asking if they carried bottles of Collier's Civil War Lager, the affirmative response thrilled him. "Gotta warn ya 'fore I open it, though," said Ray. "'Tis the most expensive beer in the place. Three bucks."

You've never been to Manhattan, have you, Ray? "Bring it on, sir, and a glass please, if you'd be so kind."

The libation was supplied, and the first sip tickled the Writer proverbially pink. *I guess I'm an alcoholic, but I suppose it's appropriate to share company with the likes Ernest Hemingway, Sherwood Anderson, and Dylan Thomas.*

"Fella that has a fancy beer show on cable make that beer with his wife. They come in here ever now'n again 'cos they own a bunch'a bars and restaurants. *Holy rollers,* they is, if that don't beat all. But they give us a discount per case and they tip good, and I tell ya, that wife'a his"—he whistled off-key—"a fuckin' *fireplug* she is. That ass she fill them tight pants'a hers with make ya wanna shout, and she got tits stickin' out like ta make ya pump a great big cock-hock in your shorts."

Cock-hock, the Writer considered, amazed. "Well, I must say, this is a finely crafted beer, produced, I suspect, via the old Czech recipes that were brought here in the early 1800s."

"Yeah, but ya know what? That little holy-roller spinner, she were eyeballin' me fierce, she was, like just *lookin'* at me was gittin' her juicy 'tween the gams."

"Ah, Ray, I swear more *shit* come out'a your mouth than all the cow-butts on Charlie Fuchson's farm!" Neenie interjected. She continued washing pitchers in the triple-sinks, which required her to bend over. This pose made it impossible for the Writer too avoid the vision of her un-bra'd breasts showing in the gap of her low-cut blouse. He thought of two white socks with a baseball in each toe. "That woman weren't lookin' at you in a million years, and it's a good thing, 'cos what would you do with her anyway? That dick'a yours ain't been anything but limp as a wet noodle for a blammed decade."

"What'choo talkin' about, woman? My dick's hard as gnarled oak, like I prove to you ever' damn night!"

"In your dreams, Ray!"

"No, no, in *your* dreams, Neenie, and me'n my pecker'll make 'em *all* come true!"

"Only dream'a mine you could make come true is ta *quit!*"

Listening to this less-than-illuminating discourse made the Writer feel like a fencepost being sledge-hammered into the earth, yet he maintained a congenial expression in order that he not offend his hosts. And relief embraced him a moment later when Ray took his himself and his mouth toward some other customers down the bar.

The vague buzz of the well-bodied lager seeped pleasantly into his being. *Now we're talking...*He even slipped the ever-present pen and white index card out of his top pocket, for he fancied he felt like jotting some notes for the novel. It would be thrilling to write an entire novel based on that mysterious first page. Still, he felt certain that when he did, along with his simply being in this town, his memory would return. He anticipated this event as one who was close to picking the lock of a treasure chest found in the attic.

A brilliant sentence popped into his mind, and, as most writers could relate, the need to writer it down immediately was imperative; otherwise it would be forgotten forever. The excitement blazed in him body and soul, and he applied the pen-tip to the paper and began to—

"Eeeeeeeeee-yabbadabba-DOOOOO!" a voice exploded after the entrance slammed open. "I am HERE, folks, so now the party can START! How my favorite rednecks doin'? Well I'm OUT of the joint and ready to PAAAAAAAAAAAAR-Tee! BOOM-shockalockalocka! BOOM-shockalockalocka!"

This egregious distraction disintegrated the Writer's brilliant sentence before the pen could move. He smoldered. *Out the window now, gone as vapor in a breeze.* The Writer was not inclined toward hostility in any fashion, and entertaining violent thoughts, even in fantasy, he was not capable of fathoming. However, at just that precise moment, he ground his teeth and involuntarily thought *Who ever that HORSE'S ASS is, I'd freely deliver my soul to Osiris to stave his head in with an iron cudgel!*

The "horse's ass," he saw upon turning, was a fat redneck in a leather sleeveless vest and frayed leather hat, dressed so similarly to Ray the Barkeep that he could only be Ray's son. *Pox be upon thee. Give me back my sentence, you reprobate hooligan!*

"Line me up some shots, daddy!" the ex-con reveled. "You put 'em down, I'll put 'em away!"

Ray smirked. "Money up front, son, and we all know you ain't got none so why don't you just split?"

"Aw, shucks, daddy. I just got out'a jail! That ain't no way ta treat your only son!"

"The way I *ought'a* treat my only son is to kick the snot out of him. Your dear departed mother'd be damn 'shamed seein' how you turnt out. Now git'cher useless ass out'a here and get a fuckin' job."

"Awww, daddy..." When the son left, the bar applauded.

"Must'a had dog shit on my dick when I knocked his momma up with him," Ray remarked, shaking his head.

The Writer sat deflated. And just when he tried to refocus on writing, pinball machines began to ring, billiard balls clacked, and then the *Snap! Snap! Snap!* of the air hockey table. Rowdy patrons poured in through the entrance. All at once this dive bar was in full swing, and a quiet evening in a sedate contemplation was suddenly beyond the Writer's reach. The only thing missing were nails across a chalkboard.

What am I doing here? I don't remember this place, and I don't remember ANYTHING since I got to town. The logical action would be to leave, but—

At least one more beer seemed absolutely requisite. *If I leave, where will I drink?* Nothing could be more inadvisable than wandering around an unfamiliar place in the dark. Just to look for another bar that would almost assuredly be as unsuitable as this one. *And I'd be a sitting duck for muggers...*

He cringed for Ray or the woman so he could order another beer, but neither was in sight. Bar clamor crowded his brain; he wished he had ear plugs. What more proof of alcoholism was needed? *I need just ONE MORE BEER so bad, I'm going to continue to sit in this tavern-version of Dante's Ninth Ring rather than leave.* His chin settled in his hand. *What a self-revelation.*

Eventually Ray reappeared and a new beer was provided. The bar stools were filling up but no one sat beside the Writer. *Am I anathema?* but in truth he much preferred to sit alone. If this were, say, a bar near an Ivy League school, then that would be different. Some stimulating discourse would surely be had. But here?

Not so much.

The Writer jolted on his stool when Ray abruptly bellowed: "Milky! Git'cher hand out your pants and bring up more ice! *NOW!*" Momentarily, a tall lanky bar-back lumbered up with a large ice bucket. But it was not this commonplace task that locked the Writer's gaze and seized him with inquiry. It was the bar-back himself.

Tall, stoop-shouldered, an oddly long narrow face, jutting chin, and crinkly white hair. Red eyes. He was an albino.

Undoubtedly he's a relative of Snowie and her mother... But that possibility faded when he thought more simply and fixedly: *Snowie...*

What a great body! Such a radiant aura, the picture of desirability and good-nature, truly a fun-to-be-around young woman. So what if she's got the face of a dour man...

Sparks, then, began to crackle again "south of the belt," as the saying went. And this shone more light on a deeper puzzle. Since this entire venture had begun, back in Dr. Offenbach's office, the Writer had become subject to a most acute and even aggravating sense of sexual awareness, which was clean contrary to his experience. As aforementioned, he felt himself so wrapped up in his erudite muses and aesthetic thoughts, that no room was left for desire, lust, or romantic interest of any kind, and before his memory failure he couldn't imagine that symptom was any different. A pretty girl passing by, a stunning model spied in a magazine or on a billboard, his few accidental stumblings onto erotic imagery on the internet–all this registered naught in that cerebral entity known as the Human Sex Drive. The Writer was quite content without this distraction; he wanted nothing in his mental makeup that might intercept his true philosophical nature. And though he supposed he'd "had sex" at some time or other in his life (even though he couldn't remember it!), he felt fortunate and even superior in his disregard for the ludicrous, frenetic and animalistic coupling of *intercourse* as well as all of its viscid trimmings. Even the Sin of Onan was a "once in a blue moon" occurrence for him—in other words, the hilarious and self-depreciating practice of "beating off." As for women, the Writer no more wanted to put his penis into a malodorous, hair-rimmed hole of flesh than he'd want to put it into the drain at the bottom of a dumpster. Likewise, he couldn't understand what would motivate a woman to admit into her mouth the exit spout of a man's bladder, so as to let him "come in her mouth," not to mention actually *swallowing* the product of the orgasm. When such a revolting thought occurred to him, he'd visibly shiver. And the very idea of applying his *mouth* to the egress that a woman urinates through, bleeds through, and pushes babies through...That was all a great big *YUCK!*

Now, though?

Now?

Something's happening to me, he knew. That next beer was already half gone in these cruxing reflections. *I'm hornier than a jackal full of spanish fly. I'm NEVER like this? But right now?*

He eyed the barmaid. Reenie? *Right now, if she wanted my penis in her mouth, by George, she'd have it! And if she wanted intercourse, why, I'd nail her to the floor, tube-sock-breasts and all!*

This bar excursion was not going well. He felt annoyed by himself, betrayed and embarrassed by these newfound emotions, and his pants were...uncomfortably strained. *Time to pay the man and retreat to my room. And who knows? Maybe I'll run into Snowie. And if not, I should at least have occasion to get another glimpse of that GREAT set of tits on her mother...*

He was all set to flag Ray for his tab when a wisp of

fragrance caressed him, then so did a pair of anxious arms. "I *knew* my friend'd be here!" a hot female breath thrilled in his ear. "My ma said you looked like a man lookin' for a drink when you left the inn!"

He turned to find, of course, Snowie practically climbing on him as if he were a jungle gym. "Why, Snowie, how delightful to see you. I was just thinking about you, believe it or not."

"I hope they was *nice* kind'a thoughts!"

"Indeed they were," he said, his erection flexing, and immediately she took the next stool, jerked it closer to him.

Her right hand rested on the inside of his left knee. The Writer nearly ejaculated in his pants.

"Can you buy me a drink? I don't git paid till next Friday and—"

"Say no more. Get whatever you want."

The heat of her body, the presence of her next to him, and that blasted soap or shampoo or whatever it was...A blinding thought struck him: that he'd have no choice but to go to the men's room and masturbate. *In the name of Valhalla, give me strength!*

"Ray, this here's my friend, _____," she told the barkeep. "He's a famous *writer!*"

"Dang, really?" said the barkeep. "There goes my good tip..."

"I'm not really famous," the Writer hastened, but then all thoughts stalled. "And the misunderstanding before? Forget it." He turned. "Snowie, when did I tell you I was a writer?"

"You didn't, ma did. And, Ray, I'll have what he's drinkin'." She grabbed his sleeve and pulled him towards her. "Always wanted to have me that Collier's stuff but 'twas too expensive!"

The Writer ordered another for himself as well.

Questions crowded his mind, which he burned to ask, but it was impossible not to keep glancing over at Snowie. Those formidable thighs in her jeans, that bosom—braless, he believed—beneath the magenta blouse. He couldn't be positive but no panty lines appeared against her jeans, and all he could imagine was pubic hair the same unique white-yellow as the hair on her head. *Am I REALLY going to excuse myself to the men's room just to masturbate?* There was no urbane way to say it: His erection was leaking like a faucet with a bad washer, and it didn't help matters when Snowie squeezed his knee for no perceivable reason.

He struggled to push his cognizance through the lust-daze. "Snowie? Do you know how *your mother* knew I was a writer?"

When she shrugged, her awesome breasts rode up a few inches, then dropped. "I figured you told her."

The Writer nodded non-committally. "And have you by chance...seen anyone who resembles me around town?"

"You kiddin'! I'd fall down in the blammed street if'n I saw any fella even *half* as good-lookin' as you!"

She MUST have vision problems. He hoped he didn't blush, but one thing he was sure of: upon her stating those words, a good deal more pre-ejaculatory fluid pumped out of his penis. "That's, uh, that's very nice of you to say, Snowie."

She leaned closer. "I'd really like to know what it is your write about!"

At least his stock answer would take his mind off the heavy, heavy aura of sexuality pouring off her like smoke; and the entirety of this answer was based on what he formulated by reading all of his novels—which he didn't remember writing—and by his philosophical ideologies—which were innate. "I'm a *writer*," he stated with emphasis. "I travel all over the country. I need to see different things, different

51

people. I need to see life in its different temporal stratas."

"Stratas," Snowie repeated.

Or is it STRATUM, for the plural? Or, no! Stratum is the singular and strata is the plural! Damn! Stratas is incorrect! He went on, "I come to remote towns like this because they're variegated. They exist separately from the rest of the country's societal mainstream. Towns like this are more *real*. I'm a writer, but in a more esoteric sense I'm a *seer,* because what I write is the re-invention and re-interpretation of what I experience, and the provenance of all experience is *seeing*."

The pretentious and, actually, *preposterous* summation of himself seemed to put Snowie on the verge of melting. Her pink eyes locked on him, and the mouth on her almost unnaturally narrow face dropped open; it was as though his stodgy, phony-intellectual answer had had the effect of a love potion. *This certainly has turned into the most bizarre several hours of my life,* it occurred to him. Would the hours of the *rest* of his stay in this town prove just as bizarre?

She stared at him so intently he believed she was about to lean forward and kiss him. The Writer knew he must maintain control of himself. After all, he had to be thirty years older, if not more; plus, pleasant as it would be, if she *did* kiss him, he surely *would* release a spontaneous ejaculation in his pants. *I can't let that happen!* The wet spot would be impossible to conceal.

He had to snap her out of her lust-trance-stare. It was growing uncomfortable, and the hayseeds packing the bar were probably noticing. "Oh, let me ask you. Your mother mentioned that a popular...*evangelist,* or something of that sort, would be staying at the inn?"

The fog went out of her eyes. "Huh? Oh, yeah. He came early, were checkin' in just as I git home from work. His name's Pastor Tommy Ig...Ig-something or other. Got his own TV show. I reckon he's rich 'cos he gotta fancy black car, a Cadillac, I think."

"Hey, thar, Snowie, honey," said the bar-back. He was still raking ice over the troughs of beer bottles.

"Hey, Milky," she said, only half-aware of him. "Don't work too hard."

"I never do, sweetie."

The Writer jumped on the diversion. "Might he be a relative of yours?"

She was finally coming out of her daze. "Oh, you mean 'cos we both be albinos—well, yes and no. We all part of the Howard Clan. Ain't but two relatives attached to any of us, but that was, dang, I don't know. Years'n years'n years ago." She sighed; her fingers tightened on his knee. "It's a long, borin' story, and I'm shore you don't wanna hear it."

"Oh, but I'd like to hear it very much," he insisted, leaning closer.

"I think it go back to, like, the '20s. Ma's actually the best one ta ask." She seemed to involuntarily tighten her pectoral muscles, the action of which highlighted the contours of her bosom in the most fascinating way.

The Writer wanted to moan aloud.

"Guess there be 'bout forty or fifty us spread out in these parts," she went on. "Ever time a Howard male knock up a reg'lar gal, a albino come out, and ever time a Howard gal git pregnant by a reg'lar guy, same thing. The baby's always a albino. Strangest thing, but it's always been that way since way on back then."

"Not that uncommon at all," spake the Writer. "The union of those two progenitors back in the '20s produced what's known as a *dominant* gene. And, Snowie, you're just as 'regular' a person as a non-albino; in fact—and if you don't mind my saying so—if anything, your albinism makes you even more beautiful," after which a Dunce Alarm went off in his head. *What did I just say? She's going to think I'm patronizing her! She's going to think I'm trying to soften her up with corny pick-up lines!* He prepared to apologize but—

Her head was bowed, her fingers wiping at tears in her eyes. "That's-that's the nicest thang anyone ever say to me..."

The Writer was paralyzed as to response. He took her hand in his lap, said, "Snowie, don't cry, I only—"

But then she braced up, sniffled, wiped her eyes. "You are just the sweetest man," and now she leaned over and it was clear that she would kiss him—

But—

—with her lips an inch away from his, the gesture was severed like an ax through a lampcord, by a nearly blaring, upbeat boisterous tune. Snowie's cell phone lit up.

"Awwwww, *fuck!*" she voiced an obvious displeasure. "Damn, it's Dawn. I'se sorry but I gotta take this."

"Oh, please do," because though the Writer's kiss had been hijacked, he was overwhelmed anew by this exciting element to ponder. Snowie's *ringtone.* The Writer winced, wringing his brain. *What was that tune?* He knew he'd heard it a million times but he simply couldn't summon it up. An inconsequential thing, yes, but it absolutely nettled him. One side of his brain struggled for the name of the tune, the other side took great pains to inconspicuously eavesdrop on Snowie's conversation with this Dawn person...

"—damn, Dawn, I'm *busy,* I'm with a friend, *dammit,* and I don't wanna leave. What—*when?* A couple minutes ago? Aw, shee-it, girl! Was it a county ambulance? You kiddin' me? I didn't even know Luntville *had* a ambulance! They've never brought 'em before, have they?"

Ambulance? the Writer's curiosity was piqued, yet that other half of his brain power continued to compute

54

the identify of that ringtone tune. *It's right on the tip of my tongue! What IS that ringtone?*

"But, Dawn, I told you LAST WEEK, we can't to any now 'cos Tubesteak's not here. I TOLD YOU!"

The Writer's brain-flexing abated for just a moment, to consider: *Tubesteak...*

"He took his two sons to the Boy Scout Jamboree at Boone's National Park. Damn, girl, you don't listen to a word I say! So we got no one ta–ta...you know..."

Whatever these cryptic comments regarded, the Writer couldn't imagine and didn't care. Just now, he worried that he'd never fall asleep tonight if he didn't recall that blasted ringtone.

"You don't know that. All you gotta do is tell Augie not to come till *next* week..." A pause, some vaguely heard yammering on the other end. Then she paused once more, as if contemplating. Meanwhile, the Writer continued to contemplate that ringtone. Then, like an arrow from a crossbow, it hit him—

The Munsters! he rejoiced. *It's the theme song from the Munsters!*

Snowie said, "All right, I'll do everything I can to make it happen. See ya soon," and she hung up.

"Snowie," he blurted. "How do you know the Munsters? You're way too young to have seen them."

She looked crookedly at him. "Huh? Oh, my ringtone? Yeah, I love the Munsters. Ma and I watch 'em all the time on cable. S'my fave-rit show, in fact."

"How fascinating!"

She leaned over, squeezed his hand again. "I gotta go to the ladies room, then I need to ask you to do somethin', okay? It ain't no big deal, and there's somethin' in it for you, believe me."

She jumped off her stool and disappeared for the rest room.

Her request sideswiped him. He was thinking about that wacky, wonderful Munsters' theme. That theme song drenched up memories of the most pleasant sort: watching the *Munsters* every week during his adolescence, and other great shows too, like *Addam's Family, Gilligan, the Rat Patrol,* oh, and begging his parents to let him stay up late for *Outer Limits.* What wonderful times those had been!

Then, next, stared into space, and came a sensation like a wrecking ball through a house of glass...

Praise the great King Zeus! I just remembered something, specifically and with detail, about my childhood! TV shows, on black and white TV, and then the big color RCA when Dad got that raise at work! The house in Bowie, the Ford Fairlane station wagon in the driveway! It had "fly" windows!

Surely, this was the beginning of the trickle that would eventually lead to a full recovery of his memory..

But, *What did Snowie say. She wants me to do something? What on earth could it be?*

She returned at that moment, with a tense expression on her narrow face.

"Snowie, I'm very curious. What is it you'd like me to do?"

She fidgeted. "Just want ya to go with me to my friend Dawn's."

Seemed harmless enough. "I see, because you'd prefer not to walk alone at night."

"Naw, that ain't it. Just, just, trust me."

"Of course, I'd love to accompany you anywhere but do I have time for one more beer?"

"Well, no, see, see...just trust me. We gotta go now."

"Ah, I understand." But after all those hours in the bus, wasn't he a bit tired for a long walk? "How far is Dawn's house?"

"Uh-uh, well, we ain't goin' ta her house, we'se goin' ta where she works, and it ain't but a five minute walk."

The Writer nodded agreeably. "And where does she work?"

Her epochal breasts stood out in unrestrained grandeur. She sighed. "Dawn works at the Luntville funeral home..."

As much as he enjoyed spending time with her, this was beginning to take on a tint of oddness that was prickling him. "Well...what exactly is it you'd—"

"Just come with me please!" came her whispered plea. "I done told ya, there's somethin' in it for you. Wanna know what it is?"

"Why, certainly."

She whispered lower. "Dawn'n me, we'se'll give ya a double blowjob. We'll both suck yer dick so hard, yer eyeballs'll come out'cher peehole..."

Common sense took a powder. This was all wrong yet the Writer turned, raised a finger. "Sir? Ray, if I may? I'm afraid I must trouble you for my tab."

The vested, silly-hatted redneck nodded. "Comin' right up—"

"Oh, but, Ray? Would it be at all possible for you to also ring me up for a six-pack of Colliers to go, please?"

Ray stopped in place, went bug-eyed, and approached in a movement so rapid, it was alarming. "What'choo want me to do, mister? Sell you alcohol to go when we ain't got no package license? That's against *the law!*"

"Oh, I'm terribly sorry, I didn't realize—"

Ray slapped the bar. "I'se just jokin' with ya, mister! A'course you can have a six to go!"

Wow, the Writer thought. *I guess I need a sense of humor...*

He paid in cash, left a ludicrous $50 tip, and rose from

his stool. "Thank you, Ray. I'm sure we'll soon meet again."

The barkeep's face seemed to warp. "Thank *you,* mister. In thirty-some years'a tendin' bar, I ain't *never* got a fifty buck tip."

"Tell me something, if you will," the Writer went on, ever distracted. "You mentioned that a man who looked like a younger version of me came here recently and—"

"And run out on his tab after downin' a bunch of our best single malts, the rat fuck motherfucker. Hope I never git *my* hands on him."

The Writer didn't quite know how to phrase it, nor could he guess why he was even asking, yet he asked anyway: "I'm merely curious, you see? But...how much was his tab?"

"Can ya believe it?" Ray said. "T'was $126!"

***

Coincidence, he urged himself to believe. What else could it be? *So what? My bar tab here twenty some-odd years ago was the same as the guy who looks a little bit like me?* Meaningless. He shut the reflection down while walking alongside Snowie on the main street, away from the town center. Several more strips of shops lined the road; the infrequent street lamps seemed to grow darker, and the only activity was up ahead–a Wendy's hamburger place. *Is that the place that makes square hamburgers? Why not curvilinear triangles? Why not trapeziums?* A strange deja vu, again, made his neck hairs prickle. Even though he was being led by a perfect stranger in a strange town, to a *funeral parlor* at close to midnight (a potential circumstance for danger) the Writer felt buoyant in a satisfaction dissimilar to anything he'd ever felt. *The Munsters!* he thought. Snowie's ringtone had triggered his first memory of import. To him, it was an earth-shattering event, and he could only suspect it was the tip of an iceberg. *More memories are no doubt on their way. The combination of little things, such as a ringtone, plus this environment no doubt, were the catalysts...Dr. Offenbach was right!*

Only now did he realize Snowie was holding his hand as they proceeded down the ever darkening street. She'd promised a lewd reward for making this "trip," hadn't she? *Oral sex from two women!* But wasn't he too cultured to take them up on it? *In the name of Washington Irving, I hope not!* Further descriptions of his current state of sexual receptivity need not be included here.

"So now...we're going to meet your friend Donna—"

"Dawn," she corrected.

"Dawn, of course, at...a funeral home? Have I got this right?"

"Yup, and I knows it sounds strange but—" she squeezed his hand and smiled in the streetlight. "Trust me, it's best I explain it all when we git there. You's're doing us a great service like you wouldn't believe."

Cruxing, yes, but fascinating. *What "great service" could I be implementing* by *going to a FUNERAL PARLOR?*

Further considerations weighed on him. Was she drawing him into this unseemly trek for some *other* purpose? Were miscreants waiting at the other end of it, preparing to rob a suspected "rich novelist?" or some variation thereof? It was a sensible supposition...Yet on he went, hand in hand, lugging a big six-pack. The next street lamp cast their shadows on the asphalt. *What TREMENDOUS breasts,* he noted of her silhouette just as they passed the Due Drop In. Dim yellowish lights shone in all the windows and now a long car seemed to be pulling up at the front drive, a black Cadillac.

"There's Pastor Tommy," she remarked. "Ma loves it

when he stays here, bein' that she's kind'a sweet on him. Handsome man. And *rich?*" She whistled.

Thus far, an interesting cast of characters, the Writer mused. The observation suddenly lit a creative fuse. *I can fictionalize this town, and these people! A veritable Peyton Place of the poor white South!*

Had that been what he was doing when he'd written that first page all those years ago?

These thoughts followed him when a break appeared in the next line of closed shops, revealing a segment of gravel-pocked dirt, rocks, weeds, and lots of empty beer cans. And—

He stopped, squinting. "Is that a *car* parked there?" A sudden surge of his heart then, when he thought he saw a male figure on the portly side standing next to the car, but—

No, just a trick of light.

There was no figure, just some trees, some shadows.

"Shore is," she said and turned toward it. "Come on, I'll'se show ya. 'Tis just a junker, been sitting there over near twenty years. Since you's a writer you might 'preciate some'a our local legends."

"I would indeed!" the Writer enthused. "Does this vehicle here pertain to such a legend?"

"Yeah, it does. 'Twas the fastest car in the county they'se say. T'would blow the doors off the state police pursuit cars and the ATF unmarkeds." She took him right up to the heap of a vehicle, a two-seater with a hardtop and long back bed like a pickup truck. "Belonged to a 'shine runner named Dicky Caudill, not very nice. He hanged out with a dude even less nice, named Balls Conner. They'd run 'shine from here inta the Kentucky dry counties, never got caught. But they also raped'n murdered a whole lotta girls—and fellas, too, I heard—just fer fun."

A couplet of sociopaths, the Writer figured. *Akin to Lucas and Toole, Bianchi and Buono.* "I see. And what became of Mr. Caudill and Mr. Conner?"

"Got kilt, both on the same night. Got kilt horrible's what they say, up where the old Catholic chapel used ta be."

"Chapel?" the Writer questioned. "For Catholics? Considering the demographics, I would've presumed everyone here to be protestant."

"Don't know nothin' 'bout that," she said. "But it weren't just a chapel, 'twas a hospital or somethin', for sick priests'n nuns. Ever' one calls it the old abbey, on account that's what it was years and years ago."

A Catholic abbey, here of all places, thought the Writer. *How curious.* He was looking at the car now, a ruin on long rotted tires, a once-fine finish effaced by years of weather. He recognized the make and model at once: "A 1969 Chevrolet El Camino," he said.

"Wow! You know about old cars?" she asked.

He reflected on the question. "Actually, no, I know absolutely *nothing* about cars and have never been interested in them." He scratched his beard. "Strange that I'd be instantly familiar with this one..."

Was it another buried memory seeping through? *Maybe I saw this car when I was here in the early '90s...*

That must be it!

"Folks don't come by this spot much, and they'se won't even tow it away," she went on. "Sometimes ya can see Dicky's ghost standin' there, which I know sounds like a bunch'a horseflop, but, well, I seen it a few times myself..."

The Writer found himself keenly interested in such things. "Have you now? Can you describe him?"

"Fat fella, crew cut, pudgy face. 'Tis always a-rubbin' his crotch, just like he done last time I seed him in real life when

I was little. Lookin' at me'n grinnin'. Rubbin' hisself there."

The Writer's mental stasis stretched on. The figure he thought he'd seen had indeed matched the same description, hadn't it? Sans the crotch-rubbing?

Hmm.

"'Tis said anyone who tow this car away'll be cursed and his whole family with him. And there be another legend too..."

"What might that be?" the Writer eagerly asked.

Snowie seemed to undergo a mounting distress, and at once the Writer thought that possibly this Dicky Caudill man had maybe raped or molested her long ago. "On second thought, Snowie, I can see that the matter bothers you, so you needn't tell me anymore."

"Well, okay," she said. "Suits me actually to get away from this place," she retook his hand to navigate him back down the street. "I'll tell ya some other time."

The Writer liked being in suspense, because it forced him to devise his own creative conjectures. *I've only been here a few hours, and already I've got a surplus of material for the book!*

Another strip of darkened shops appeared, made even more desolate since the last of the streetlamps were now behind them. The tiniest glint of light appeared in one front window, and when he looked up he could just make out the tell-tale chimney. *Crematorium,* he knew. *This must be the place.* Letters like those carven on a gravestone spelled:

WINTER-DAMON FUNERAL HOME

The Writer was surprised by his lack of hesitancy.

Odd how Snowie had a key to the establishment's front

door, which she turned in the lock, but—

"Oh, dang, I feel bad at least not tellin' you the rest'a the story. I mean, you's bein' a writer an all, probably gits your goat when someone starts tellin' a story but don't never tell the whole thing."

"You mean about the legend of Dicky Caudill's car? As I said, please don't recount anything that brings you distress," but in truth the Writer was anxious to know all about it, anything at all.

"I'll tell ya that part later, but I mean about Dicky'n Balls thereselfs, and how they died."

"Ah, yes, you mentioned they were both killed at some abbey or clerical hospital."

"Yeah, see, and these days folk's will say some ATF cops finally got hold of 'em and just took out in the woods'n kilt 'em, or Clyde Nale, the biggest corn liquor maker in these parts kilt 'em fer stealin' their product."

"Either possibility seems quite plausible," however, the Writer sensed something else by her expression and pose.

"How Dicky'n Balls was *really* kilt was they run inta, well, a monster in the woods, and it teared 'em both apart bare-handed. Pulled Dicky's *spine* out his *butthole,* it did."

"A monster, I see," the Writer went along.

She smiled. "Oh I kin tell ya think I'm pullin' yer leg—"

"No, not at all. It's my bounden belief that *dis*belief in what one has never seen is a fool's tenet."

She sexily cocked a hip. "Let me just say I *know* it's true."

"You mean you *saw* the monster yourself?" the Writer posed, trying to maintain an acumen that suggested no mockery.

"Yeah I did, I swear on my poor daddy's grave," she said. Now she seemed oddly excited. "Didn't see it back then, a'course, but I seen it after." Her eyes narrowed like slivers of glass; she smiled again. "And you'll get to see it too."

"*What?*" He no longer knew how to perceive this. It was nonsensical. "You're telling me I'll get to see the *monster* that killed Dicky and Balls all those years ago?"

"Uh-huh. Oh, don't worry, it's dead, and it's, well—" she jabbed a thumb over her shoulder, indicating the funeral parlor. "It's in there. And you'll git ta see it, but'cha gotta do somethin' fer me'n Dawn first."

The Writer frowned. "What *exactly* is it I must do?"

"We'll tell ya, but ya gotta agree first. Otherwise I cain't take ya in."

She smiled at the Writer more intently now, while he stared back, perhaps for as long as a full minute.

This was too much, and hypothetically very hazardous. Anything could be awaiting beyond that door, and it wouldn't be any "monster," it would be someone with a gun, the final end of the ambuscade he originally considered. He was about to decline, when she went on:

"The monster died in—I'm not sure, '96, '97, thereabouts, and its body, well, its body's been stored here ever since."

The Writer continued to stare.

"And it had a name, see? Folks all over called it the Bighead," she finished.

The mental impact of the name jolted him like driving fast over unnoticed train tracks. And not only had he seen it scrawled in the bus john but he was now eerily certain he'd seen it elsewhere too.

A thrilling chill went up his back.

"You've got a deal," he said.

Snowie opened the big paneled front door, the hinges of which creaked spectacularly.

He followed her in.

***

Even a brain as "brilliant" as the Writer's was faltering in its ability to process all the data, speculations, and observations that had been thrust at him since he'd gotten off the Greyhound. A bodiless voice with an absurd reference to Gummy Worms; the cryptic graffito in the bus john about "Bighead" that was said to have killed the psychopathic owner of the 1969 El Camino the Writer had just seen and which was undeniably familiar to him; evidently an entire clan of albinos all with the same facial characteristics of the unsettlingly familiar sketch portraits located in the old hotel he'd checked into tonight and had clearly checked into over twenty years ago but didn't remember; the slow seeping of what could only be genuine memories long forgotten (including the *Munsters!*); a man who looked similar to him who'd run out on a bar tab for the same amount that the Writer himself had paid in the early '90s; and—

And—

Now I'm following an albino bombshell I just met, into a FUNERAL HOME, at night, because she told me I'd get to see the body of this–this Bighead, a MONSTER, she says, but only after I DO something she refuses to define, he added up.

Nevertheless, on he went.

The threshold was crossed, the prodigious door shut behind him and locked. He followed her, in pin-drop silence, his eyes wide on everything. Beneath a veneer of age, faded colors, and disparate decay, some relic of stateliness remained: the fittings and atmosphere of an old fashioned funeral parlor, circa 1900. Antique furniture, sedate if smoke-stained wallpaper, brass-stemmed table lamps with stained-glass shades. Carpeted stairs rose to the right, a sitting parlor opened to the left, lit by modest yellow lamplight; the Writer spied a closed coffin.

Is there someone in it?

Snowie conveyed him down the quiet entrance hall, which was lined by aged photographs, mezzotints, and tintypes of dour moustachio'd men in high collars and bow ties, all in wooden oval frames. The only thing distracting him from all this fascinating decor was the voluptuous shape of Snowie's rear-end just ahead of him, and occasional side-glances of her momentous bosom.

"Why is it," the Writer began, "that you have a key to this establishment? Do you work here when you're not at the store?"

"I...sort of. I don't really work for the funeral parlor, I just, well, help out...Dawn...with...Some stuff..."

The chopped up reply told more by what it didn't say than by what it did. *But I have a feeling,* the Writer felt sure, *that some answers will be soon forthcoming, and they'll likely be some "royally fucked up" answers," to use the parlance of the day...*

She unlocked another door, on which a plaque read NO ADMITTENCE, and the Writer, naturally, winced. *They spelled admittance wrong!* This next, heavier door closed behind them, and the sound of Snowie relocking it echoed as if in a large, hard-walled space. They stood in darkness but up ahead was a bright light over a table–a table with a sheet-covered figure atop it. *Corpus delicti,* thought the Writer. *But surely this isn't the monster, the Bighead.* If anything the figure beneath the sheet appeared thin, frail, not much more than five feet tall. Hardly a monster.

And did the Writer really expect to see a *monster* in any case?

A door behind the table banged open, a figure approached

but quickly turned to silhouette once the bright light was behind it. "Thank God, you brought beer!"

"Hi, Dawn," Snowie greeted. "How's my favorite carpet muncher?"

"I don't know. If your dad was here, you could ask him."

"Yeah, well last night when I were a-suckin' off *your* dad, he say I do it *much better* than you."

"Well, what *your dad* last told me, when he paid me to put diapers on him and ass-bang him with a two-foot zucchini was that he was fucking *your* mouth before you even popped all the way out your mother's pussy. And he did it three times a day till you were five. He said he'd be damned if he'd spend good money on baby food for a baby *that* ugly. 'My cum's good enough for her,' he said."

Snowie retorted, "Yeah? Well how's 'bout I stick this whole six-pack up your dirty pussy? We both know it's big enough."

"Yeah?" Dawn came back, "and how about I put my foot so far up you corny ass you taste my nail polish?"

"Which foot? The real one or the metal one?"

"Both, and it'll be the best action you've had since the last time you went to the dog pound."

"Oh, yeah? Well—"

"Ladies! Ladies!" the Writer interrupted, for he'd had enough. "I thought you were friends! For Elysium's sake, you sound like mortal enemies!"

But now they were hugging. "Aw, we'se just funnin' with each other. Dawn's my best friend in the whole wide world," Snowie said. Then, "Dawn, this here's _____ ___, who's stayin' at the inn."

Dawn shook hands, still submerged in dark. "Hi, and thanks for the beer."

"My pleasure..."

The shapely silhouette continued, "You must be the writer I've been hearing about."

The Writer wilted. "Evidently, though I'm at a loss as to how *anyone* knew I'd be here."

But the oddity was forgotten. Dawn ordered, "Snowie, open three beers and put the rest in the fridge, and make it snappy."

Snowie's jaw dropped. "Who you think you'se're talkin' too, you bossy hussy? Just 'cos you was in the Army durn't mean you can order me around."

"No, it *durn't,* you uneducated hayseed. *I'se're* sorry. Make it snappy *please.*"

"That's better," and Snowie took the six-pack through another door.

Dawn led the Writer to the table where the light enabled him to discern her details. She appeared 30ish, five-foot-two or three, curvaceous and plush, just short of chubby–a woman with some "meat on her bones," the locals might phrase it. She wore Army pants—BDU's, he believed they were called—and an OD green t-shirt stretched impressively by breasts that rivaled Snowie's. Dark hair was pinned into a lump behind her head.

And she'd *limped* to the table, which recalled Snowie's remark about "which foot."

"So," Dawn said, "you're Tubesteak's stand in, huh?"

The Writer's eyes widened but fixed on nothing. "I, um..."

"Me and Snowie'll do most of the dirty work, you just gotta raise the lumber, if you know what I mean. And that ain't easy, especially if it's your first time. But don't worry. We'll get you up, then we'll cock ring you. The rest is cake. And there's a fifty in it for ya."

The words she'd spoken may as well have been Old

Gaelic. The Writer could only open his mouth but could give voice to nary an utterance.

Dawn's expression sharpened. "Snowie told you, right? You *do* know what this is all about, right?"

"To be precise," the Writer managed, "no. But I'm starting to get some inklings that I'd say are...discomfiting. Snowie only told me that she needed me to do something urgent, but didn't say what."

Dawn's face inflamed. "Damn her," she muttered, then yelled, "Snowie!"

"Comin'," came Snowie's nonchalant voice as she walked in with three opened beers. She smiled calmly, passing a bottle to each of them.

"Honeybunch?" Dawn asked. "Did you tell your friend here what we needed him to do?"

"Well, yeah," Snowie said, then, "I mean, no."

Dawn's lower lip jutted and her eyes bulged. "'Yeah,' but 'no?' Did you hear what you just said?"

"I didn't *'zactly* tell him, on account I thunk it best fer you to."

Dawn fumed. "Well you *thunk* wrong, you illiterate jizz for brains, pink-eyed bunny rabbit with tits! Why did you bring him here if he didn't say he'd do it!"

"Well, well, he did say he'd do it...kind of!"

The Writer raised his finger as an intercession. "If you will, please allow me to append. Yes, I *did* agree to do whatever this thing is you want me to do, in order to be let inside, but you never specified what the task was. And as I recall there was a condition or two."

"What conditions?" Dawn barked.

"Well, for one, I was promised I would receive, a—a—" but it just felt wrong for a refined Ivy League scholar to speak so crudely in front of women.

"A-a *what?*" Dawn demanded.

"A double blowjob," Snowie answered.

"Is that all? Well that's in the bag, no problem, but...," Dawn paused, eyeing the Writer intently. "That *isn't* all, is it?"

"No, it most certifiably is *not,*" the Writer answered. "Snowie also told me I would be shown what I presume to be the preserved cadaver of something of a *monster.* A thing or being known as the Bighead."

"YOU TOLD HIM *THAT?*" Dawn's voice thundered so loud that Snowie's yellowish-white hair billowed. "Did you drop your BRAIN in the fuckin' TOILET the last time you took a SHIT?"

"Quit yellin'!" Snowie yelled back. "We can trust him. He's a good friend."

"Good friend?" Dawn limped right up to Snowie and jabbed a finger into her chest. "So how long have you known this *good friend* of yours?"

Snowie shrugged defiantly. "Two hours at least, probably more like three."

"You *asshole!* Let a perfect stranger get you drunk and now you've spilled the beans on everything! Why, I oughta—"

"Oughta *what,* cripple?"

The two "best friends" lunged, and what ensued can only be described as a Redneck Chick Fight in the grand style. They collapsed to the concrete floor, grappling amid sundry curses and insults. The Writer could almost see Batman and Robin-style legends blooming over the scene: *BAM! POW! Kuh-KRACK!* Interesting as this spectacle may have been, the opportunity could not be resisted; the Writer could get out of here now and they'd be none the wiser. *As I believe the idiom goes: it's time for me to blow this pop-stand,* and he stalked for the door, turned the knob but—

70

Locked! And no inside catch!

He sighed and returned to the melee, where Dawn struggled to keep Snowie's clacking teeth from biting her face. Then she expertly rolled the albiness over and—

"Oww!" Snowie bellowed.

—bit Snowie hard right on the breast.

"Fuck this shit, bitch!" Snowie pledged. "I'm killin' ya!"

"Only thing you could kill is a pack of cockroaches with your b.o.!"

Snowie replied to the remark by eye-poking Dawn so hard she fell backward, a hand to her face, howling. Snowie guttered laughter, wrapped her legs around Dawn's right leg, and started yanking on her ankle.

"You cunting whore!" Dawn bellowed.

"You're *hoppin'* home tonight, honey!"

Dawn's right pant leg had been pulled up to her knee, revealing a metal rod with a shoe on the end—a prosthesis, her real leg being gone several inches below the knee. Snowie grinned like an Africa devil mask as she endeavored to detach the artificial limb.

True, the Writer still had very little memory but he thought it was a good bet that never in his life had he witnessed anything so absurd as this: an albino with large breasts struggling to remove the artificial leg of an amputee who also had large breasts, all on a mortuary floor.

He set down his beer which he hadn't even had time to sip, pulled Snowie backward by her hair, and shouted, "Ladies! Ladies! Stop right this moment! This is maniacal and no way for two adults to engage themselves, much less two friends! For goodness sake, there's enough fighting in the world already. You girls ought to be ashamed of yourselves!"

Both women pouted at each other.

"Apologize, both of you," the Writer demanded in a rare

display of authority.

"Well, shee-it," Snowie said. "I'se sorry I called ya cripple."

Dawn gulped. "And I'm sorry I bit your tit and said your face could stop an M1 tank with no brakes."

Snowie mulled it over. "But...you never said that."

"I was about to."

Both girls erupted laughter and were hugging and kissing moments later.

Are all women like this? the Writer wondered. "Excellent. And now that that's settled, we need to get back to the matter at hand."

"Oh, yeah," Snowie said. She and Dawn both looked at the table.

"Just let me out of here so I can go back to my hotel and get some sleep," the Writer said, retrieving his beer. "Whatever it is you need me to do, I'm afraid you'll have to do it without me."

"Well, there's a big problem with that," Dawn began. "We're in a pickle, Snowie and me, and if you don't do this for us, Snowie and me'll have to leave town right now."

The Writer was befuddled. "Why on earth would you have to do that?"

"Because if we stay, we'd both probably be dead by early morning."

The Writer took a good hard pull on is beer. *Ah, the pause that refreshes!* "I just don't understand. How would you come to be *dead?*"

"There's no time to explain! What's the big deal? All you gotta do is"—she turned, grabbed the sheet, and flapped it off the mortuary table. To no surprise, a corpse lay beneath. The Writer's eyes froze on it. The decedent was a female, and from the neck to her toes quite attractive. The legs were long, sleek; the breasts full, high, barely subject to gravity; the pubis a delicate pink groove rimmed by blond fur. "See?" Snowie said. "She ain't bad lookin', huh? Just...durn't look at the face."

But the Writer *was,* and the face was but a charred, crisped mask. Burned. And all of her hair was burned off as well. "Snowie, this is the woman those four brothers raped and set on fire at the general store!"

Snowie made a stray glance. "Yeah, shore is. But like I said, she got what was comin' to her. I hate druggies. Give our fine town a bad name."

The Writer jerked his gaze back to Dawn as if to beseech her.

"I'll put it all out in black and white, mister. We need you to fuck this dead chick. Now. While we videotape it."

The Writer could only stare, which seemed reasonable.

Then Dawn said the strangest thing. "Hey, Snowie, did you..."

"Uh-huh," came Snowie's very slow reply.

"You're a genius!" and then they were hugging and kissing again.

Meanwhile, the severity of this outrageous circumstance began to...dwindle in the Writer's awareness, while at the same time he began to feel very, very good. He slid his hand over his crotch and noted that his penis was growing very, very erect.

Wow...

It didn't occur to him that he'd been drugged until both women were at his sides, slowly lowering him to the floor. "Careful he doesn't fall," Dawn instructed. "We don't want to the poor bastard hitting his head..." The Writer looked open-eyed at the ceiling, and found it intriguing.

Both women were back on their feet. They looked down

at him much like two mourners looking down into a grave.

Next, Dawn said, "Get his pants off. I'll get the camera..."

The Writer's consciousness floated happily away into darkness.

***

He was wandering, aimless yet content, through a dense forest, and immediately thought of Robert Frost. *Whose woods these are I think I know...*His footfalls took him over the forest's carpet of twigs, leaves, and detritus, all without sound, and that's when he realized there was no sound at all, anywhere–an impossibility. How could this be?

But, of course, it was all a dream.

On he went, then, in this pleasant and utterly silent oblivion. It occurred to him that no tree in this wood had ever felt the blade of the ax, and no human had yet traversed this space. Next he thought of Henry David Thoreau living on Ralph Waldo Emerson's land and writing *On Walden Pond.* What luxury there was in true transcendentalism! The Writer thought back: *Wasn't there an alternate title? A Life in the Woods?* Oh, how the Writer would embrace such a life...No people. No machines. No hypocrisy and—and—and—

No cellphones!

***

But here the comfort of stray musings ceased, for suddenly there was a sound, and with it a potent redolence. The sound: footfalls, steady, deliberate, and clearly bipedal. The redolence: the musk of the human female.

The Writer backed up against a stout tree, suddenly trembling, suddenly asweat. *Sounds like it's going to pass right by me,* but then he caught a breath in his chest. Why had he instinctively thought *it* and not *she?*

And why the sheer terror?

The footfalls grew louder, that steady crunching over the forest floor, and as they neared, they brought with them something like *impact.* The Writer feared that his teeth might chatter aloud, or like the Poe story, that his heart might beat loud enough to be heard...

The interloping woman stalked right by him as expected, but—*Heaven be praised!*—she did not notice him. Why would he be so fearful of a woman?

One glimpse assured him that fear was more than reasonable: she was nude, erotically curvatured, with long toned legs, a buttocks like a work of art, yet in each hand she grasped a severed head, while her own head was not human at all but horned and, indeed, bovid.

The head of an ox.

The creature disappeared amid the trees in moments. *Like the Minotaur in the tale of Theseus saving Atticka, only THIS was female,* he reckoned. *Not a Minotaur.*

A Minotauress...

More footsteps locked him in rigor against the tree; these were quicker, more shambling. Would it be the male counterpart, pursuing its mate?

No. No, it would *not.*

Sheer terror notwithstanding, the Writer clamped a hand to his mouth in order not to laugh. What ventured past him this time was, to put it forthright, a giant erect penis on two human legs. A great sack of flesh dangled as it plodded forward, satcheling two testicles slightly larger than basketballs.

Now the Writer sighed. *Of all the preposterous things.* No fear struck him when more rustling approached. Another, a third beast of the forest was coming and the Writer had a funny feeling it would be not terrifying but, instead, ridiculous.

And ridiculous it was.

He frowned, shaking his head, as a butterscotch-colored rabbit hopped by. It was the size of a St. Bernard.

I'd say I definitely stumbled down the wrong rabbit hole today...

Disgusted with the nonsensical waste of time his sleeping brain was inflicting on him, he continued his desultory wandering, hardly caring now about the beauty of the woods and the luxury of transcendentalism. *FUCK Robert Frost, and FUCK Thoreau!* he thought with an ample ire. *Shit, Thoreau ate dinner at Emerson's house every night. That's not living off the land! Walden's Pond is all bullshit!*

All he wanted now was to walk out of this dream...and in a sense, he did. From out of hackneyed nowhere, he was standing before a water's edge, and a lake of substantial dimensions. Hillbilly rock and roll jangled from a boombox ("I'm gonna buy me a graveyard of my own, kill everyone who ever done me wrong...") next to a cooler full of beer. The thought of beer enlivened him...until he saw a score of crushed cans lying about. *Ugh!* Keystone Light. But a turn of his head showed him a matter far more grievous than undrinkable beer. He was instantly watching an unwatchable scene, and witnessing events that were indescribable.

However they will be described nonetheless...

At the water's edge there sat parked a gleaming jet-black 1969 Chevy El Camino, with an expanded hood in order to house a street-illegal engine. On the multi-lacquered hood rested the open-mouthed, open-eyed severed head of a blond woman, before which stood a portly young man with a crew cut. His jeans were down to his knees, and he masturbated with what could only be called *precision,* intermittently glazing his corona over the tip of the head's lolling tongue. The Writer knew immediately who this man was: Dicky Caudill.

Another denim-panted man knelt on the ground and was engaged in an activity far worse than Dicky's exploit. It was a long-haired, wiry, muscular man with chopburns, wearing a ball cap that advertized chewing tobacco. *Balls Conner,* the Writer knew at once. Before "Balls" lay a headless woman divested of all garb, and easily eight-and-a-half months pregnant. Her thighs had been tied together so to prevent miscarriage. Balls, pants opened, straddled the corpse and was slowly inserting and withdrawing his erect penis in and out of an obvious wound in the lower quadrant of the woman's belly. A bayonet on the ground told the tale of how the wound had come to be.

"Fuck, Dicky, I'm gonna bust right away, feels so good, it does!" Balls related with enthusiasm.

But Dicky hadn't heard, too focused was he on the task, literally, at hand. He quivered, rose to tiptoes, while his love-handles jiggled beneath a double extra-large t-shirt which read BASTIN SAWKS CACK. The fat man's back began to arch as he grunted "Uh-uh-uh-uh!" in a comical sight, and when the crisis arrived, he shucked his penis like a corn ear, doing his best to ejaculate into the severed head's mouth.

Balls' crisis arrived almost simultaneously. He palmed the great gravid belly before him, thrusting, thrusting, then– "Ahhhhhh, there she blows, Dicky! I'se a-fillin' this here preggo creeker the fuck *up,* I is!"

Dicky faced the spectacle now, for some reason pulling on his now-flaccid penis. He giggled as an over-excited retarded person might. "Yuh-yuh-yuh shore did, Balls! Yuh shore did!"

Now Balls was standing and pulling his flaccid penis as well. He seemed to ponder an overwhelming question. "Gee, I'se wonder if...well, if the baby in 'er is a girl, I wonder if maybe I knocked it up..."

"Could be, Balls," Dicky said, impressed by the possibility. He put the blond woman's head in the beer cooler, no doubt, for partying later.

Balls was hitching up his pants. "Yes sir! Nothin' like a good ole fashioned belly-fuckin.' Gettin' a good nut an' doin' society a service at the same time! These cracker bitches all the time gettin' knocked up on purpose just so's to git the welfare."

"Dang straight, Balls, dang straight." Dicky put the cooler and boombox in the vehicle's back bed.

"Yeah, way I figger, 'tis any man's patriotic duty to belly-fuck these knocked up trailer trash 'ho's ands cut off their heads. Keep down the surplus population, and helps fix the deffer-sit." Before he zipped up, Balls urinated for an unimaginably long time on the pregnant, headless corpse. "And what they'se knocked up with is anyone's guess. Mexakins, Colored, Injins, Moozlims—shee-it. Only white dudes ta ever knock *these* hosebags up is their daddies 'er brothers. What's the world comin' too?"

Another minute more ticked by in Balls voiding his very full bladder on the headless woman. The belly shined like a wet, white beach ball (well, in a manner of speaking, since beach balls weren't generally tattooed with the words FUCK ME TO HELL'N BACK!) Balls started to zip up.

"Dang, Balls," Dicky pointed out. "Cain't believe ya wasted yer pee like that. You ain't yerself lately."

Balls cut a sneer. "What'choo talkin' 'bout, Dicky? Ain't *myself?*"

"Guess you're too worried 'bout the 'conomy'n the

welfare'n all. See, any other time you wouldn't'a thunk twice. The Balls Conner *I* know would never've peed on a gal he just belly-fucked. He'd've peed in the hole he fucked her in."

Balls looked at the glistening corpse, then slapped himself in the head. "Dang, Dicky! What the hail's wrong with me fer not thinkin' of that!"

"'Twas just sayin', you know? Stands ta reason, ya just done come all over that baby inside, might as well pee all over it too." Dicky chuckled. "Bet her belly'd git all swole up like a water balloon."

"Shee-it! I'se *hate it* when I forgit important shit! When we'se done at the Crafter House, we gotta find us another preggered gal! "

"Shore thing, Balls. 'Twon't be too hard, not 'round these parts."

"Dang right. Come on, let's git," said Balls, dejected with himself. Both men got in the car. The doors thunked closed, then the earth shook when Dicky started the 750hp engine and sped off, leaving a screen of dust.

Was it just the veil of the mechanism called dreaming that made the Writer certain he'd known these men?

Or did I know them for real?

He contemplated abstrusions, orphic enigmas, and oblique strategies, all while exerting every effort not to look at the dead pregnant woman. He could swear that something had moved beneath the belly...

Yes, he knew full well that he'd seen those two men before, long before they'd died. For real, not merely in the dream. And he knew something else...

He knew he'd heard of the Crafter House, and a name to go with it: Ephriam Crafter.

But in the next blink, all musing disintegrated when

suddenly he was gagging, surrounded by a stench like the worst body odor imaginable, intensified a hundredfold. He was about to collapse to his knees but alarm prevented it. His temperature dropped, his sweat chilled. He felt a massive, almost palpable shadow cover the ground in front of him.

It was no man who looked down at him; it was a malformed *thing,* seven, maybe eight feet tall. It had a hand-breadth the size of a dinner plate. Through the horrific stench, the Writer noticed that the thing wore overalls and had a huge bulge at its crotch. Then it palmed the Writer's head like a basketball, lifted him aloft, and opened a black maw for a mouth rimmed by what looked like a dog's teeth. When that mouth closed over the Writer's face, he either lost consciousness or died...

***

Who was credited with the infamously hackneyed line, *It was a dark and stormy night?* The Writer wasn't sure for he'd read very little horror fiction but he thought it must be *Last Days of Pompeii* author Baron Edward Bulwer-Lytton. Perhaps then the Baron was credited too with the equally hackneyed line, *He awoke in a cold sweat.* At any rate, that's exactly how the Writer awoke on his first morning in Luntville. His head felt stuffed with cotton; his eyes took no short time to focus. Then he realized he lay fully clothed atop his bed in Room 6 of the Due Drop In. His long hair was pasted to his brow, his boring white button-down shirt was pasted to his body with sweat. The horrific dream wheeled back into his mind, and he thought he might scream aloud.

Those two sociopaths—Dicky and Balls—and what they were *doing...*

The Writer was trapped in the notion that he'd met them before. He was *certain* of it. And he was certain of something else:

I know damn well I've been to the Crafter house...

Grim as the nightmare had been—not to mention that mammoth, rotten-meat-stinking thing that had been one heartbeat short of eating off his face—he knew that this was cause for celebration.

More memories are returning!

Memories from long ago, yes. But what of those of the shorter-term variety?

He sat up in bed, confused. *What happened to me last night?* He remembered being at the tavern, and he remembered talking to Snowie, but...

That was it.

Must've gotten drunk. Great way to make a first impression. He could almost feel his body creak when he got up and staggered to the bathroom. He had to urinate like the proverbial racehorse, but when he opened his pants to engage in the task—

The memory lodged in his head with the immediacy of a bullet.

Once again in a rare departure from sophistication, he thought *Holy mother-fucking-SHIT! Those girls drugged me and made me fuck a corpse!*

What triggered this decidedly horrific recollection was nothing more than this: the black rubber ring he discovered on his penis when he extracted it to urinate. A woman's voice, sharp as a violin string, penetrated his mind's ear: *We'll get you up, then we'll cock ring ya. The rest is cake.*

Cake, indeed!

A stupefying smell wafted up, and when the Writer reckoned its source, his stomach began to convulse as though a hand were opening and closing over it. Of course, the revolting smell was that of the one-night-old remnants of what could only be defined as "pussy-stink," which in this case was far worse than the usual sort because *this* "pussy" was *dead.*

Would the Writer actually vomit from the smell and the recollection of how it got there?

Yes!

He fell to his knees with a painful *double-thunk and* vomited like a hand-crank bilge pump into the white porcelain receptacle.

Up it all came, up and out of him, one urp after the next. Ropes of vomit-flecked slime dangled off his lips like jungle vines; the bug-eyed reflection of his face in the toilet water was not fortifying to contemplate. *I am absolutely MORTIFIED!*

He showered in an enraged fog, scrubbing his privates like an excessive-compulsive. *My penis was in a DEAD woman last night!*

It seemed his shear anger had burned off the hangover. *Have I EVER been this mad before?* He was dressed and out the door without a second thought, nearly bumping into another guest. "Pardon me," he said in a rush. "Of course, brother," replied the guest. He was thirtyish, longish styled hair, in blue jeans and a sports jacket. "But remember, God pardons us *all,* for *all* our worldly sins, as long as we beseech Him. He's the great King above all gods–do you hear me, brother?" "Indeed," the Writer responded, rushing by. "Consciousness, or the subjective awareness known as qualia, proves beyond all doubt that God exists. The tenet is called Cartesian Dualism."

"But, my friend, have you heard me?"

No doubt this was the televangelist, Tommy Something.

"Yes!" the Writer nearly yelled. "It's all elemental! The egg *had* to come before the chicken! Therefore, only a Supreme Being could have invented the egg! It's called the Law of the First Cause! Read Kant, and Descartes! Read St. Anselm, read Leibniz!" and then the Writer took long strides to the stairs, leaving the guest slack-jawed.

I am so fuckin' pissed! the Writer thought, nearly stumbling down the steps. He passed the framed sketch of the long-faced man without so much as a glance. Foreboding looks from other dour portraits seemed to follow him down. No one tended the front desk. *Who to confront first?* he wondered heatedly. *Snowie or Dawn?* Snowie was probably at work at the general store, which was too far to walk. He considered renting a car but then remembered that in spite of his license, he didn't really know how to drive. So...

Dawn it is...

He pounded out the front doors and strode down the street in the direction, of course, of the funeral home. The town looked not quite so desolate in daytime but his anger circumvented any possibility of his taking note. All he *did* notice, however briefly, was the trashed lot between the two strip malls, and the corroded 1969 El Camino sitting there on long flattened tires. *I saw that same exact car in my dream— brand new! Fuck! What a fucked up dream!*

He trod determinedly down the main drag. Several passersby shot him curious looks; the curtains in several windows opened, paused, then closed. All the Writer could see with any clarity was the tincture of his anger. He was not a man generally given to any kind of emotion, nor the kind to "break bad" or to pursue confrontations. Instead, his nature was that of an inert spectator so that he might observe the emotions and confrontations of *others,* then analyze them for his writing.

Not so today.

The ornate funeral home door shook when he pounded it with his fist. It flung open quickly to reveal an exasperated Dawn, who whispered fiercely, "The door's open! Don't knock it down!" only to pause upon recognizing the knocker. "There he is! The man of the hour!" She gave him a big hug and lengthy kiss.

The Writer's tirade stalled when he noted her appearance. Gone was the dowdy green Army t-shirt, and no more were the baggie camouflage pants. Now she dressed smartly in black shiny-cotton slacks, a pair of mid-heel black pumps, and a dark cardigan which made no secret of her eminent bosom without being too forthright. This new look was finished by modest eyeliner and makeup.

"Why, you look quite fetching today," the Writer said, taken aback.

"Thanks," she said, eyes fluttering. "Had to play dress-up this morning 'cos we had a viewing." She led him in and he noticed two men in work boots putting the casket in the viewing room on a roller. "Let's go to the office," she said.

Halfway down the sedate hall, the Writer remembered why he was here; he grabbed Dawn's arm, turned her around in a near-violent action, and said, "I'm mad as hell! You girls drugged me last night and made me have intercourse with a cadaver, didn't you?"

"Why don't you say it a little louder so the transport guys hear you!"

"You did, didn't you?"

"Yes! So what?"

His eyes crossed. "So *what?* Is that what you said?"

"In here!" she snapped, pulled him into a non-descript office, and closed the door. "We had no choice! Those psychos would probably have killed me and Snowie if we hadn't."

"Psycho? Who? You mean those men moving the coffin?"

Dawn sat down at a desk, wincing. "No, no, not them. Paulie and Augie. Jeez, didn't that moronic bleach-faced bumpkin tell you *anything?*"

"You mean Snowie?"

"Of course! You know any other moronic bleach-faced bumpkins? We had a clip to deliver, and if those two psychopaths came out here and we *didn't* have a clip, they'd use *us* in the *next* clip! You know, snuff films, torture and rape clips, shit like that."

The Writer's eyes bloomed on her. "I have virtually *no conception* of what you're saying."

Dawn's impressive bosom rose when she took a long breath. "This is the scoop, all right? Listen. We got this *thing,* see? For *money,* see? We got this *deal* with these two guys my boss introduced me to but now my boss is in a fucking nursing home so I have to run the whole gig. See?"

"No, I *don't* see," spake the Writer.

"There's no economy in this shit-bucket town. No jobs, no way to earn cash. There's a minimum wage Wendy's, a couple piss-ant stores, and that's about it. Only reason Snowie's got the job as the general store is 'cos the owner's one of the albino clan. Corn liquor's covered by Snot McKully and Clyde Nayle, and anyone tries to compete with *them,* they disappear. And anyone stupid enough to sell drugs in these parts, the Larkins brothers take care of them. Food cards and Section 8 housing, that's what keeps this ass-crack from dying out completely. I do workups and funerals here but that amounts to peanuts, couple hundred a month, if that. I get two grand a month from VA for my leg, but every penny of it goes to my father's meds because fuckin' Medcaid won't cover the shit. So I got *no choice,* see? I *have* to do side work for Paulie; otherwise me and my father would be homeless. I can't leave him, and I can't move 'cos he's too sick to travel."

*A commendable sacrifice...*But she'd mentioned that name—Paulie—several times. The Writer tempered himself against the steaming swath of confusion. Very slowly he asked, "Dawn? Who the FUCK is Paulie?"

She consulted a desk drawer and produced a fifth of whiskey: Black Velvet. "I need a shot," she said as if desperate. "You?"

"No. No, thank you. Whiskey in a plastic bottle goes beyond my limits of tolerance."

She shrugged, down a shot, and sighed. "Paulie," she repeated. "A.k.a Paul Vinchetti the Third. He's a mob boss with the Monstroni, Leone, Vinchetti crime triad. *Mafia.* Get it? It ain't just the Godfather and Johnny Depp movies. There really is a Mafia, and they're all over the place. Paulie controls all the smack in the big cities around here. Charleston, Parkersburg, Huntington, those places. Pills, too. Vicodin, Oxy, Roxy, that shit. It's all counterfeited from China and Iran and Canada. Big business. But Paulie also handles all the Hard Underground on the east coast, I guess 'cos he's one of the few mob bosses sick in the head enough to handle it."

"Hard Underground?" the Writer questioned. "You mean pornography?"

She laughed. "Pornography is xHamster, Clips4sale, and Bang Brothers. Hard Underground's what the feds call felonious pornography. Snuff, Scat, KP, 'wet' torture, and nek." She stared the Writer down. "Snowie and me don't have anything to do with hurting or killing people. We only do nek clips."

Even in his sheltered naivety, the Writer instantly deduced, "Nek. Necrophilia."

"Uh-huh, and what's the big deal? No harm, no foul. The only victims are dead people, dead *criminals.* So my conscious is clean, and my father and I don't have to sleep under the interstate bridge."

So it was that simple? The Writer kept staring. "You had no right to drug me—"

"You're right, and we're sorry, but we had no choice," she said matter-of-factly. "Paulie knew the chick's corpse was here because the ambulance drivers are on his payroll, see? So he calls me from a blind phone and tells me to do the clip and have it ready for pickup by morning, see? I told him no problem because I didn't know Tubesteak was at some fuckin' Boy Scout thing with his kids. Snowie said she told me that last week but the stupid skillet-head left the message on my old phone, and we got no way to call Paulie back to tell him it's a no-go. So it boils down to this, see? Either me and Snowie provide a clip of someone banging the dead girl, or Paulie puts me and Snowie in the cremator, alive, and films it."

An untoward perspective, he thought. But then: "You should've just called the police!"

She downed another shot. "Don't make me laugh. The police won't *touch* Paulie Vinchetti, not even the state troopers. They're *afraid* of him. Last guy to fuck with Paulie? Was a captain with the sheriff's department. Paulie had the guy abducted, brought him here, and...Can you guess what happened? Paulie put the guy in the cremator, alive, and filmed it."

"Oh...dear..."

"Then he emailed the clip to every police headquarters in the state. So you tell me. What would *you* do? You have the choice between fucking a dead girl or going into the cremator, *alive,* what would you choose?"

The writer was at a sore loss. "I'm incapable of arguing against logic so multifarious, but..."

"And I still don't see what you're complaining about," she said. "First guy I ever met to complain about a free piece of ass."

The Writer exploded, "It was a DEAD piece of ass!"

Did her hair really fly back at the gust of his outrage? "For fuck's sake!" She jumped up, tore out of the room, but returned a moment later, relieved. "We're lucky those transport guys are gone. Listen, you can't tell *anyone* about this. It's a first degree felony."

"I'm guilty of no such thing. I was drugged unconscious and manipulated against my will."

She chuckled. "You fucked a cadaver for money. 'Nuff said."

"What money? I never—"

"I told you you were in for a fifty. We put it in your wallet. Didn't you check?"

"Of course, I didn't," he began to shout, but then discovered a double folded $50 bill in his wallet. *Oh, for the sake of Robespierre!*

"So just forget it," she went on. "We'd be dead if it weren't for you, and I can tell you, me and Snowie *take care* of anyone who helps us out of a jam. You wanna see the clip? We always make a dupe for a safety. It's great!"

The Writer's eyes bugged, as they'd been doing a lot of late. "No. I *don't* want to see the clip—"

"*Perfect* cream-pie, man," she reflected. "I had two cameras pulling the g-y-n shot, one was my macro. When Snowie pulled the dead chick's hips off your wood? Fuck! Never saw so much nut from one shot in my life! That was *some* rod work, I'll tell ya. Hand's down, you were the best dead-girl cream-pie we ever filmed."

This arcane terminology: "g-y-n shot," "dead-girl cream-pie," "rod work," "nut." He supposed he could estimate their definitions but, like Melville's "Bartleby," he simply preferred not to. Questions of a more incise nature occurred to him next. "What drug did you use to render me unconscious?"

She reconsulted the desk drawer, and handed him a small glass bottle, which he read with scrutiny: *ORAMORPH MS-IR, 5 mg/mL, Xanodyne Pharmaceuticals.*

"*Liquid heroin!*" he railed.

"Yeah. Colorless, tasteless, odorless." She grinned ever so minutely. "You were out like a light, *big* smile on your face. Then we pulled your pants down, lifted Little Miss Dead Junkie off the table, flipped her over, and lowered her onto your cock. We've done it many times. When the job was done, we took you back to the motel in Snowie's mom's car, and dragged you up the back stairs to your room. You really should lose some weight. I've carried wounded G.I.'s in full field gear over my back who weighed less than you. No offense."

"None taken!" the Writer spat.

"Then I detoxed you with an IM injection of Naloxone. Opioid blocker."

"Diabolical. And how is it possible that I managed *sexual intercourse* with this...*decedent* while in a state of unconsciousness? How could an erection be possible, since male arousal is dependant on not only physical stimulus but also synaptic activity in the brain that sends messages to the penis to effect erection? If a man is drugged unconscious I wouldn't think erection to be possible."

"I don't know about all that," she dismissed, "but you were hard as a fuckin' Coke bottle. I also put a few drops of Sildenafil Citrate oral solution in your beer, but you were obviously pulling wood even before you started drinking it."

Intriguing, he thought despite the full-blown ludicrousness of this conversation.

"You'd be a natural for this gig if your cock was bigger," she added, then, "Er, no offense."

He ground his teeth. "None taken..."

"Relax, stud. In the corpse-fucking business the size of the dick doesn't matter much. It's all about the size of the *load.* And, man, you cum more than Peter North."

The Writer's face screwed up. "Peter...*Who?* Isn't he the majority leader in the Canadian Parliament?"

"Never mind. Jut trust me, you shoot huge loads, I mean, one of your loads is like two of Tubesteak's on a really good day. *That's* saying something."

What has my life come to? he wondered. *My seminal volume is being compared quite favorably to a man named TUBESTEAK...*

"And like I said," she went on, "The boner was no problem. Your junk sunk right into her cooze like a champ, then you blew the gusher load, and *still* kept your wood. We cock-ringed you after that just to be safe, then you had another go. You came that time too. It was *beautiful.*"

This overflow of insane information was warping the Writer's perspective to near incognizance. *In the name of Caesar Augustus...Another GO...*

"Guess you haven't been laid in a while, huh?" came her next crudity. "That was a *lot* of spunk you had built up."

Her observation reached deep into his mind; he stared at it through narrowed eyes. *I don't remember EVER having sex, and what if I haven't? What if I'd gone 58 years without ever having sex and now...*His hands began to shake. *I've lost my male virginity to a cadaver...*

He shook his head violently to try and dislodge some of this madness. "So. You filmed me. You filmed me having sex

90

with a corpse. Have I got this right?"

"Yep."

"And people will see this demented video clip?"

"Of course," she said. "Paulie sells them for big money."

"Ah, so...My *face* is on this clip, in the act of a heinous first-degree felony? For all the world to see?"

Dawn frowned. "We're not idiots, man. Of course not. Snowie and me are in these clips too. We all wear *masks.* I'm Herman, Snowie's Grandpa, and you're Eddie."

The Writer's mouth hung open. Herman. Grandpa. Eddie. "The-the *Munsters?*"

"You got it." Another reach into the drawer and next she displayed the plastic Halloween masks.

That's them, he thought, amused for the first time of the day. Herman Munster, Grandpa Munster, and Eddie Munster.

She began, "It's an old TV show from the—"

"I *know* what it is!" he snapped. "It was my favorite show as a child. So you're telling me that no one will see my face in this, this, this—"

"That's right," she assured him. "No one will see *you,* they'll see *Eddie* putting the blocks to that corpse. Shit, I used to be a big trivia fan. Who's the actor who played Eddie? Billy Mumy?"

"No, no, that was from *Lost in Space.* Eddie Munster was played by a boy named Butch Patrick."

She thought a second. "You're right!"

Of COURSE I'm right, he finished in thought.

"So, see? Everything's cool."

But yet another thought pricked him, one with some sting. "Things are hardly *cool!* Do you have any idea of the health hazard you subjected me to last night? A dead drug addict and prostitute? Probably full of untold pathogens and bacteria!"

"Gimme a break," she smirked. "Snowie and me have to *go down* on these dead chicks. We have to lick their *ass cracks* for the camera. I PC every square inch of these dead tramps."

"PC?" the Writer asked.

Once again she resorted to the desk drawer and was next showing him a green spray bottle the size of a 409 bottle. The Writer was flabbergasted by the label on it: *PATH CLOUD, the world's leading brand of cadaver disinfectant!*

"There. Happy now? We gotta fuck with these corpses too. That girl last night? I pumped her stomach, lavaged her entire g.i. tract, sanitized her from head to toe, and douched her out with the PC. There wasn't a germ on her. That was the cleanest her pussy's been in, like, *ever.*"

Oh. Well. That's good, I guess. It seemed the Writer was running out of things to be infuriated about. *What's done is done, and like she just said. No harm, no foul. I guess.* "It's a curious irony, though, if you think about it. The hapless woman who is being interred in her coffin right now was engaged in intercourse with me not twelve hours ago."

Dawn made an uncomprehending face. "Huh? Oh, you mean the coffin those guys were taking out of here just now?"

"Why, yes. I presumed that was woman I...the woman from last night."

"No, no, that was Mr. McGillicutty. Twisted old fuck. That old crinkle-faced bastard lived ninety-two years, and he raised hell for every single one of them. Heart attack a few nights ago, did the town a favor. One of his sons paid for the casket and funeral. Not too long from now that stick-in-the-mud'll taking the dirt nap forever. Good riddance, I say."

The Writer raised a finger. "So...what happened to the girl I...the girl from last night?"

Dawn raised both brows. "Let me put it this way. She

entered the building through the back door. She exited the building through the chimney."

*My God. They cremate the evidence...*But still, there was something..."Wait a minute, miss. The way I see it, you and Snowie owe me a, well..."

"We gave you your double blow job last night," she said.

"I was *unconscious!*"

"Quit bellyaching, will ya? All right, we'll give you another one later."

He raised his finger again. "Well, that remains to be seen, and you're skirting the more salient issue, aren't you? Wasn't I promised something else as well?"

Dawn calmly downed another shot and finally put the bottle away. "What do you mean?"

"I was promised I'd be shown the body of the *thing* known as the Bighead," the Writer declared with resolution, "which is somewhere in this facility, according to Snowie."

"That stupid cunt." Dawn released a long sigh. Then she stood up. "All right. A deal's a deal. Come on."

If the word *flabbergastment* existed, then that was the look on the Writer's face. "You're—you're telling me it really is here?"

"Yeah, come on. You wanna see it, fine. I'll show it to you." She opened the office door.

The Writer followed her, stumbling. "So you're—you're *serious?*"

"Serious as the Black Death," she said, leading in a quick limp. "Come on, let's get this over with. I hate looking at the thing."

This was more confounding than all else. He'd never really believed there was a monster...had he? "But it's not really a monster, right?" he asked desperately. "It's got to be just, like, a man with some grievous deformity. Right?"

"No. It's a monster. And you can't tell anyone, *ever.* You got that?"

"Of course, but—"

They passed through the work-up room, passed the now unoccupied morgue table, went through another door down a dark, chemical scented corridor. A small bare bulb was mounted over a very large metal door bordered by bolted steel struts. No knob was visible, just a heavy circular keyway.

Dawn produced a key, was about to insert it when–

"But-but," the Writer continued to stammer. His hesitation was a surprising occurrence. Was he afraid that the myth was true, and that his conception of reality might be damaged beyond repair? "I—I...wait—this is happening too fast. I need to assimilate potentialities. I have to prepare myself, you know, for the limits of cogitability and reckoning—"

Dawn winced. *"What?"*

"More information is needed," he struggled. "Like what exactly *is* the thing behind this door? Where did it come from? Why is it here?"

"That's a two-hour story, man! Do you wanna see it or not?"

Before the Writer could answer, the front doorbell rang.

She glanced at her watch. "Fuck. That's Wally Eberhart; his wife is about to kick from liver disease and he wants to coffin-shop. I gotta go." She withdrew the key from the lock, unturned, then was nudging him back down the hall and out. "I'll see ya tonight."

"Tonight?"

"Yeah," she said. "You can meet me and Snowie at the Crossroads and buy us drinks with that fifty you earned." She winked, then abruptly lassoed her arms around his neck and kissed him on the mouth. She ran the tip of her tongue across the seam of his lips. "And if you're a good boy, you'll get another double blowjob," and then she was scurrying away as best she could. "Go out the back door," then she called out ahead, "Be right there, Mr. Eberhart!"

The Writer thought that yesterday had to have been the most bizarre day of his life, but now he knew better. And once again his libidinal hormones were in heavy fluxion, a trait quite the opposite of his normal experience. The physical product of the uncanny arousal left him *uncomfortable.*

I should just go take a nap, came the idea as he walked out the back fire-exit. Outside, the sun blazed through distant trees. Along the rear brick wall rose the iron vent which was no doubt connected to the crematory. His dead paramour from last evening had escaped this mad world through that same vent, and with her, no doubt, so had some minuscule traces of his DNA. Reverted to smoke and now part of the sky...

Some tiny square thing at his feet gained his notice. *What have we here?* He picked it up: an SD card, for computers and such. He'd never used one but he believed that his laptop possessed the proper slot (or socket or receptacle of whatever it's called) to accommodate this type of miniature storage device. *Finders keepers,* he thought and put it in his pocket.

What now? He began to traverse the rear of the building, to regain the main street. He supposed it would be most practical to return to the Due Drop, unpack his laptop, and begin his book, picking up where that mysterious first page had left off. *It will be exhilarating!* Of course, not remembering writing any of the dozens of novels he'd written seemed to propose a high-order quandary. Yet the Writer was undaunted; he had *no doubt* of his ability to compose creative narrative. *I can sit down at that keyboard and start right away, without missing so much as one step.* It was a feeling of unprecedented satisfaction.

The satisfaction shattered after a few more strides.

A man was standing at the edge of the building, grinning. Like the Writer, he wore blue jeans, sneakers, and a white dress shirt, had longish hair and trimmed beard. *Unlike* the Writer he was slim and fit.

And his face looked *exactly* like the Writer's, minus the accrual of twenty or so years of age.

There he is! The guy who looks like me! "You there!" he called out.

The grinning face was pulled back out of view, its grin nearly leaving an after-image.

I'll get to the bottom of this right now! he resolved, and he started to run at the top of his speed, and after less than ten yards, he could run no longer.

Oh for pity's sake!

He huffed and puffed around the corner of the building and made the street. Sucking wind, he looked back toward town, and there was his double, jogging away. The man turned, noticed that his pursuer was too fat and old to pursue, and began to laugh.

Of all the brazen insults! I'm being laughed at, by ME... "Wait! Please!"

The double apparently lit a cigarette and moseyed on down the road, puffs of smoke in his wake.

The Writer sat down at a bench in front of a closed barber shop–*long* closed judging by the cobwebs in the window. *Drat!* he thought. *I grow old. I shall wear the bottoms of my trousers rolled. I have known the evenings, mornings, and afternoons. I have measured out my life with coffee spoons...,* he thought by way of T.S. Eliot–truly a melancholy verse. Then he simply thought, *Fuck!*

Eventually he was back on his way down the street. No sign remained of his younger twin, but the Writer had to wonder if he'd existed at all. *Side-effect of being drugged last night...* He was parched now and found himself approaching a lone soda machine in front of a closed Shell station. The machine was humming, which was a good sign. He dropped in four quarters, and an instant later, a can on Diet Coke clunked down the chute. He turned with a start—

A woman no more than twenty and likely younger was standing right next to him, provocatively dressed to say the least. Skin-tight pink shorts and a lumescent-yellow tubetop hammocking two pert breasts the size of breakfast muffins. A brunet bob with streaks of red and yellow dye. Large light-green eyes. "Hi, mister," she said. She was counting a handful of nickels. "Dang, I'se fifteen cents short. Ya think ya could loan me—"

"Certainly," the Writer said, and dropped four more quarters in to save time. He stepped aside and bid the machine.

"Why, thanks!" she enthused, and hit a button. "Don't you want none'a this?" she asked meaning the nickels in her hand.

"Not necessary. My treat."

"What a nice fella! Not many men like you 'round here." Her brows rose. "But you *ain't* from here, are ya? I'll bet you're the writer ever-one's talkin' about."

The Writer shrugged. "Evidently so. I'm traveling, I like to see different places to fuel my creative processes."

"Oh, ya mean fer books'n all."

"Exactly. For a novelist, locations work the same way different colors work for a painter."

"Cool! My daddy was a painter—painted houses. Let's go this way," she said, and he followed back toward the town center. "I wanna show ya wear I'se work. Oh, and my name's Junie, by the way."

"Pleased to make your acquaintance, Junie. My name is..." He frowned. "Just call me Writer. It's easier to pronounce." He could not help eyeing her lithe, creamy legs glowing in the sun as they walked along. *Damn!* "And where do you work? The Wendy's?"

"Naw, see, they's already on the leanest kind'a part time. I work for my ma at the spa. June's Spa it's called. June's my mother."

He indeed recalled the glowing neon sign her seen last night. "Oh, I see. Therapeutic massage, I take it."

She smiled. "Well, see, what'cha do is ya pay forty and ya git a table shower and massage, for a whole hour."

The Writer had precious little interest but enjoyed the small-talk which gave him an excuse to steal glances at her. *She's adorable!* "That sounds like a formidable bargain."

"Oh, shore, and then, see, ya pay twenty more to git'cher willy whacked, and if ya pay ten more on top'a that"—she held up her index finger—"you git the corn-finger."

The Writer's mouth opened. *CORN-finger? Probably NOT a new James Bond movie,* but after a moment's more thought, he got it. "Ah. I, uh, see. The corn-finger."

Junie chirped a giggle. "My ma, she's so funny! She say the way to a man's heart is through his stomach, but the way to his wallet is through his butthole!"

The Writer struggled for response. "I must say, your mother is a veritable font of wisdom."

Junie errantly grabbed his arm (which unsurprisingly steeped up his already cringing arousal) and said excitedly, "Oh, and here's somethin', but only if you can keep a secret."

"To you, Junie, I pledge my utmost confidence." *Probably just local gossip,* he suspected, *But where would, say, To Kill A Mockingbird, be without such gossip. Where would Anderson's Winesburg, Ohio have been? Domestic and social dynamics provide the flesh of any important novel, imparting a symbol of the times.*

"There's this preacher fella just come to town, got a room last night at the old Gilman House—"

"This would be Pastor 'Tommy?' I spoke to him briefly but it appeared he'd checked into the Due Drop In."

"Oh, yeah, they'se the same place. Used to be called the Gilman House on account a family named Gilman used ta own it but they all dead now so's it got sold..."

At once the Writer's brain was working. That name—Gilman—rang a note of familiarity. *I wonder...if that's where I'd stayed those twenty-plus years ago? The same building I'm staying in now!*

"Anyway, Pastor Tommy real late last night, he come inta the spa ta see my ma. He been here a bunch'a times and always stops in 'cos my ma take such good care'a him." Junie squeezed his arm and talked closer to his ear. "He paid a extra hunnert, plus a hunnert dollar tip, 'cos my ma strapped on a rubber dong and butt-banged him! Ain't that somethin'! A TV minister!"

"I suspect he's not the first to be on that manner of a 'receiving end.'"

"You should'a *seen* it, the rubber dong, I mean. A foot long at least!"

"My gracious, that's the corn-finger and *then* some."

Junie's spew of chirp-like laughter enlightened the Writer to hear. First, it was "erotic as hell" and, second, a lovely counter to this laughless age of hate, terrorism, and crime. "This pastor, too—clearly exhibiting himself as a vassal of God—might want to consult the second volume of the *Summa theologiae* of Sicilian Saint Thomas Aquinas who strongly suggested that it was a sin of serious import to seek the admission of things into the "back door," as they say."

Junie made the cutest little face of absolute disconcertion. "*Wwwwwwhat?*"

"Oh, never mind, I'm rambling which is something I do in abundance," he said cheerily. Without thinking, he did something that his scholared refinement and taxonomy of etiquette would never before have allowed: he put his arm around her, so comfortable was he with her company and the situation.

Until he came to the full realization that he'd just put his arm around not really a woman but a girl whom he was possibly three times older than.

She made no gesture negative whatsoever.

"You're a such a nice man," she said dreamily and put a hand on his arm.

"Thank you, Junie, and you're very nice as well—say, I'm curious, how old are you?"

"Just turnt sixteen!" she said and gave his arm another squeeze.

For the love of... That made him three times *plus* ten years older than her. But the Writer was thinking of no such sexual endeavor. Instead, he marred the implication: "What a wonderful thing youth is. Revel in it, Junie. Never take it for granted."

But the cozy aura collapsed; she tensed up, almost terrified. "Can we git on the other side'a the road? I always get the heebie-jeebies on this side."

Their approach was taking them close to the junked El Camino. "Ah, you mean Dicky Caudill's car?"

She stopped, astonished. "You *know* 'bout him?"

Not only do I know ABOUT him, I have this very low feeling in my psyche that I knew him PERSONALLY. "A friend of mine mentioned it, and mentioned that there was some local legend about this car..."

She was edging him toward the other side of the street. "Yeah, there's a legend, all right. Shit, I swear I seed his ghost a couple times."

"You don't say?"

"Oh, I know, ya problee think I'se just a silly girl who believe ever-thang she hear."

"Not at all. And I'll be honest with you, Junie. I'm fairly certain I saw Dicky's ghost myself, last night, right here."

"Really?" She almost squealed the word. "I'm so glad ya don't think I'm some stupid backwoods rube."

"It would be an impossibility for me to think *any such thing.*" They stood askant from the corroded vehicle, and, given the angle, he thought he noticed something on the windshield—something incongruous—but he was unable to clarify that due to the glare of the sun.

"Dicky was a bad, bad man. He died couple years afore I were born," she said in a voice that sounded like an enthused dread. "See, Dicky and his buddy Balls was *so evil* that their spirits is said to have *cursed* this whole town, and you's kin believe that—the town bein' cursed and all—'cos their ain't been anything good *ever* happen here. Ever-one get sick, no one got money, folks got jack-shit fer a life so's they just drink thereselfs to death. It's on account'a Dicky and Balls, and that damn *car.*"

"I'm intrigued, Junie. But how can a very old car be responsible for the ill-fortune of Luntville?"

"Mr. Writer, there is a whole lotta really bad shit that go on in this town'n always has, 'cos of what that car represents. You know, what it *symbolizes.*"

The Writer was impressed by her articulation. "Way my daddy tolt it to me was, a long long time ago, like dang near a hunnert years, this town weren't much more'n a piss-poor village, ever-one killin' each other and hatin' each other'n all that, even worse stuff. Then what happened is, well, this *man* pass though, see? From up north ever-one say. And he done somethin', not sure what, but he did somethin' very, very brave and all the folks here, they see that, and it lifted their spirits, it did, and it show ever-body here that they ain't shit but all of 'em is good people just like this man, and they all's have the power ta rise up from their shitty lives and do *good* and be *happy.* "

A fable in the works! I need to know this for the book! "Junie, what exactly did this man—this savior—do?"

"I dun't know 'zactly what, but it was somethin' that really put a fire under ever-one's ass and showed 'em that if you's got *faith* in yerself, you can do anything, juss like he did." Junie sighed, gripping the Writer's arm harder, and leaned her head against him as if in a tremendous relief. "And from that point on, ever-one raised thereselfs up, and lived by the 'zample'a this man, and for years'n years, this town turnt inta a great big bunch'a God-lovin', life-lovin' folks, helpin' friends in need and lovin' their neighbors as thereselfs, and things become just wonderful 'round here."

An incise, powerful local ballad, the Writer thought. *Ah, but incomplete...* "So, Junie, what—"

"What happen after that? Well, I kin tell ya what my daddy say. He say ever-thing was beautiful until, well, until Dicky Caudill'n Balls Conner was born. It were like Satan hisself just up'n take a *shit* on this town, and his two biggest turds was Dicky'n Balls."

An exceptional lower-economic hinterland allegory, I'd say, the Writer reckoned.

"Word is they done shit ya cain't bear ta ever *think* about, so bad they was," she went on. She was trembling at the recital, a very impressionable girl. "And I'se mean even when they was little kids. Robbin' folks, raping gals, killin' people, just for fun. If'n that ain't evil, I don't know what is."

Child sociopaths, the Writer diagnosed. "But, Junie. I'm not clear on something. How does the regrettable return of bad things—the curse through Dicky and Balls—relate to this car sitting before us?"

The girl seemed depressed by the topic, just as Snowie had been. The Writer hated to press her...

But he *had* to. He had to *know.*

"'Tis said by many folks that that damn car is like a *anchor* of the bad stuff that go on here since Dicky'n Balls died. But 'tis also said that one day—no one know when—some man, some stranger, from afar'll come to Luntville, and he'll sit his butt in that old car, turn the key...and it'll start." She looked up at him, wide-eyed. "And from that day on, goodness'll come *back* to Luntville just like it did way back when."

"That's *quite* a legend, Junie," he said. "Thank you for taking the time to tell it to me."

"The man who start the car, they all call him The One."

The One...

"See, he who starts the car is The One, and from that point on good luck will befall him and the whole town as well. And the curse of Dicky'n Balls will be banished forever." She looked to the sky, ponderingly. "I sure hope The One comes soon, 'cos I shore as hail could use some good luck..." Then she half-laughed. "A'course, I don't guess it could ever be started on account that car been sitting near twennie years. 'Tis true, the key's still in it, and many'a man turn it, but... nothin'. Problee what my ma calls codswallop. How can a car run if it all gone ta rust and got no gas?"

"Don't discount what you can't materially understand," the Writer proposed. "Can a man part the sea by prayer? It's said that Moses did indeed do that when his tribe was being

103

pursued by the Egyptian army. Many witnesses beheld Christ raising the dead, just as many witnesses watched Mohammad supernaturally quench the thirst of thousands of his soldiers at the Battle of Tabouk. We regard these things as mythological fabrication today. But there's archaeological and historical evidence that all these events occurred. My point?" He smiled at the girl. "*Anything* is possible. Belief is a powerful thing."

Of course, the Writer was merely trying to offer some positivity.

"I don't know," she pondered. "I ain't sure if I really believe or if it just be somethin' I *wanna* believe."

"Everyone wants to believe that a savior is coming, be it spiritual, materialistic, economic, or ideological," the Writer theorized. "Please don't ever stop believing, Junie."

It was a poignant moment. "Oh, I won't," she said, and perhaps there was a tear in her eye. "I'se guess what you're sayin' is that *belief* can make good things happen?"

"Without a doubt."

"Great! Now I'm gonna go ta work and *believe* that I get me at least five customers, 'cos Lord knows I need the money!" She looked at him with expectation. "I like you, come on. I'll gives ya a discount even!"

"No corn-finger for me today, Junie," he said. "I'm quite busy with my work. Perhaps another time. It's been a pleasure talking to you."

"'Bye! Hope ta see ya again!" She trotted happily off. It seemed that the Writer's words had enlivened her.

And now this, he thought, now that the preambles of cordiality were finished. He walked immediately across the asphalt to the car. And he was right.

The different angle of his view altered the windshield glare, and he saw that there was indeed an incongruence. No, not a crack. It was *writing.*

In the film of dust on the glass someone had scribed, as if with their finger:

START THE CAR

The Writer stared. He knew who'd likely written this—his doppelganger. But was the writing real? He couldn't be sure, just as he couldn't be sure this double of his was real either. He inspected the writing more closely. It looked freshly made and very real, someone had drawn their fingertip through the dust and film right down to the bare glass.

As for the tale of the El Camino and its accommodating details, it could only be—as Snowie's mother would say—codswallop. A stranger—a savior figure—can only relieve the town's curse by starting this cursed and quite unstartable vehicle. *Just a variation of King Arthur assuming his rightful place as heir of Uther Pendragon to be England's sovereign leader.*

Codswallop, yes, but amazing that some rustic redneck had summoned the creative ingenuity to devise such a manipulation of Arthurian legendry.

He opened the car door, which groaned and grated. *Can't hurt to try. If William of Normandy hadn't attempted a third and seemingly impossible assault on Senlac Hill at the Battle of Hastings, then all of history since then would be grossly different.* His joints groaned as rustily as the door when he sat down behind the wheel. It was a bench seat, not "buckets," with a prodigious gear shift protruding from a hump in the floor. Upholstery, as might be expected, was cracked and torn. Several beer bottles (Icehouse, he noted with distaste) lay in the passenger footwell, along with various redneck litter like food and candy wrappers, cigarette butts, and small sticklike things which he presumed were petrified french fries. Also, expended bullet casings and some live cartridges. He picked one up and squinted at its flanged base: E . 17 I. No indication as to caliber but it appeared a half-inch thick. From under the passenger side of the seat he retrieved, first, a faded, mold-caked magazine from 1995, *All Hands On Dick!,* whose cover depicted a photo of several nude caucasian women all reaching up as if worshiping the preposterously large erection of an African America body builder. The Writer tried to open it in order to make visual appraisal of what the forum might offer in the way of photographic composition but, no, the pages were all stuck together. Second, he pulled out a yellowed but modern No. 10 envelope, on which was handwritten *voynich p. 238.*

The Writer's hands trembled, for in his scholastic pursuits of the uncommon, he already knew what the reference was to, and when he unfolded the vanilla-colored sheet of vellum, his brows rose. On it, in hand-written ink, were lines of circuliform letters that belonged to no language he was aware of, and a colored-in drawing (like that of, say, a teenager) showing naked Rubenesque women standing expectantly upon an occultish diagram and all gazing at the same point off the page. *This appears to be a page of the infamous Voynich codex from the early 1500's,* he thought. *If it's original and not a forgery, it's worth tens of thousands.* The Voynich was a hand-written and illustrated manuscript, c. 240 pages, scribed in an unknown language. To date only a dozen or so words have been deciphered by the world's most expert cryptographers, and several pages are known to have been pilfered.

"Why," he said aloud and very pointedly, "is this colossally rare codex page under the seat of an abandoned hot rod in Luntville, West Virginia?" It would be akin to finding a Gutenberg Bible in a Used Books 'R Us.

He carefully refolded the sheet and put it in his pocket. The last exploratory attempt under the seat yielded this:

A severed hand, mummified.

This he did *not* put in his pocket.

Time is wasting, and time is life, he thought next, then misquoted Shakespeare. *Time is but a walking shadow that struts his hour upon the stage, and is heard no more.* In other words, a pretentious writer's way of telling himself to stop wasting the day, because he didn't know how many more he might have left.

He knew that the car would not start, that it was an impossibility. The battery would be corroded and incapable of holding a charge, the belts and hoses long rotted to dust, that last of the fuel siphoned or evaporated years ago.

He turned the key and the car started instantly.

He urinated in his pants.

Then he got out of the vehicle and walked very quickly and very wide-eyed back to the Due Drop In.

***

Exhaustion followed him back along with his alarm, and he fairly ran up the hotel stairs to his room. *No no no no no no no,* he thought. *Too much weird stuff is happening here too fast. There's no time to assimilate anything! And-and...I'm too fuckin' old!*

Back in his room he changed his pants and at once lay down on the bed. *Just take a nap, go to sleep.* Then he could re-examine his perspectives. Sleep claimed him at once, only to catapult his mind's eye into the belly of a particularly morbid nightmare, which starred none other than the four Larkins brothers. The stage of this nightmare was a spacious barn fitted with a wooden floor, and into this floor was bolted a curious metal chair, clearly hand-made via some mode of expertise. Ah, and in this chair sat a rather scrawny naked woman with large eyes and dark unkempt hair. She was strapped in place quite securely by various leather bands, and secured further by chains which crisscrossed her shoulders and were bolted to rings in the floor. "What'cha got goin' here, boys?" inquired a pinkened faced man in his '60s with a gray crew cut, pot belly, and short sleeve white button-down shirt. Several cigars occupied the breast pocket. "Looks interestin'." "Oh, it's interestin' all right, mayor," a brother said. "'Twas Clyde who thunk it up, and he'n Gut made the chair and built the rig. We call it "long-neckin.'" "Long-neckin', huh?" said this cross-armed mayor man. "I think I'm beginnin' to see how's it works. Who's the gravy boat?"

"She one'a the bitches tried ta run out the meth shack we'se got wind of just past the Governor's Bridge." The brother chuckled, then so did all his siblings. "Clyde kick in the front door, then ever-one inside run out the back, six, eight of 'em. Who's countin'? A'corse we was a-waitin' out back with our pumps. Most was fellas out first and we put deer slugs through 'em, made holes the size'a one of Claire Marson's tits! This one here were last, so we'se snatched her. Buck nek-it, she was, which tells me she's a meth-whore givin' the rest a place ta dump their cum for some free crystal."

"Ain't no doubt," the mayor agreed. "Kin tell just by the look of her. You burn the place, right?"

"Hell, yeah, sir. Went up like a hay bale, then blowed up just dandy!"

"Speck-tack-a-lur!" said another brother.

Why bother trying to tell them apart?

The mayor strode over to the girl in the chair. She was gagged, by the way. "Git that gag off her, Horace. And git'cher lighter," then he pulled down his zipper.

"Let me go, please, I didn't do nothin'!" she shrieked the

instant the gag came off. "I'se beggin' ya!"

"Ah, hush now, sweetie. Time to pay fer the error of your ways. One thing we cain't tolerate 'round here is the drugs." The mayor extracted his penis. "Listen, now. You's're gonna hold yer mouth wide open and let me piss in it, and you'd best swallow, or else—"

Horace grabbed her by the hair, flicked the lighter, and held the flame under her ear lobe.

Naturally, the woman bucked in the chair as if hit with a shark-prod, and she screamed blood-curdlingly.

And she opened her mouth as wide as she could.

The mayor began the urine-shower at her splayed crotch—"Better warsh this pussy out a tad, to tamp the stink down"—then lifted the steam up slowly to her mouth. Slowly, because, well, there was *plenty* in reserve. The poor woman did her best to gulp it down, and it was assumed by everyone not to be too arduous a task considering all else that her career as an addict had accustomed her to swallowing. Then the mayor shook off the last few drops and zipped up.

"Aw, my God," she groaned, dripping. "Okay, untie me. I swallowed your piss so you're gonna let me go, right?"

The mayor ignored her query and walked to a work bench to fetch a beer. It was another brother, Gut, perhaps, who answered, "Oh, we'se gonna let'cha go, honey, but problee not quite the way you got in mind," and then he winked at another brother—was it Horace?—who swung round a noose of stout rope which rose to a pulley-wheel in the ceiling and trailer down to an iron capstan of sorts mounted into the floor. Her fitted the noose around her neck. Near the capstan was a ratchet—device through which the near-end of the rope was threaded.

"We'se gonna long-neck ya, ya dumb ass," Gut informed her.

"*Huh?*"

One of the others began pulling down the ratchet bar. Slow. Maybe one tooth per ten seconds. Each click (it should go without saying) tightened the rope in modest increments.

"What it does, see, is it very slow pulls yer neck out longer till yer neckbone break, but we don't stop there, no sir! We keep ratchetin', see? If'n it's done good and slow, it stretch yer neck out. A foot, sometimes even two feet. And you'se'll stay alive fer a lot of it on account even though yer neck is broke, the rope keep all the blood up in yer brain, so you git a see it all!"

"See it all!" she yelled, through another click of the ratchet. "That don't make no sense! What'cha talkin' 'bout, ya fat cracker?"

"No need fer insults, hon," Gut said. "Words hurt, ya know? Kin hurt folks' feelin's, it can, and it just, well, it ain't nice—"

Everyone honked laughter as *click!* went the ratchet.

Another brother rolled over a long mirror on wheels, and propped it right in front of the unfortunate woman. Now she could watch her own murder.

And what an extraordinary murder it was!

By now no slack remained in the rope and her neck had been tautened to its normal anatomical limit. Her face seemed to swell, blushing due to the constriction of the blood vessels; she managed to blurt, "Why? Cain't ya just shoot me in the head'n git it over with? Why you doin' this to me?"

Gut or Horace or whoever it was simply shrugged and said, "Why? Well, on account it's cool ta look at."

After another click, the woman could respond no longer. Her hands and feet jiggled. Her mouth formed frantic but silent outrages. And her neck was indeed—

click!

—getting longer an inch at a time.

"It's cool ta see a gal with her neck stretched out a couple feet. We done it several times and we'se gittin' it down. See, if'n ya stretch the neck slow, then the neck muscles don't tear. Give it time in 'tween each pull an' it git longer. Guess you never seen that, huh? Well, keep lookin' at that there mirror and you will!"

More laughter joined him.

"Shee-it, mayor," another one complained. "Watchin' this gits my dick up'n barkin' like a pit bull at a meat wagon. Know what I'se mean, seein' her little titties jigglin' like that, and her all convulsin' and shit? I got a fixin' ta beat me off a dinner-size load right now, yes sir!"

"What's stoppin' ya, son?" the mayor replied. "Ain't gotta ask my permission, fer shit's sake. 'Tis a natural act any man got a right to do anytime he want. Gives me a thrill, in fact—the thought of a gal gettin' a wallop of cock-snot flung inner yap same time she's bein' kilt all slow'n fancy like."

"Git it, Tucker!" one cheered. Ah, so his name was Tucker. "Whip up a batch just fer her!"

"Yeah, show the bitch ya really *care!*"

"'Fraid so, fellas," Tucker said. "And I'se just *love* the idea'a the last thing she ever taste afore she dies is my cum!"

Tucker's right hand got down to business, while the other three brothers high-fived. The mayor, apparently a man of foresight, retrieved a screwdriver and used it to pry open the girl's mouth, since by now the tension of the noose was forcing her jaws closed. "There ya go, son. Go fer the gold."

Tucker huffed and puffed and...since it would institute an indulgent narrative irresponsibility to describe the act in any detail, it will be said only that the moment of climax was achieved, and after positioning himself properly and quite comically, the quadruplet successfully ejaculated with more than fair accuracy into the woman's mouth. The mayor withdrew the screwdriver, the woman's jaws snapped shut, and—

click!

—her neck extended another inch.

Her hands and feet continued to jitter, her face going bright red. Her eyes were seen rolling around and blue veins beat furiously at her forehead. The five spectators observed with the raptness of a family gathered round the television to watch the first moon landing.

After two more clicks a grisly *pop!* was heard which was the signal that the victim's skull had been officially separated from her spine, most likely at the vertebra designated Atlas C-1. Yet death did not yet claim her as the spinal cord had not yet been severed. The tension, now, was attempting to pull the brain down through the hole at the skull's base called the Foramen Magnum.

Her neck was now nearly a foot long.

A few more *clicks!* would exert so much unnatural pressure in the brain that massive strokes would take place and cerebral function would eventually cease. The watchers were delighted to note that she was still alive, conscious, and watching the reflection of her neck lengthening in the mirror.

Her face was blue now, her cheeks puffed, and the whites of her slitted eyes were becoming infused with crimson. And after two more clicks?

Massive convulsions took place within the chair's strictures, and then—

Lights out, as they say. Then a few more clicks, and a few more inches.

"Well gawd dang," a brother celebrated, astonished. "Best long-neckin' we'se ever had!"

"Shore is, Clyde, shore is."

The mayor, arms still cross in an attitude of authority, said, "Why you boys talkin' like it's over? Leave her set a hour, then give a few more cranks, and another hour, and a few more cranks. When yawl git my age, ya learn that patience makes profit. Shee-it, one time when I were a kid I 'member findin' a old box full'a my great great grandpappy's pictures. He were in the Civil War, served with General Caudill. They captured these Yankee field nurses and stripped 'em, fucked 'em, and strung 'em up in double-quick time. And took *pitchers* of it all—see, my great great grandpappy were the division *photographer,* and this was way back when takin' pitchers was a new thing, none'a this fancy citified cell phone shit'n digital what not."

"That's mighty cool, mayor," Gut or Horace said, "but what that got ta do with patience?"

"I'm gittin' to it, boy, I'm gittin' to it. See, what he done is he take a *before* shot right after they hang these northern cunts, then he take a *after* shot the next day. And after the passage'a that much time, ya could see in that after shot that them Yankee bitches' feet was *touchin' the ground.* Their necks was a *yard long.*" The mayor lit a White Owl. "Moral'a the story, boys? It takes *time* ta do job right."

"Wow!" several brothers said in unison.

"Now come on, let go up the 'Roads and get us some beers," the mayor ordered, puffing cheap cigar smoke. "I'm buyin'," and amid celebratory hoots and hollers, the five of them filed out of the barn. Now the poor woman's neck was close to two feet long—

—and the Writer was vaulted out of sleep to lurch awake in, yet again, a cold, sticky sweat.

He sat up, in confusion, disgust and a sopping dread. He cursed his own subconscious mind for fabricating such a hodgepodge of atrocity. He was no stranger to heinous and/ or absurd dreams lately but this was too much. *Can't even take a nap! I don't need this shit!* he thought. He still had yet to be in town a full twenty-four hours and his experience thus far could only be described as impossible, insane, and ludicrous. Witnessing those "Larkins" brothers last night had clearly provided the grist of this nightmare but...*Do I really BELIEVE that those men "dead-dicked" a drug dealer at the general store? Do I BELIEVE that the girl they raped and burned later appeared on the mortuary table and that two women had forced me to copulate with the corpse and "cream-pie" her? Do I BELIEVE that my doppelganger is running around town? Do I BELIEVE this Paulie man exists and that there is a MONSTER being stored at the funeral home, and that I just started a car that's been rusting for ten or twenty years?*

DO I really BELIEVE I was here over twenty years ago?

"No," he determined. "It's got to be some affliction of delusion or a *grand mal* hallucination combined with hysteria and probably some organic brain defect. I'm too smart to believe ANY of this..."

He recalled some of the fiction of Dr. Montague James, a Cambridge scholar and England's primary authority of medieval manuscript translation. In his off-time, little that there was, he composed ghost stories in which a scholarly protagonist regularly doubted his sanity, with lines similar to this: "The truth is (perhaps if I write it out I will view it in its true proportion) I am seeing things. This, as I know full well, is a universal symptom of incipient decay of the brain. Yet I suspect I'd be far less perturbed to know with assurance that this was the case, rather than to know that it was not."

Yes, brain aberration can be the ONLY cause of this indicia, the Writer conceded, *so I might as well forget about it. I've little interest in brain surgery.*

That decided, he retreated to the bathroom to "brush up," splashed some water in his face, and felt infinitely better. *I'm a writer,* he reminded himself. *What would any good writer upon realizing he was insane? He would WRITE about it!*

He unpacked his laptop or notebook or lapbook or whatever it was called, whistling that wonderful little novelty ditty from the Roaring Twenties, "Yes, We Have No Bananas," (first coined by Long Island grocers in response to a banana blight in Brazil. Little did they know that bananas would be the least of their concerns a few years later when the Great Depression reared its head.)

Computer tucked under his arm, he left the room, turned, then stopped, wide-eyed, as the word "Asshole" registered in his consciousness. It seemed to generate on his left side, as if someone's lips had spoken an inch form his ear, but when he turned there was nothing.

Worst part was, the word seemed to have been uttered in *his own voice.*

"Don't panic," he told himself aloud. "I've already come to grips with the idea that I'm insane. So...work with it." He carried on his merry way toward the stairs, and at mid-landing impulse forced him to stop at the sketch-portrait of the sullen long-faced man in an out-dated sports jacket and thin necktie. The sketch work was the product of no unskilled artist, while that notion of creepiness seeped back in. *Who IS this man? He looks SO familiar...*

No matter. *I'm nuts. So what? It's...interesting. Guy de Maupassant was insane later in life, so was Kerouac, Hemingway, Swift, Poe. I'd say I'm in quality company!*

Downstairs at the lobby desk, Mrs. Howard smiled at him. "Hi!" she said, standing for some reason on her tiptoes, which only delineated the robustness of her bosom. Had she made the gesture on purpose. "How you doing this fine day?"

"Couldn't be better, Mrs. Howard," he, well, circumvented the truth to a degree. "I have my portable computer with me, as you can see, and I was wondering if it might be all right for me to sit in the lobby and write a while. It's a lovely creative setting for a writer. A touch of the grandeur of better days gone by."

The idea seemed to thrill her. "Oh, go right ahead! 'Twould be a honor to have a famous *author* work on his latest masterpiece in our sittin'-room!"

I'm not that famous, he thought. *But a MASTERPIECE I can promise. A literary chronicle of a writer's insanity! It'll be better than Thomas DeQuincey!* "Why, thank you, Mrs. Howard."

"And if'n ya need some aspirin, I'se gotta whole bucketful here."

"Aspirin?" he queried.

"I should'a warned 'bout drinkin' with my daughter and her friend Dawn. *Those* gals? They can drink most *fellas* under the table. See, I couldn't help but overhear that last night, you, uh, got in a bit 'in yer cups,' as my momma used ta say."

The Writer shivered. "Yes, I'll admit I had a number of largish beers, Mrs. Howard"—*And then your genteel daughter put HEROIN in one of them!* "But, uh, is that, uh, *all* you heard?"

Mrs. Howard honked a high laugh. "A'course! What? You's 'fraid she tattled on you fer doin' somethin' naughty?" and another high laugh.

Lady, I "cream-pied" a cadaver last night. Does that meet your definition of naughty?

"And fer fear'a sounded like a busy-body," she went on, "she tolt me you and her got a date comin' up, and I cain't tell ya how's thrilled I am to know that my dear sweet daughter's takin' up with a *famous writer!*"

Fuck, the Writer thought. *I forgot about that.* "Yes, yes," he blathered. "You can rest assured I'm looking forward to it. And now I'll retreat to my writerly solitude and engage in some work."

She batted her fascinating pink eyes. "I hope it all goes just dandy!"

Fuck, he thought again. Laptop cradled in both arms, he moved deep into the lobby corner which was furnished with some couches and old armchairs. The far corner pleased him, for it was angled with high bookshelves, and it occurred to him that any literary novelist should perpetuate his craft whilst ensconced by the works of others.

He sat before a scroll-footed table, set out his laptop, turned it on, then realized how much he *hated* it, especially when that annoying Windows jingle ensued. It just seemed *wrong* for a writer of true art to compose on these contraptions; allowing all that technology to exist between the writer's brain and the final product was enough to make James Fenimore Cooper squirm in his grave. So far, all he'd managed to get down on this thing were notes and ideas. He felt that he should be writing fiction on a *manual* typewriter. Many 20th Century novelists regarded manual typewriters the same way that Jay Leno regarded fancy automobiles. Many collected them like baseball cards. No quad-core processors there, no sir. No SSD drives or DRAM or graphics cards or SD card slots. With a good old manual typewriter, the novelist achieved his art the old fashioned way: he *earned* it.

However...

Now that he'd thought of SD card slots, he remembered he'd found such a card today, hadn't he?

Or maybe I didn't. In fact I PROBABLY didn't. He'd already reconciled himself to the acknowledgment that he was insane. Therefore, he knew there wasn't really an SD card in his pocket.

Was there?

He stuck his fingers into his shirt pocket and withdrew an SD card.

Oh, dear, he thought.

Still, he might very well be insane. What proof was this of the opposite? As he ruminated inserting the card into his computer—

"Good afternoon, Paster Tommy!" Mrs. Howard nearly squealed from the desk.

"It is, that, ma'am," said the man the Writer had met in the hall earlier. He wore the same "hip" tailored jeans, smart tan sports jacket with elbow patches, and cowboy boots. "A good afternoon to praise God Almighty!"

"Amen!"

Then he glanced into the corner. "Brother? Are you ready for some good news?"

"Indeed, I am, pastor," the Writer replied. "Please, go on."

"'For the wages of sin is death, but in the gift of God is eternal life in Christ Jesus our Lord!'"

"Name the book, chapter and verse," said the Writer.

The pastor stalled. "Why, I believe...it's Revelation 3, um, 20."

"No, that's the 'Here am I. I stand at the door and knock' line. Yours is Romans 6:23."

"Amen, brother! Whilst thou join me at church come Sunday?"

"I whilst not, pastor, for I hath always serveth my reverence within the temple of mine own skull. And woud'st thou alloweth me a parting note, young man?"

"Bring it on, brother! Bring it on!"

"Nihil sub sole novum nec valet quisquam dicere ecce ho crecens est iam enim," the Writer enlightened the pastor.

Pastor Tommy's mouth turned to something like fish-lips. "Amen, brother! Amen!" and then he stalked out of the lobby very quickly.

I suspect he may be venturing himself to June's Spa for a little—if I may be so crude—"backdoor" action, the Writer thought with a half-smile. *I suppose that's the best way to shut him up: quote Scripture in Latin.*

Now he installed the SD card into the slot. Immediately a message read: WOULD YOU LIKE TO UPGRADE NOW TO THE NEXT WINDOWS?

"No!" he muttered under his breath, and made an effort to manipulate the cursor-thing to NO.

Next, another message blinked on: HOW WOULD YOU LIKE TO OPEN THIS FILE?

He winced. *I don't know! Shouldn't it just come on automatically? This motherfucker cost two grand!*

He resolved to return to this techno charade later and wisely decided to begin the new novel. But in only moments he found himself doing what most writers do in the same situation: he procrastinated. He was out of the chair and taking visual inventory of the many volumes on the shelves of books. It was a comfortable thought, and again he paraphrased Dr. James from some story of his or other, something the likes of "Any one who spends a lion's share of his time with reading or writing is more apt than most to take notice of large accumulations of books. A walk along the shore finds him squinting at the paperbacks being consumed by sunbathers; a pass by a book shop will invariably cause him to stop and peruse the window selections; and if a library or bookcase stands nearby, he need not rely on any host to provide entertainment."

From a distance, the lobby's shelves appeared enticing, but closer up this was not so much the case. Ranks of ancient Harlequin paperbacks faced him, as did much Zane Grey and Louis L'Amour. Another shelf housed hardcovers but all equally uninspiring: gardening, regional cooking, Reader's Digest condensations. *For the love of Johan Fust!* Nothing that appeared to be at all readable seemed to exist on the shelves. At the shelf nearest the floor, more old hardcovers stood, no doubt more mass-market fodder. He was too fat and lazy to get down on a knee for closer examination, but had he done so, he might've noticed the yellow dust-jacketed *Dracula* and a signed copy of the first edition of *Moby Dick,* each worth at least $10,000.

One very old hardcover appeared on the next row, at eye level. *In Defence of Episcopacy.* Author: Archdeacon John Benwell Haynes; publication date: 1817. "Could be interesting," the Writer muttered to himself, opened to a random page, read it, frowned, and closed its old cover.

Pushing the book back into its slot, he noticed the first book on this particular shelf was half-withdrawn.

He was certain it hadn't been a moment ago.

*More weirdness...*He took the book out, a newer hardback, but found it titleless. Clearly it was an empty journal of some kind, a curio, for all of its pages were blank.

Or...All pages but one, the very first.

MEET ME AT THE CRAFTER HOUSE, ASSHOLE. BRING A SHOVEL

The Writer gulped. Again the name Crafter had sprung up, along with its disturbing familiarity. *My doppelganger strikes again,* he supposed. He began to contemplate the matter more deeply when—

"Come on, honey," a tinny voice blurted behind him. It was coming from his laptop. "Give Mr. Ed somethin' to smile about, and don't take all day, or I'll be stompin' a mudhole in your junkie ass. You get lazy on *us,* you wind up in the Hudson."

The Writer's eyes shot wide, and Mrs. Howard looked up abruptly from the desk. "Ever-thing all right over there?"

The Writer rushed to his laptop and turned the volume off. "Very sorry, Mrs. Howard. It's one of those infernal *pop-up ads* on my computer."

"Oh, I'se see. Thought I heard sumpthin' 'bout *Mr. Ed.* What a great old TV show!"

"Yes, uh, yes, a great show indeed," the Writer blathered. By the time he'd gathered himself behind the laptop, it was a demented scene and then some which greeted him on the screen. Obviously, while he'd been surveying the bookshelves, the SD card's video file had finally opened on its own.

On the screen, an emaciated, naked white woman was—

Oh, no. No no no...

—kneeling below the belly of a largish horse—a white horse with black patches—and she was masturbating the shining pink/black bone of the beast's penis. She did this with her left hand, while her right positioned a clear plastic pitcher, of the kind Kool-Aide might be served in. The Writer edged the volume up just a tiny bit.

"Come on, Charger," the girl coaxed dully, "be a good horsey and cum for me, because for fuck's sake, if I don't shoot up soon, I'm gonna fuckin' hang myself."

A man stepped into view, chuckling, a big man, broad shouldered, short salt and pepper hair, wearing a suit and tie. He was also wearing a rubber Popeye mask with the mouth area cut out. "You hang yourself, bitch, you'd better tell us first so's we can film it."

Another male chuckle resulted, off screen–obviously the cameraman. "Yeah, like that time we strung up that commissioner's teenage daughter, and took turns beatin' her back and forth with the bat like a fuckin' pinata! And then Micky Motormouth fucked her while she was still twitchin'! Man, Augie, wasn't that great?"

Popeye looked right at the camera. "You fuckin' empty-headed dago. You got linguini and clam sauce for fuckin' brains? How many times I tell you *never* to use real names in the flicks? Now you'll have to waste time cutting that shit out in post. And lemme tell ya, J.J. Fuckin' Abrams you *ain't*."

"Aw, shit, Aug—I mean, sir, I'm really sorry."

Popeye shook his head and returned his attention to the "action," where the nude woman slid her hand vigorously back and forth over the animal's member. "Come on, you dirty hype! This horse usually comes like a hair-trigger. Guess he's sick'a lookin' at your scrawny tits. Give his balls a squeeze. Didn't your daddy ever teach ya that?"

She muttered something, did as ordered, stroked a few more times, then the horse whinnied and began to fidget. Just as the ejaculation commenced, the Writer took grim notice that the pitcher was already half full, and judging by the other pastured horses in the background, more that a few equines had already made a contribution. (On an incidental note, however, and a datum unknown even to the Writer's eidetic intelligence, the average human ejaculation was about 10 milliliters; the average *horse* ejaculation averaged 100-300 milliters, every 100 milliliters equaling 3.4 ounces, while "stud quality" specimens or "breeder" horses were known to belt out as many as 500 milliliters. "Charger," part of a Mafia stud farm, was very much a breeder, and delivered every milliliter of the 500 to the pitcher.)

"Good Charger! That's my good, good horsey!"

The Writer willed to move his hand to the cursor pad, to turn off this infernal "movie" but the commands of his brain had been intervened. His finger froze above the pad...

"Squeeze out the last of it, toots," ordered Popeye. "It's like the fuckin' coffee, good to the last drop."

"Huh?" said the pallid girl, frowning.

"Just milk all the cum out of the horse's dick, ya jizz-head, or I'll turn ya inside out through your pussy with a boat-hook."

"I'm milkin', I'm milkin'," she whined, and milk she did, till the last of it was in the pitcher.

"Now come on..."

The camera tracked Popeye and the girl back across the pasture. In the background, down a green hill, some sort of arrangement of wooden buildings stood out. Farm structures? Stabling? It wasn't clear. But it was a considerable compound, surrounded by high mesh fence. It appeared to be abandoned, and initially the Writer suspected that this was where the film's participants were headed.

But not so.

They turned up a path instead, a path that served as a driveway which wound up to a small, single-storey house with a brick front and sagging roof. The Writer guessed the house to have been erected in the '50s. A scrubby front yard hadn't been mowed in a while but the sound of a lawn mower revealed that the task was being undertaken at that moment.

Pushing a Briggs & Stratton mower close to the front door trudged another pale-white naked woman. She wore sneakers. Greasy strings of dark hair wagged in front of her face; her pallid flesh shined tackily from perspiration. She was even skinnier than the woman holding the pitcher: flaps for breasts, a sucked in abdomen, ribs showing like window blinds. On she trudged behind the mower, never even looking up when the troupe passed. Wide-eyed, the Writer thought of Baudelaire's "Skeleton Laborer" in *Les Fleurs du Mal.*

The camera followed Popeye and the horse-girl into the house.

"Fuck, man," complained the girl. "Can you carry the pitcher please? It's heavy as fuck."

The camera roved to the pitcher and its Egg-Drop-Soup-like contents, full to within an inch from the top. The girl's arm straining to hold it looked like a broomstick painted white.

"Too heavy, huh?" said Popeye. "Then I guess you better lighten it up. Take a chug."

A hold on the girl's face. "Whuh...chug?"

"You dense? Take a good long chug for the camera."

"Aw, fuck no! Come on, man!"

Popeye stared her down. "You don't, I break your legs, drag you outside, and make your girlie-friend mow *you.*"

"He ain't kiddin', honey," said the camera man off screen. "I seen him do shit like that and worse."

"Awwwww, man..."

The camera framed her hollow-eyed face. The girl gripped the pitcher with both hands. Her hands *shook.*

"Oh, and toots? You drop that pitcher, I'll turn you into a four-hour snuff-flick, and I'll make sure you're still just a little bit alive when we drop ya in the dog pen. Clients pay good money to watch that stuff."

The girl was pouting, tears streaming down her cheeks. Shakily, then, she brought the pitcher to her lips, took in a mouthful, and—

gulp

—swallowed.

"That's my girl," Popeye approved. "How 'bout one

more for the road?"

The girl went bug-eyed. "Aw, come on!"

"Ya better do it, hon," advised the cameraman. "What's the big deal? Horse cum can't taste any worse than human, and you've chugged *plenty* of that."

"Aw, fer shit's sake!" she wailed, steadied herself, and—

gulp

—fulfilled the order.

"Cool. Turns out you're good for somethin' after all," and Popeye took the pitcher. "Come on, let's get this freak show done." The cameraman followed Popeye and the stultified nude woman down a dark hallway—

The Writer, stultified as well, managed at last to get the cursor to the STOP box and click it.

He sat at the table, frozen in place, staring. Summoning reactive thoughts defied his capabilities at that moment; he felt as though he'd just trudged a mile uphill. The silence, indeed–after watching the hellish debauch—was golden.

"Good gawd *dang,* Hazel!" a hickish voice cracked the silence. "You hear what Mitt Waller just found out on the Tick Neck Road?"

"Why, no, Jimmy," Mrs. Howard replied. "Hope it weren't somethin' bad."

"Oh, it were bad, all right." The speaker was 50ish, in the sort of work apparel one might wear in a machine shop or garage bay. "'Twas just past the deadfall near ole Jake Martin's shack. It was a nekit *girl,* Hazel, deader'n my shop anvil."

Mrs. Howard brought a shocked hand to her bosom. "Why, of all the—I hope it weren't a *local* gal."

"Naw, not local'n fer that we can be grateful," said the man. He was leaning on the front desk. "A druggie, it looked like, barely more than skin'n bones and fulla the tattoos."

Mrs. Howard shook her head. "That's shore what it sounds like. Them drug people is always comin' here from other towns tryin' ta git a foothold here. Thanks God fer the Larkins boys."

"Amen to that." Jimmy scratched his shaggy head. "Worse part were how she was found. Her blammed *neck* was *three feet long*."

Mrs. Howard almost dropped her coffee. "Say *what?*"

"I seen it myself, Hazel. 'Twas like this gal were a Gumby doll, and somebody done stretched her neck THREE FRIGGIN' FEET!"

"My word. Those Larkins boys—what'll they think of next?"

"Sends a strong message to all them druggers out there," speculated this man Jimmy. Oh, and I'll tell ya another thing—"

"*What?* There's *more?*"

The Writer, of course, was in earshot, and the news of this dead girl with the three-foot neck left him paralyzed. But there was more?

There was more.

"Jest, well, weird." Jimmy, clearly, was eyeing Mrs. Howard's breasts. "Mabel Croy who live up top of al the old Chinamen's cleaners? She up'n *swear* she heard someone start Dicky Caudill's hot rod."

"Oh, my Lord..."

"Uh-huh. Lotta weird stuff's goin' on of late..."

I need a drink, the Writer thought. His nightmare of the Larkins brothers had evidently been premonitory, and someone had heard him start the El Camino which meant...

He wasn't insane.

Fuck. Just when I was getting used to the idea...

He almost fell out of the chair when his cellphone rang,

and he had an idea that he may have made some sort of suppressed exclamation because Mrs. Howard and Jimmy both shot him peculiar glances.

"Hello!" he barked.

"Wow, you shore sound grumpy." It was Snowie. "I'm stuck at the store. Was just callin' ta see how you're a-doin'."

He could not forego a little sarcasm. "How I'm a-doin'? Oh, you mean after you and that crafty bitch Dawn drugged me and made me"—he lowered his voice—"fuck a junkie corpse!"

Snowie giggled. "Sorry, 'twas life or death. You saved me'n Dawn! You're our hero! And, holy moly, you done made fer the best cream pie we ever filmed."

"So I've heard. I wouldn't call that accomplishment a feather in my cap."

"And now Paulie and Augie are off our backs. They was *real happy* with your work."

"You make it sound like a research paper! And—wait a minute. How did you get my phone number?"

"Took it off your phone. Didn't think you'd mind."

"So you took my *phone* out of my fucking *pocket?*"

"Well, yeah. When I'se took out'cher wallet to put the fifty in."

Of all the gall! But I better get to the point. "Look, Snowie. There's something I need to tell you."

"What! You love me?"

His nose crinkled. "Well, no."

"Ah, shit. Well, what then?"

"I was walking in town earlier and I passed Dicky Caudill's car, and, well, just for the sake of sport, I—I—"

"What, honeybunch?"

"I—I—I sat behind the steering wheel, turned the key, and, uh, well...the car started."

A squeal thrilled in his ear. "Are you *shittin'* me?"

"I assure you, I am not. I assumed I was merely going insane but...well, now I'm not so convinced of that."

"Did you drive the car back to the inn?"

"Well, no. It didn't occur to me to do that, and, besides, I couldn't."

"Why the hail not?"

He shrugged unseen. "It's a manual transmission. I don't know how to operate a stick shift."

Snowie's cup of enthusiasm was overflowing. "My goodness, gracious! That car is the symbol of Dicky and Ball's curse on the town. 'Tis always been said anyone who tow it to the scrap yard would double the curse, but 'twas also said—"

"Yes, I heard. According to the legend, some day a stranger would come—The One—and start the car, thereby terminating the curse of Dicky Caudill and Balls Conner." *How had the sixteen year old Junie phrased it?* "Once he starts the car good luck will befall The One and befall the entire town."

"That's right!" she continued to thrill in his ear. "Has any good luck come to ya today?"

The Writer laughed. "No, indubitably not."

"Well, it will. If you really started that car, it will."

The Writer smiled.

"Look, I git off in a few hours. Meet me at Crossroads. And don't tell anyone 'bout you starting the car," she insisted. "I never drove nothin', but Dawn has—she drove tanks and shit in the Army. She can tell you how to work the stick."

He resigned to it. *Why not? I've got nothing better to do except forge ahead on my career.* "Ok, Snowie. Call me when you're getting off work and I'll meet you there."

"But, wait!" A pause. "Don't hang up yet."

"Yes?"

Her hushed, wet voice whispered, "I really like you," and then she hung up.

Terrific. Now he *really* needed a drink, and just as he prepared to close up "shop" here and adventure himself toward the bar—

Wouldn't you know it?

The SD card's video file came back on...

Turn it off! he commanded of himself. *Throw the whole fuckin' computer out if need be but DON'T WATCH ANYMORE OF THAT HORROR SHOW!*

But of course his "Imp of the Perverse" had again taken possession of his will, leaving him no choice but to let the screen take hold of him. He edged the volume back up just enough to hear...

The film, if one could call it that, resumed with the cameraman following Popeye and the horse-girl down a dark hall and into a room.

Lengthy descriptions of the room's purpose, and its lone inhabitant, exist as an impossibility. It shall only be said that— no surprise—the room's "purpose" was unspeakable and involved a mode of misogynistic degradation, imprisonment, and abuse that constituted genuine, undiluted horror. There was a small television, now tuned to a cooking show where some fussy French chef was preparing Sole Meuni Re in Beurre Noisette with Pommes Souffle. A nude woman sat splayed-legged in the corner. A metal collar girded her throat, attached to which was a stout chain secured to the ceiling. This gave the girl (if she chose to walk about, or if she even *could*) a margin of freedom of maybe ten feet. In the floor was a square hole, the utility of which was clear.

"You lazy cunt!" roared Popeye. "This place smells worse that a bum's ass-crack! I told you to always put the board over the hole after you use it!"

Split infinitive, the Writer somehow thought.

The sunken-eyed, droop-mouthed girl looked up in a slow stupor, blinked, then crawled a few feet and pushed a board over the hole. When she'd moved forward, she did so not on her palms but on her fists.

Cameraman off-screen: "Hey, boss. What's wrong with her hands?"

"We turned 'em into hooks. Had the Doc come here when we first knocked her up and he cut some special nerve in each arm. Can't have her hangin' herself before she pumps the kid out."

An overlooked detail: the woman, though her arms, legs, and face were skeletally thin, she was egregiously pregnant. The Writer would've been surprised if the bloated belly and its pre-natal contents comprised the majority of her total body weight.

"Why are you doing this to me?" said the woman in a parched whisper.

"Doin' what?" said Popeye, then he laughed. "Oh, you mean why did we make you preggo and feed you nothin' but horse cum for the last eight and a half months?" He paused, perhaps for effect. "Because we *can,* baby! We *can!*"

The pregnant girl began to cry. "What did I ever do to deserve this?"

Popeye shrugged. "You tried to run out on us. And no one, and I mean *no one,* runs out on *us.* Somebody could hide you in a bank vault and put it on the bottom of the sea and we would find you."

"You're sick in the head," she muttered.

"Hey. *I'm* not sick in the head. It's those people out there who're sick in the fuckin' head. They're the ones who *pay* for this shit. You think I do this 'cos I want to, 'cos I get a kick out of it? Believe me, honey, I'd rather be home tossin' the ball back and forth with my kids, or watchin' fuckin' sit-coms. It's *commerce,* toots. It's about filling a need in the marketplace, that's all. People wanna Three Muskateers? They go to the fuckin' store, pay money, and get one. Same thing here. People wanna see a knocked up junkie get force-fed horse sperm for her whole term, they pay money. To *us.* If they weren't paying for it, we wouldn't do it. It's called capitalism."

So much for the macro-economic thesis. Popeye said next, "Open up, you know the drill," produced a plastic tube—obviously a manual-feeding tube—and expertly slid it down the girl's throat. After that he dragged over a hand-lever pump of some sort, attached the free end of the feeding tube to it, then carefully picked up the pitcher. "Come on, honey. You gotta be told *everything?* Don't piss me off."

"Yes, sir!" replied the horse-girl and she was at once on her knees at the pump. Her dead eyes implored the pregnant woman. "I'm sorry I have to do this all the time, but if I don't, you know, they'll kill me."

"No," said Popeye. "We won't kill ya. We'll make ya *wish* we did."

The pregnant nodded tearily, and–

"Start pumping." Popeye slowly poured the pitcher's contents into a funnel atop the pump, while the horse-girl....

Pumped.

The camera deftly captured the horse semen moving up the tube and into her throat.

"Shit," Popeye remarked. "You gotta wonder. What's a baby gonna look like that ain't been fed nothin' but horse cum the whole time he's in his mama's belly?"

The sperm kept pumping down the tube—

pump pump pump

131

—then the video ended.

Unnumbered minutes elapsed with the Writer staring at the blank screen. As badly as he wanted a beer, or several, he resolved to go lie down again. Drinking on top of the images he'd just digested would surely lead to spontaneous vomiting. He took the SD card out of the computer, put it in his pocket, and would soon throw it away. He was just about to turn off the laptop when the cellphone rang again.

"Yes?" he droned.

"Hi, Mr. ___, it's me, ___ at Scribner's. How are you today?"

The caller was his editor. The Writer gulped—still envisioning that manual feeding tube—and said, "I've been better."

"I'm sorry to intrude, Mr. ___, but there's an urgent matter I'd like to talk to you about, sir."

This was, at the least, idiosyncratic. His editor *never* called him "Mister" or "sir." The Writer let a wave of nausea pass, then consented, "All right."

"Since you don't have an agent, sir, I feel privileged to give you some information you may not be aware of. Sir. Has...any one else called you, I mean, any other publishers?"

The Writer frowned. "No. What's this all about?"

"Word has gotten around in the publishing circles of New York, Mr. ___."

"Word about what?"

"Why, about you, sir. And the word is this: you're back. The prodigal of the neo-post-modernist lit scene, after disappearing unheard of for years. Yes, sir, the word is you're *back,* and working on a new book. I believe you told me some days ago that you had a new project in mind."

"Yes, I do," he said irritably. "The continuation of that single page you gave me, which I have reason to believe is the last thing I wrote, way back in the early '90s."

"Yes, sir, 1991 to be exact. And you're calling it *White Trash Gothic?* Is that what you said?"

He was getting a headache, and he couldn't stop hearing "Popeye's" voice. "Yes."

"A brilliant title."

"I know," the Writer barked. "Now, really, it's not my nature to be testy, but I'm rather ill today, and you seem to be meandering to your point. What is it? Please."

"Very well, sir. And I apologize. Scribner's and Sons has just wired one million dollars to your bank account, the first third of a three million dollar advance for *White Trash Gothic.* I trust that is enough to the point, sir?"

The Writer didn't hear the last sentence because he was on the floor, which he hit with a groaning thud.

"Mr. ___? Are you there?"

"Yes," he said without bothering to get off the floor. Instead he just lay there, phone to ear. "This is unfathomable, in fact, I don't believe it."

"Believe it, sir."

Just then, his phone beeped and a text message flashed. THIS IS A BANK OF AMERICAN WIRE TRANSFER NOTICE. $1,000,000 HAS JUST BEEN WIRED TO YOUR SAVINGS ACCOUNT. THANK YOU FOR BEING A VALUED BoA CUSTOMER.

Holy shit. "I don't understand. I can't see how you regard my next book as being worth a million dollars."

"*Three* million, sir. The first million is just the advance."

"But...what about the contract?"

"Check your email, sir."

The Writer still didn't feel like getting up, so he clicked his AOL tab. With much squinting, he clicked the attachment box, and there it was. "I see. Here it is. I suppose I should have it printed out, sign it, and mail it to you, yes?"

The editor laughed. "It's a Docu-Sign file, sir. Click the OK button, then your facsimile signature will be applied, then click send."

"Really? Technology certainly has come a long way," said the Writer, momentarily astonished. He followed the two-step instructions.

Several seconds of silence stretched across the line, then the editor said, "Got it, Mr. ___. Thank you very much. Remember now, sir, if I may, you've just signed a binding contract with this company. Should other companies make offers..."

"Of course, I understand. The book is yours, and so, evidently, is my ass."

"Is a six-month deadline feasible?"

"I don't see why not." He pondered a moment more. "So that's it? I click a button and now I'm a millionaire?"

"Yes, sir. Congratulations. And I thank you doubly. You may not understand this, but you're hot property now. If I hadn't retained you, I'd have been fired."

"Well, I'm glad *that* didn't happen." He laughed, still absurdly on the floor.

"Call if you need anything. Would you like a new car, perhaps a new Corvette? A cruise? A holiday in Europe or anywhere else? I'm prepared to offer that as a gesture of my company's appreciation for your loyalty."

"Uh, no, thanks. I think the million is sufficient."

"Three, sir. *Three* million. Happy writing, and...welcome back."

The call ended, leaving the Writer understandably dizzy. *Did that just really happen?* With more than a little effort and more than a few grunts, he got back into his chair, and wiped sweat from his brow.

Either that just happened, or am I, indeed, insane. He couldn't decide which. Then he recalled what he'd found under the seat of Dicky's car: the Voynich manuscript page. He removed it from his rear pocket, looked at it, acknowledging the unmistakably unknown language it had been scribed in, as well as the colored drawings of Ruebenesque nude women looking at something off the page.

Laptop stashed under his arm, he walked to the front desk. "Mrs. Howard? Might I ask a favor?"

Her odd face and pink eyes lit up. "Of course!"

"I forgot to bring my reading glasses," he lied, "so I'm wondering if you'd be so kind as to read this piece of paper to me."

"I'd be happy to," she said, donning glasses of her own. She placed the page on the desk and leaned down to inspect it, or perhaps more so to elucidate her cleavage for the Writer's viewing pleasure.

And what a pleasure it was.

"Well, now, I cain't read *nothin'* on this—"

"Is it blank?" he asked, knowing that if she answered "yes," then he was insane, which, as he considered it, might not be a bad thing.

"Why, no, it ain't blank. It got a bunch of circle-like scribbles on it, all lined up proper. And some fairly randy drawin's of nek-it gals."

Shit. I'm not insane. Well, then, it was settled. His nightmare of the long-necked girl *did* come true, the atrocious video clip *was* real, and...he really *was* a millionaire.

He took back the sheet. "Thank you, Mrs. Howard, and have a good night."

"Ta-ta!"

Back to his room he went, dragging his feet and oddly un-impressed that he now had a million dollars in the bank. He'd always been a qualitative being, and more in line with Baruch Spinoza's treatises Monistic ethics and Immaterialism. In other words, money meant little to him (as long as he had money for beer). But a spark of responsibility fizzled in him. *I have a six-month deadline for a three million dollar novel I've only written one page of.* He'd best get cracking.

And again, when he'd turned the computer back on, and activated his word-processing program, he could only stare, uninspired, at the glowing white screen and throbbing cursor. *This just isn't right. Harry Crews didn't write on a damn laptop, and neither did Theodore Dreiser! So, damn it! Why should I?*

Real writers used *typewriters.*

I don't even think they MAKE typewriters any more...

He left the door ajar and suddenly there came a gentle knock. He could see Portafoy in the gap.

"Please come in, Mr. Portafoy," he said.

The well-dressed, elderly man entered and nodded. "Beg pardon, sir. But I just came on duty and thought I'd ask if you needed anything."

"Actually, Mr. Portafoy, I need an old thrift shop, junk store, or antique store. Are there any in town?"

"In better times, yes there were, sir, but no longer. I suppose you'd have to go a bit out of your way to find one. Is it anything in particular you're needing?"

The Writer almost laughed. "Yes. A good old fashioned typewriter."

Portafoy pinched his chin, speculating. "I seem to recall...If you'll excuse me a moment, sir," and then he left the room.

The Writer shook his head. *What? I expect the man to come back here holding a fuckin' typewriter? Don't make me laugh.*

But it was not the night-porter who barged in, it was—

"Dawn! What a pleasant surprise...I think."

Still dressed in her earlier business clothes, she seemed stressed. "Snowie told me you were here."

He frowned. "Did she now?"

"Yeah, and, shit, was she bullshitting me? Did you really start Dickey Caudill's car?"

"Yes, I did, or at least I think I did. Well, I must have. I was beginning to think I was insane but..."

She disregarded him. "Look, I don't know what you're talking about but I need your help—"

An alarm bell blared in his head; he pointed at her like a gun. "No more cream-pies!"

"That's not what I mean," she rushed. "Augie called me just after I signed the deal for Wally Eberhart's coffin."

"Augie...," he mused. "Wasn't there an Augie Doggie cartoon in the '60s?"

"I'm in deep shit, man!" she yelled and actually grabbed his collar and shook him. "Augie called me and said he thinks he dropped an SD card at the funeral home. It's got some hard underground shit on it. I spent the last couple hours looking high and low for the motherfuckin' card but so far, ziltch. I need you to come and help me look. If I don't find it, that goomba psycho will come back to the parlor and tear the place up looking for it." She leaned closer, imperatively. "I can't let him find that big door!"

"Big door?"

She kept hold of his collar, shrieking, "The big metal fuckin' door where we keep the Bighead's body!"

The Writer didn't mind being violently shaken by this very interesting and robust woman, for her breasts nearly pressed his face. "Ah," he said. "So there really is a monster corpse behind that door you showed me?"

"Yes!" she said and shook him some more.

"Tell me, then. This man Augie you've mentioned before. Is he Paulie's boss?"

"No, no, other way around. He's Paulie's lieutenant, his muscle. He does all of Paulie's wet work. He's big as a linebacker and has fists bigger than croquette balls, and harder. When he's pissed off, people get killed in bad ways! I don't want to be one of them! Please, help me look for the SD card! Snowie's coming too, when she's done at the store."

The Writer looked up pointedly. "Might Augie be a man with a penchant for Popeye masks?"

She released his collar, shocked. "How the hell did you know that?"

"I found this in the parking lot behind your place of employment." He fetched the SD card and gave it to her. "I suspect it's the object you so direly seek."

Her eyes bugged from her head. She popped the card into his opened laptop, waited, watched, then shrieked, "Yes! Oh my God, thank you! You saved my ass again!"

"It was nothing," he said, then, "Now, if you'd kindly leave, I'm waiting for Mr. Portafoy after which I intend to take a nap."

She grabbed his collar and began shaking again. "Fuck that! Snowie said you need me to show you how to drive stick! Let's go!" But then she paused in a long-staring moment. "Wait a minute. The legend says when the One starts that car good luck—"

"Good luck shall befall the One and all who live here," he finished. "I heard the entirety of the legend."

"Well, lemme tell you," and she held up the SD card. "Without this I'd probably be having my tits cut off and stuffed up my ass tonight. But you just handed it over to me!

138

You granted me luck!"

"I think coincidence is a more likely explanation," he said.

"Bull-fuckin'-shit! Has anything good happened to you today, since you started that car?"

The MILLION DOLLARS suddenly in his bank account left the answer unchallenged. "Well, um, yes. I can't deny that."

She wrapped her arms around him, pushed her lips to his, and was marauding his mouth with her tongue. At the same time, she pawwed his crotch. "Let's fuck! Come on!" She muscled him down onto the bed, much, much stronger than he. "You really *are* the One!"

"Dawn, please," he tried to stave her off. "This is hardly the time or place."

She was jamming her hand down his pants. "I won't even make you use a rubber. I *want* your cum in me! If I get pregnant, I'll have the kid and I swear I won't even sue you for child support! It'll be our love-child!"

"No, no, really, I'm far too old for such spontaneity," he pleaded.

Just then, Portafoy backed into the room, his arms heavy laden with some bulk. "Pardon me, sir, but I'd like to show you this and see it if might suit your needs."

Embarrassed (and erect) the Writer nudged Dawn away. "Great Hadrian's ghost!" he exclaimed. "Where did you find that?"

Dawn collapsed, defeated, on the bed. "Hi, Portafoy."

"Miss Dawn, a pleasure to see you," the elder man said, held an involuntary glance on her bosom, and set something down on the desk. This "something" was a very old manual typewriter. "I've noticed it in the custodial closet, sir, many times. I'm told it's been here since long before I came on."

The Writer jumped up, ecstatic. "I don't believe it!" he exclaimed; he knew it at a glance. "It's a Remington Standard Typing-Machine No. 2! Mr. Portafoy, this is the Mona Lisa of typewriters!"

The porter eyed the bulky machine. "Someone may have told me that a guest left it here back when the Gilmans owned the property; but I wouldn't get my hopes up, sir. It appears to be very old—"

"I'll say," remarked the Writer, gazing at the prize. "This model first came out in 1874!"

Portafoy's white-gray eyebrows rose. "Well, that's something, sir, and it seems well-constructed; perhaps it's still in working order."

The Writer inspected it with a jeweler's intrigue, and found the machine's parts to be clean and well oiled. The type-stems and strike-faces may even have been customized replacements. The platen rubber, too, was new. "It's completely maintained and refurbished," he whispered, mouth agape. He rolled his Greyhound receipt into the paper tray and—

clunk, clunk, clunk.

It worked!

"These were with it, sir," the elder said, offering a small cardboard box full of cellophane-sealed metal capstans.

"Ribbons!" the Writer rejoiced. "Brand-new!"

"I'm happy you have found satisfaction with the machine, sir. Feel free to use it as much as you like. The manager can't possibly object."

"Thank you, Mr. Portafoy!" The Writer hugged the man. "You're a Godsend! This is my lucky day!"

"And mine as well, sir. After my first rounds, I'm off to the bank. Today I received a letter from an estate attorney from Wilbraham, containing a check for no less than $10,000. An inheritance, from a distant relative I've never known."

"I couldn't be happier for you, Mr. Portafoy!"

"Thank you, sir. Ring for me if you need anything, sir."

The cultured porter left before the Writer could even think to provide a tip. *Wow! First I get a million dollars, and now THIS!*

Which left Dawn, in her smart dark funeral hostess apparel. She stared in awe. "The legend really is true. You really *are* the One."

"I doubt it, Dawn. But it's amusing to think that I just may be. All mythologies are rooted in some filament of truth."

"You ain't kidding," she said, grabbed his hand, yanked him out of the room, closed the door, and hauled him to the stairs. "We're going to Dicky's car, *right now!*"

"But-but, I have to take a nap!"

"Fuck naps!"

"And I have an obligation to my editor—I have to *write!*"

"Fuck writing! Come on!"

***

Proceeding to the El Camino was rather like running the gauntlet, not of a violent mob, but of throes of onlookers and inexplicably exuberant townsfolk. It's not in order to provide every detail of the unlikely duo's trek to the mythical car, but it should be conveyed that much data of a curious nature was gleaned. Awed whispers such as, "There he is!" and "Is that him?" circled round. Many persons were actually teary eyed, others hysterical with joy. It seems that no fewer than ten of these people had recently purchased Scratch Off tickets, and had won thousands of dollars. Henry Wheeler's SSDI had just come through, and so had Mrs. Dexter's Medicaid, which had been thrice before denied. And just an hour ago, Wally Eberhart's wife, who'd been diagnosed with terminal liver problems, had been informed that she'd undergone a miraculous remission. It looked like that coffin order was premature! Wally himself had lunged through the crowd to actually hug the Writer, and babbled incoherent thanks.

Dawn held his hand fast. "You really, really are it."

This time the Writer forbore his usual skepticism.

Lastly, Junie, the hot-panted sixteen-year-old massage parlor girl, darted through more people to kiss him. "I *knowed* you were good luck, I just *knowed* it! I just had eleven quickie clients in a row and they all tipped me fifty! I haven't beat that many fellas off in one day in, well...never!"

"I'm so glad for you, Junie," he said, flabbergasted.

"Make way! Make way!" a stout-voiced man ordered. "Give the man some room!" and then the next phalanx of townsfolk parted.

At the end of the gauntlet, there it sat: the faded black 1969 El Camino. It seemed to be waiting for him like a dutiful mascot.

"Let's do this," Dawn said.

The crowd hushed when the Writer opened the driver's door and got in. Dawn got in on the passenger side.

They looked at each other for a long moment.

Dawn leaned over, making it impossible for the Writer not to see her plush cleavage. She pointed to the three pedals on the floor. "That's the clutch, that's the brake, that's the gas. With your right foot on the brake, push in the clutch with your left foot."

However insecurely, the Writer did so.

"Now," she whispered, "turn the ignition key."

Here is where fantasy ends, he felt certain, *and reality kicks me square in the face. Up until now, this has all been hallucination,* and then he turned the key and the engine roared to life.

"Lemme make sure we don't back over any rednecks," Dawn said, peering back. Everyone had stepped well away from them.

The Writer was getting a headache from the infernal engine noise. "What now?" he shouted.

"Let me shift." She slunked the Hearst shifter into reverse. "Very slowly release the clutch and cut to your left when we begin to move."

"I'm not at all comfortable with my responsibilities here, Dawn!" he said frantically.

"Don't be a pussy! Just do it!"

He did and the car jerked backward in hitches. Were people laughing? *Of course they are!*

"Now cut the wheel to your right and drive!" she yelled over the engine cacophony.

"Drive where?"

"To the fuckin' gas station! We got no tires and no fuel!"

A capital idea...

Maneuvering the beastly vehicle less than a hundred feet into DeHenzel's Hess station was no easy feat. But eventually he managed to park—rather crookedly, in front of the mechanic's bay.

A smudge-faced tall blond man approached, wiping his nose with an oil rag. A tag on his stained overalls read DAVE. Here was another whose jaw dropped at the sight. "You gotta be shitting me. This thing's been sitting over there for damn near twenty years."

The Writer groaned getting out of the low driver's seat. "I'd like to engage your services, sir. I'll need you to completely refurbish this vehicle to a state of perfect working order."

The attendant, Dave, chuckled. "That's a lot of money, mister."

The Writer simply looked at him.

"I mean, thirty, forty grand maybe."

"And I'd like it soon, if you'd be so kind," the Writer said. "How soon can you have it finished?"

"Dave" kicked the tireless rims, and laughed. "Depends on how many men you can afford to pay me to hire on. This is a total overhaul. And we're talking fifty an hour per man."

"I'll pay a hundred." The Writer scribbled a check on the car hood. "And I'd like it painted white, if you will."

"Ten coats of jet lacquer?" the man inquired. "That's what Dicky Caudill put over the black paint back in the day."

"Ten coats."

Dave shook his head. "And if it needs a new engine?"

"Get it."

"What kind of tires you want?"

"The best."

"But, uh, sir, the very best tires for this car'd be over five hundred apiece."

"Ring it up." He gave him the check. "Here's a forty-thousand dollar retainer. Call me if you need more."

Dave dropped his rag. "Forty *thousand?*"

"Forty thousand. The remaining details such as trim, upholstery, etc., I leave to your professional judgment," the Writer said. "And now, thank you, sir, and good afternoon."

He grabbed Dawn by the hand and led her away, leaving Dave staring speechless.

"Wow," Dawn said in a hush. "What a *man.* You really walk it like you talk it."

"Not really," he admitted. "But I do seem to have taken on a newfound sense of confidence since I first started that car."

"Fuck. You've got me dripping like a fuckin' busted washing machine hose."

"Spoken with laudable eloquence, and if you don't mind," he said, "can we quicken our pace? After all the entails of the day, I *really* need a beer."

***

However badly the Writer needed a beer, that need would not find solvency at the Crossroads, not tonight. The dirt parking lot was *full,* and some were actually parking in the woods. "This cracker shit-hole is *never* full," Dawn said. "I wonder what the occasion is?" conjectured the Writer, whose hopes for several Collier's Civil War Lagers just sank as surely as the USS Monitor. "I know!" Dawn said as if struck by an epiphany. "*You're* the occasion!" "Me?" "Sure. You ended the town's curse! I'll bet every single Gomer in there won or received money in some way, and they're in there celebrating. And they're probably hoping you'll show up, so they can thank you!"

The Writer didn't necessarily put much stead in her supposition but he didn't want to risk it being true. He *hated* being sociable. "Where else can we drink?" he demanded rather testily. "I *need* to drink."

"Sallee's strip-joint'll probably be the same, and so will the other shit-pot bars." She paused for rumination. "I guess we could grab a couple six-packs to go and drink at the funeral parlor."

The Writer's psyche flared like a match-flame. "Oh, let's do that!"

The diversion of their course and their business at the local 7-Eleven clone was the work of but several minutes. Each lugging two six-packs of the coveted beer, they re-embarked, but something immediately snagged the Writer's eye. Graffiti, which was his wont to notice, was easily discerned on the coinbox plate of a long-disused pay phone. "Dawn, look at this!"

What had been written there, in magic marker, was something familiar:

THE BIGHEAD WILL GET YOU IF YOU DON'T WATCH OUT!

"Rather sinister, don't you think?"

Dawn rolled her eyes. "That shit's written all over the place. No different from 'Kilroy Was Here.'"

"Ah, I see"–his eyes darted lower. "But this, this scrawl here?"

He pointed to another graffito, which read:

I GIVE SARA JEAN A HEADER!

"What might the meaning of this be?"

She seemed to quaver. "You don't want to know. Now come on."

***

In no great expenditure of time (but very much in an unnecessary expenditure of *words*), the pair was soon situated in Dawn's office at the Winter-Damon Funeral Parlor, three bowling-pin-sized bottles of beer opened, and the rest stowed in the refrigerator. *Three* opened bottles, because within the most brief interim, Snowie had joined them. "You know you're the town hero, don't'cha?" the albiness asked, and kissed him sloppily on the mouth.

I've gotten a surfeit of tongue today, he thought. "So I've gathered."

"After you tolt me 'bout you startin' Dicky Caudill's car, I thunk sure I'd get me some good luck like damn near ever-one else I talk to today—"

"But you didn't?" Dawn asked with some surprise.

"Well, no." She seemed to hesitate for effect, then squealed in delight. "Until I was gettin' off work and Tobias tell me he's given me a *five dollar a hour* raise!"

"That's wonderful news," the Writer said.

"You sure that just wasn't for all the free blowjobs you give him?" Dawn spoiled the moment.

Snowie jabbed a finger at her. "Don't *make* me open up a can of whup-ass on you!"

"The only thing you're opening a can of anytime soon is dollar store dog food—for dinner—"

Snowie lunged with astonishing agility, landed on Dawn in her chair, and toppled them both to the floor, replete with the sounds of fists smacking faces. Disgusted, the Writer hauled Snowie off, by her hair, and yelled, "Girls! Girls! Stop this at once!"

Both women chuckled moments later. "We'se just funnin'," Snowie said.

Dawn added, rubbing her jaw. "You'll get used to it."

And in the *next* moment, Snowie was sitting in Dawn's lap, and they were voraciously jointed at the lips. The wet smacking sounds were plentiful, and so were shining pink glimpses of their tongues plowing into each other's mouth. *This really is the oddest couplet of friends I've ever imagined,* the Writer thought, sipping his beer, and shaking his head.

At the interlude's cessation, the Writer recalled the curious note he'd found hand-written in the blank book at the hotel, and he thought he'd influence conversation in a more advantageous direction. "Girls? I've a question. Might either of you have heard of a place known as the Crafter House?"

Snowie was wiping Dawn's lipstick off her mouth. "Crafter? I don't know, might've heard the name when I was little."

"Oh, yeah," Dawn spoke up. "I remember reading his file when I starting working here. Old guy, early '80s I guess. He had a weird first name, I think. Abraham, Amberham?"

"Ephriam," the Writer knew.

"That's it." She blinked at him. "Why are you asking about his house?"

What could the Writer say? *Well, I MAY have known him, or I may have known other people who knew him, and I have an uncanny notion that I've been to his house in 1991, but of course, I have no FUCKIN' MEMORY!* He couldn't say that. Nor could he say, *Well, my doppelganger made it very clear that I should go to his house and...bring a shovel.*

"Do you by chance, know if he was buried at his house?" he asked.

"It would be in all the records, but they've all been scanned by now," Dawn said, wiping Snowie's lipstick off *her* mouth. "I don't have the access to the older files any more."

The Writer cupped his chin like the Thinker at Columbia University. "Hmm. Let me ponder these elements a moment while I fetch another beer—"

"I'll get it for ya!" Snowie volunteered.

"No, THANK you. I prefer my beer to be free of all additives, including morphine and liquid Viagra."

The two women giggled in chipmonk-like glee when walked down to the "lab." The room's expected adornments greeted him with little interest. Anatomical charts, a periodic chart, and a hand-santizer and a rubber glove station, along with strange tubed machines and many bottles of chemicals, including an inverted bottle like an office water dispenser labeled JORE'S SOLUTION. He considered the best mode of locating this mythic Crafter House, which he had in mind would be most likely an old mansion. *Ask Mrs. Howard, or Portafoy?* he wondered. *Ask passersby in general?* But he much preferred anonymity, and he could easily afford it now. *Why should I canvass the neighborhood for this obscure information when I can get Snowie and Dawn to do it?* He had a funny feeling they would be benefitting from his sudden "millionaire" status, and something else occurred to him as well: *Those two loose-screw bimbos are essentially my only friends...*Fresh beer in hand, then, he returned to the office, but before he could say a word—

The sight of the two of them, now, stopped the Writer in the doorway.

If he had seen a 500-pound woman in an 18th Century Hessian grenadier uniform juggling tractor seats and whistling the theme from "Leave It To Beaver," or, say, Anderson Cooper, in a bunny suit, briskly using Shake Weights over a basket of Pet Rocks and Little Debbie Oatmeal Pies—that would've been just as unexpected as what he *did* see, which was this:

Dawn, nude from the waist down, back flat on the desk, her hands pulling her knees back to her armpits. One bare leg stuck up, as did one stainless-steel artificial leg, all to the effort of baring her vagina as blatantly as possible. Sexual anxiety reddened her face as she took in and released rapid breaths. Snowie leaned over from one side, her tongue roving fervid circles about her companion's clitoris, while her right hand was sunk to the wrist in Dawn's vaginal vault. It is not possible to effectively duplicate the variety of sounds that each girl was muttering.

The Writer sighed and sat down, sipping his beer and shaking his head. *So much for the discussion of how to locate Ephriam Crafter's house...*

Snowie's fist and forearm "pronated" and slipped deeper, and the noises of her cunnilingus could easily have been mistaken for a famished pig eating out of the slop trough. "Oooo, suck that cunt!" Dawn seethed, tensing up. "And stick it in deeper! I need my rocks off!"

Snowie obliged, managing to work her forearm in so far the Writer winced in disbelief. *How...FAR...can it go?* It must've been sheer imagination when he thought he saw a final thrust penetrate to the elbow, but be that as it may, Dawn's "rocks" were definitely gotten "off," and her vocal outcries left no doubt that orgasm has been achieved.

He may have imagined it also that the extraction of Snowie's hand had been accompanied by a "pop" sound.

Dawn laxed limp on the desk, huffing, a big ludicrous grin on her face. She was drooling. "Fuck, honey! What a great orgasm—fuck!"

"Good," Snowie said, "that should simmer ya down some." She was nonchalantly spraying her hand off with the Path Cloud cleaner, then finishing the job with a few lemon-scented Wet Ones. "You can do me later. I'm still wiped out from last night."

Dawn chuckled heavily. "Yeah, and so is he. Just ask the dead girl."

"Hilarious," the Writer said through a frown.

Snowie reclaimed her beer and sat right down in the Writer's lap. It was with no hesitation whatsoever that she mauled his crotch with her free hand. "Thought so. Hard as a piece'a pipe."

The Writer blushed.

"Not a very *big* piece of pipe," Dawn said, "but...still..."

"Thanks a lot!" the Writer barked.

"Relax, Tarzan. I'm just kidding. Your dick got us both off last night, in spades."

The Writer shrugged. *I suppose's that compliment enough.*

"See, here's the problem with cocks," the amputee went on. "The bigger they are, the more *useless* the owner is. Guys with big cocks are all assholes. Arrogant, lazy, abusive, unemployed because they live off of the floozies who fawn over them. Fuck that. I'm no sucker. I'll take a classy guy with a little dick any day," then she looked at the Writer and blew him a kiss. "A guy like you."

The Writer, again, frowned.

"Don't get your hopes up, hussy," Snowie snapped. "This one's *mine,* and don't *make* me bust your chops to prove it."

"The only chops you bust are the pork chops you shoplift from the Food Lion 'cos you're so fuckin' piss-poor."

"I am not! I got a five-dollar-a-hour raise, bitch! Slap Fight, I dare ya, ya pussy!"

Dawn flapped a hand in disregard. "Don't feel like it now. Besides, I'd win like always and you'd be crying like a baby. Like always."

"A knew it! A pussy! A chubby little scairty kat!"

"I'm not chubby!"

Snowie expanded her cheeks in mockery. "You're right, you're not. You're *fat!* Come on, I dare ya. Fattie! Fat, fat fat! Have another Big Mac!"

"I don't wanna embarrass you, 'cos I'd slap all that fucked-up albino white right off ya, and turn ya to a redskin!"

Snowie lurched off the Writer faster than the Writer could react, and—

CRACK!

—slapped Dawn so hard across the face, it left a red mark.

Unfazed, Dawn cracked back, harder, then multiple slaps were exchanged with sounds like wet leather snapping, and these exchanges ensued for a gruelingly long time. The Writer was too tired to intervene. *I just want to drink my beer and think!* At last he bellowed in a volume and tone of authority that astonished him:

"STOP THIS JUVENILE BULLSHIT RIGHT NOW!"

Both women stopped and gawped, each visibly wobbling at the toll so far inflicted by the Slap Fight.

"Listen, ladies, I'm on a serious mission here," he said, "and I need—"

"What mission?" Snowie asked, rubbing her face.

The Writer smirked. "Call it a research mission."

"Oh, for your next book?" Dawn asked, rubbing her face.

"Yes!" he snapped. "And of course, I'm aware that money, not love, makes the world go round, so I've a proposition—"

"Twenty," Snowie replied instantly, "or twenty-five if you want me to swallow."

The Writer rubbed his eyes. "That's not what I meant."

"Oh, listen to Paris Hilton over here," Dawn sniped. "The going rate for a blow in town is ten bucks, and Snowie sucks cock for five, like, *all the time.*"

"Fuck you!" Snowie turned to the Writer. "Dawn told me one time she blew *every guy in her brigade* when she was in the Army."

"Not the *brigade,* dickbrain!" Dawn bellowed, still pants-less sitting on the desk. "Every guy in my *squad.* That's three guys! You blow three guys *a day* at that hillbilly store of yours, and you suck dick for free rides home all the time, you told me so yourself!"

Snowie ground her teeth. "One more word, and I'll kick your ass again."

Dawn laughed out loud. "What's this *again* shit, you

slut-bucket?"

"Stop it!" the Writer yelled. He was *very weary* of this. "I'll pay you each one hundred dollars if you promise not to fight or argue any more tonight."

The girls both looked at each other, shrugged, and agreed.

"Wow," Snowie said when he handed her a $100 bill. "A hundred just for that?"

"He's rich," Dawn appended when she received her bill. "He just paid that pervert DeHenzel *forty grand* to fix up Dicky's car."

"Wow!" Snowie's pink eyes beamed, and she immediately and with emphasis sat back down in the Writer's lap and wrung her arm around him. "Rich men are *so* sexy. Say, since you're rich, do ya think that, like, maybe, you could buy *me* a car?"

The Writer's depressed thoughts perked up. Here was an angle he could work with. "Well, I suppose it's fully within the realm of possibility that I buy *both* of you cars. But not until you've helped me achieve the goals of my mission."

"Okay!" both of them said in unison.

The Writer finished his next beer. "First and foremost, you must discover the whereabouts of the Crafter House."

"Aw, that's easy," Snowie said. "We'll ask Great Uncle Septimus."

"He's the first of the Howard Clan," Dawn added. "Was born in, like, 1928 or some shit."

Enthusiasm riveted the Writer. "How excellent! Please call him right now and ask."

"Not possible," Dawn said.

Snowie lounged against the Writer as if he were an armchair. "He ain't got no phone, lives in the woods, in a thatch lean-to. But we're in luck, 'cos I think tonight's the night he do his fortune tellin' in Backtown. And that ain't but a twennie-minute walk."

"Yeah," Dawn remained sitting on the desk edge, her shaved pubis still impudently exposed. "We can go right now if you want."

The Writer wasn't drunk yet, and a short walk on a mild moonlit night might be just what he needed to dispel fatigue and re-engage his creative observations. "Superb, and we'll do just that, but"—he raised a finger of articulation. "There's something else we're going to do first, and I think you both know what it is..."

"Huh?" Snowie remarked, but then Dawn said, dreadfully, "Oh, no..."

"You girls are going to show me the Bighead," he insisted, "and you're going to do it *now.*"

***

For the Writer, it was an emotionally electrifying trek to that obscure backroom which featured the massive metal door; his thoughts were, indeed, abstract. What did Neil Armstrong expect just as he would be the first man to step onto the moon? What did Randal Jarrell think the moment he heard that World War II was over, or what did Edison think the moment before he flicked the switch on the new carbon-filament light bulb that would be called "U.S. patent 223,898?"

It must have been a transcendental moment indeed. It must've been CELESTIAL...

The rivet-bordered steel door now faced them. This little sub-corridor possessed an eerie yet appropriate semi-darkness, which seemed grainy, like old film. Dawn, who still had found it unnecessary to put her pants back on, faced the Writer grimly and said, "You can never tell anyone what you're about to see."

"And I never will, because," the Writer imparted, "I don't honestly believe I'll see anything. I don't believe there's a dead monster in there."

Dawn remained deadpan yet the scariest reaction of all was the expression that came to Snowie's face. She merely grinned.

"You didn't believe you'd start Dicky's car either," Dawn said, turned the key, and yanked the heavy door open.

Dawn and Snowie entered unhesitantly, leaving the Writer in the doorway, staring into untainted darkness—indeed, the manner of darkness what Lytton or Walpole might describe as "blacker than the blackest black ever espied." Then one of the girls switched on a light, a very *dim* light, dangling over a metal morgue table from a caged housing.

A covered figure lay atop the table, and that fact alone indicated no proof of "monsterdom." However, a conjoining fact projected some margin of doubt. The covered figure might have indeed been a human being, were it not easily over eight feet long.

The Writer didn't recall walking to the table; it was as if he glided there, or if it came to *him*. The girls were very casual about this, when Snowie—

POOF!

—pulled the cover off.

Now, the Writer—an acrophobe—felt as if he were standing on a 100th floor window ledge looking down. *Oh, dear,* he thought. The naked form of this "Bighead" appeared as merely a gigantic dead human being. Its feet were a foot and a half long, its hands over a foot from wrist to the tip of the index finger. Shoulder-width?

Over a full yard.

The thing's muscularity exceeded that of, say,

155

Schwarzenegger at the nexus of his Mr. Olympia days.

Of course, Schwarzenegger never had skin the color of bananas—*old* bananas just turning that slight brown tint and with black splotches. Every square inch of the man/thing's epidermis carried this tone. A network of nearly black blood vessels clearly stood out beneath this sickly, aberrant skin color.

The Writer's eyes tracked upward over the immensely muscled chest, to the—

He shivered.

The thing's head was covered with a black plastic sack of some kind—perhaps a 13-gallon "kitchen"—sized garbage bag, and the Writer felt some shuddering vagary that his was a good thing. Features of the face, of course, could not be distinguished, but the proportions of the head?

It must've been as big as a propane tank of the sort people used for their outdoor gas grills.

"We keep the face covered because we just can't look at it," Dawn said. "The rest? That skin, those splotches? We're used to that."

Used to that..."How—how much does it weigh?" the Writer mumbled. "It's got to be five hundred pounds."

"Six-something, my boss told me." Dawn stood there, legs spread–one leg of flesh, one a fascinating metal rod. Her arms were crossed as if in deep appraisal. "He needed the mini-forklift to get if out of his pickup and onto the table-scale."

The Writer stared, detached. *It appears that this is really happening, and that I'm really SEEING this, this extraordinary cadaver. It's not a monster, of course, but it certainly is evidence of an unparalleled human anomaly...*

And it made for great material in his book.

For whatever recondite reason, the Writer's visual

scrutiny had failed to so much as glance at the Bighead's genitals...until now.

"Checkin' out his junk, huh?" Dawn said. "It's hard to *not* check out his junk."

The Writer frowned. *That's a split-infinitive!* but he let it be. Well, how might Wodehouse describe *this?* A foot-long cutting of hose, and an inch and a half in diameter? A slackened tube of Pillsbury cookie dough? Whatever. It was indeed large; the greatest distraction, however, was that ill-yellowish hue, spotted by brown-black splotches. Pencil-thick black veins were clearly visible beneath the penile skin, and a snout-like foreskin shrouded the glans. Testicles—avocado-sized—lay like two forlorn lumps in a wrinkled scrotum thrice larger than a man's.

The Writer turned unwaveringly to the girls. "Ladies, as they said in the days of old, 'I must needs fetch me a another flagon of the high and might elixir first conceived by the ancient Mesopotamians."

"Huh?"

"I'm going to get another beer," he elaborated. "And then I must insist on a conclave of sorts, between the three of us, and you both shall tell me *everything you know* about the Bighead," and then he left them, assuming his departure would be a short and uneventful one.

Short, yes. Uneventful?

No.

***

A plethora of questions assailed him as he journeyed back to the ante-room of what he presumed was known as the "work-up room" or the "embalming suite." Questions such as: was it really a monster, or just a man? Reason suggested the latter, a man born with unique and staggering anatomical defects. How had it died, and under what detail of circumstances? How old was it, and who were its parents? How did it come to be in Luntville?

However, these considerations would come to quite an unceremonious halt only a second later. His thumbs tingled, which inclined him to think of Shakespeare: "By the prickling of my thumbs, something wicked this way comes," and had he been psychically susceptible, he might have called to mind the famous Raymond Chandler line (or was it Robert B. Parker?) wherein the author asserted the best cure for the novelist who doesn't know where his novel is going is to have a man with a gun barge into the room.

The door *banged* open, and a man with a gun barged into the room.

"Who the FUCK are you?" yelled a voice in a Jerseyish accent. The gun, a small automatic, was pointed in the Writer's face.

So taken aback was he, that he dropped the bottle of beer but by some miracle, it didn't break. *Thank God!* he thought.

In actuality, *two* men had barged into the room. For whatever subconscious reason, the Writer clung to his beer for dear life, to stand terrified before these two interlopers, and in the split-second paralysis that first afflicted him, he was able to make a panicked survey. Both men wore finely tailored suits, sporting conservative ties with gold and diamond stick-pins. The unarmed man stood short and darker-suited, with neatly cut black hair and a face that many might think of as rat-like (and had the writer been versed in collegiate sports—which he very much was *not*—he would've been struck by a suspicious semblance between this man and a certain basketball coach for an over-rated and oft-despised team in the south. Pardon the digression.) The other man was huge, the size of a pro football lineman, with hands so formidable that his gun-hand dwarfed the Colt .45 in it. Angular-faced and peninsular-jawwed, with short salt-and pepper hair.

The Writer could think of nothing sensible to say, so he said instead, "I trust you gentlemen are having a good day?"

"You got five seconds ta give me a reason why your brains ain't blown all over that wall," said the short one.

The large one moved the pistol closer.

"I—I—I—"

"What is this, a heist? Don't tell me you're burgling the joint."

More tongue-tied-ness prevented the Writer from any intelligible response.

"Hey, bub," said the big one (whose baritone voice immediately identified him as "Popeye" aka "Augie"), "what'cha need ta do, see, is ya need to explain to the Boss just what yer doin' here"—he shrugged massively—"or else I gotta kill ya."

"I'm friends with Dawn and Snowie!" the Writer blurted. "And please, sir, don't shoot me, I'm only a novelist."

The short man, obviously "Paulie," frowned. "Novelist? What kind'a dick-stupid job is that?"

Finally, something he could answer! "Well, sir, I would have to object with due respect that the occupation is, as you've called it, *dick-stupid*. A novelist is nothing less that another mode of artesian, no different from a sculptor, a painter, a poet, etc."

Paulie laughed in a non-too-complimentary way. "Just like poets and sculptors, huh? Yeah, *pussies*. And *painters?* Unless you're talkin' about a redneck in white overalls with a fuckin' roller in his hand, they're pussies too. Creamcakes, candy-asses."

The Writer was quite addled at this rendering. "Of course, any one man's opinion is as legitimate as another's, but I'll take the liberty of disagreeing with you, sir, and offer this for you to reconsider. Novelists, poets, and painters are *artists.* And *art* is how the aesthetic component of our population defines the human condition, wouldn't you say? Artists *reinterpret* the society around them, into new terms that kindle the imagination and incite a more complex manner of dealing with life."

Paulie stared, very darkly.

Augie roved his pistol barrel in circles. "One thing ya need ta know is, this, see. Never disagree with the Boss."

The inference registered instantly. "Ah, yes, sir, but I was going to add that the work-a-day world and those who inhabit it, truly *are* what make the world go 'round, and that artists, in the long-run, are pussies. Creamcakes. Candy-asses."

"Shaddap," Paulie said, rubbing his hands. "So you're friends with the Stump, huh?"

"The St—Oh, if by that you mean Dawn, why, yes. We are indeed friends, sir. We were just now, before you afforded me the pleasure of meeting you, having a few beers."

"A few beers, huh? Well where is she? I'll bet she's fuckin' off as usual, probably stickin' that stump up that lesbo-albino's cooze."

"I'm right here, Mr. Paulie," Dawn interrupted, then Paulie and Augie both turned and frowned. Dawn was still without pants.

"Don't get dressed up on my account," Paulie said.

"Sorry," she said. "I...spilled something on my pants."

"I'll *bet* ya did." He jabbed a thumb at the Writer. "And I still don't know what to make of this clown."

Clown? the Writer thought. *Well, sir, this CLOWN*

is an internationally published novelist who has earned considerable accolades from the most lauded literary journals in the country. And this CLOWN just made a MILLION DOLLARS today. How much did YOU make?

But he didn't say that.

"He's our friend, Mr. Paulie," Dawn pointed out. "He's the cream pie from last night."

Augie's ledge-like brow rose as if impressed, while Paulie looked outright elated. "*You? You're* the one who belted all that nut up the dead junkie? Eddie Munster?"

"The same, sir."

Paulie slapped him hard on the back. "Man alive! I sure had you pegged wrong! Hey, any guy can pump that much cum up a kicked-off skinny hype is *okay* in my book. Shit, it ain't easy gettin' up for a corpse, let alone drainin' your sack in the shit!"

The Writer stood nonplused. *I suppose...that's a compliment...*

"Okay," Paulie continued in his Jersey-accent authority. "You're off the shit-list, but that brings me to *you,*" and he glared right at Dawn.

"Me, Mr. Paulie?" came her sheepish reply.

"Yeah, you. Augie told ya about that SD card he lost, and there ain't no other place he could'a lost it but here. We *need* that card, which means you're gonna pick this place apart till ya find it. And if ya *don't?* We gonna drag you out'a here and take you upstate. And you don't wanna *know* what'll happen to ya there."

Dawn smiled. "Oh, you mean *this* SD card, Mr. Paulie? The one with the pregnant girl drinking horse cum?"

"Mama, Mia!" Paulie celebrated. "Just like that and here it is! Whaddaya think'a that, Augie?"

"Cool beans, boss."

Paulie was ecstatic (unduly ecstatic, perhaps due to some lingering hyperactivity from childhood). "Fuckin' A," he exclaimed, looking at the card, and then he looked at Dawn. "I'm so happy I could kiss ya!"

Dawn faked batting her eyes. "What a nice thing to say, Mr. Paulie."

"But a'course I *ain't* gonna kiss ya because who the *fuck* would wanna kiss a bitch who's sucked as many dicks as you!" and then he and Augie burst out laughing.

Dawn didn't laugh, however.

"Anyway, thanks for findin' this fuckin' card," Paulie said. "We'd've lost a lot of dough if it got lost."

"Oh, don't thank me, Mr. Paulie," Dawn pointed out. "Our new friend the Writer is the one who found it."

"That's correct, sir," the Writer said. "I noticed it on the pavement out back and immediately gave it to Dawn in the event it was something of importance."

Paulie's expression of joy bloomed, and he slapped the Writer hard again on the back. "Buddy, I'm tellin' ya, you must be our lucky fuckin' charm! First that primo cream-pie last night and now this!" He shot his gaze to Augie. "Augie. Tip him."

Augie stuffed a $100 bill into the Writer's breast pocket. "Ya done good, bub."

"Uh, why, you have my unheeding thanks, sir," the Writer said for lack of anything more astute.

Dawn's eye fluttered. "What about me, Mr. Paulie? Do I get a tip?"

"You wanna tip, too, sweetheart? Well, how 'bout this? Me not stuffin' your gimp tits and ass in the furnace— *that's* your tip!" and then, naturally, he and Augie burst out laughing.

Evidently, Paulie was on a roll today. In fact, next, he

blatantly rubbed his crotch and looked at Dawn. "Shit, toots, I'm so happy right now, I got wood. I need one for the road. You don't mind, do ya?"

In truth, Dawn very much *did* mind but she wisely took the more advantageous route of patronization. "Oh, Mr. Paulie, I'm so glad you asked. Nothing makes me hotter than a big dick in my mouth, especially *your* big dick."

While the Writer had no inclination whatever to witness this...ministration, he couldn't help but take note that Paulie's "big dick" was no more than three inches fully erected. *Holy National Book Award! Even MY penis is bigger than his!*

A comforting observation; however, the Writer turned immediately to Augie and persevered to engaging the man in some incidental conversation. "So, Mr. Augie. As they might have said in the 1600's, 'whence dost ye hail?'"

Augie frowned. "Huh?"

"Where are you from?"

The question seemed to plunge the giant man into a pleasant reminiscence. "Aw, shit, I grew up in Queens. Great place for a kid. My dirty cooze of a mother was bangin' all kinds of guys behind my father's back when he was at work, and...well, let's just say she disappeared one day. But anyway, it was my poor old pop who busted his balls raisin' me and my brothers. Poor old guy, worked ten, twelve hours a day at a meat-packers, never had no time for himself 'cos all he did was work to feed us. Was no fuckin' welfare and food cards back then, and pop wouldn't've taken it if there was. That's what'cha call Sicilian Pride. And see, me and my brothers never had a dime to our names but all our friends did 'cos their parents gave 'em all allowance, but, shit, we couldn't ask our pop for no fuckin' allowance, not hard as he worked. So anyway, me and my brothers, we'd all go to the big Chinatown in Flushing—"

"Oh, Flushing. I didn't know there was a Chinatown there."

"Aw, sure, best one. Brooklyn and Manhattan Chinatowns ain't shit compared to Flushing—I mean, if ya like chink food, like I do. Anyhow, see, what they had there back then were all these little nail salons, and I mean *little*. Storefronts on these joints were maybe six feet wide, no shit, and, sure, oriental ladies would go in sometimes and get their nails done every now and then, but everyone knew the real scoop."

The Writer couldn't guess beyond cat kabobs and illegal mahjong games. "And what might the real scoop have been, sir?"

Augie shrugged hugely. "They were really whorehouses, and they each had a little room in back where these gook chicks—most of 'em was old bags, and fat—would fuck guys for, ten, fifteen bucks. The Hong Kong Quickie, ya know?"

"Ah, I see," but the implication in this tale seemed to suggest some revelation that would, in time, explain whatever mode which Augie and his brothers used to earn money so that they needn't burden their working-class father. "So you and your brothers, perhaps, were hired to sweep and mop the floors or something of that nature?"

Augie winced. "No, no, man. We'd strangle the old bitches. We'd wait out back for when they came outside for a smoke-break. Then we'd whack 'em in the head, drag 'em back inside, fuck 'em, and choke 'em out. A'course, we took all their money too, and sometimes they had gook food like shrimp chips and these little jelly candies and these dumpling-lookin' things that were sweet inside. We'd take that home for pop."

The Writer stared. "Um, ah, yes. That's quite industrious, I'd say. I presume you were a teenager then?"

"Aw, no. I was, like, nine, Binny was ten, and Nicolo

was I guess twelve. I'll tell ya, for three poor kids from Queens, we were papered up like 42nd Street pimps. And ya know? They never reported the murders to the cops on account most'a them chink women were illegals. Man, I'll tell ya, me'n my brothers were go-getters." The massive man crossed his arms and nodded. "Good times, man, good times. You know, by the time I was in junior high, I'll bet I'd strangled thirty or forty'a those pan-face hoo-uhs."

"Mmm. Pan-faces, yes," the Writer offered because no other response could be conceived of. "That's quite a unique take on the rite-of-passage theme, one to rival even D.H. Lawrence's 'Rocking Horse Winner.'"

"Huh?"

Fortunately, a subverbal exclamation blockaded the need for any further discourse between Augie and the Writer. It was a guttural moan that had issued from Paulie's mouth while something clearly unwelcome entered *Dawn's* mouth.

"Aw, fuck, yeah, hun. You suck cock better than my first babysitter!"

This high praise did not seem to register with Dawn, for now she was grimacing, and was bending over the wastecan.

"Toots! You ain't gonna insult me by spittin' it out, are ya?"

"Yeah," Augie said. "Classy dames never spit. They swallow the whole pile of fuck and ask for seconds."

"And thirds!" Paulie yelled.

"Well, yeah, boss, and fourths."

"And fifths and sixths!" and then—will you be surprised?—they both busted out in laughter.

Dawn, cross-eyed now, slumped her shoulders, braced herself, and—

gulp

"Good girl!" Paulie said, pulling his zipper back up.

Dawn grabbed the Writer's beer and began chugging.

"Well, kids, it's been fun," Paulie said, rubbing his hands together. He turned to the Writer and pointed. "And *you*. I *like* you."

Augie winked at him. "That's a good thing, bub."

"You're my new good luck charm!" Paulie railed, then the two mafiosi left the room.

Dawn waited tensely with crossed fingers. She may even have been murmuring silent prayers, like a suppliant pleading forgiveness...until the back door slammed shut.

"My God, if I have to suck that psychopath's little dick just *one more time,* fuck! I'll climb in the cremator myself."

The Writer could've collapsed from relief that the previous brain-anesthetizing interlude had ended. "I thought they'd never leave. I think I was even preparing to die," the Writer said. When Dawn handed him back his beer, he refused. "No, no, you finish it."

She sneered and snapped, "What, you think I got diseases or something?"

"That's not it at all, Dawn. But given the fact that Paulie just *ejaculated* in your mouth, it's undoubted that there are now molecular traces of his semen on the bottle. I'd simply prefer not to transfer those traces into *my* mouth."

"Fuck you," she said, and chugged the rest of the bottle. "Next time, *you* can suck his dick."

The Writer refrained from further comment and, armed with fresh beers, walked back to the Big Door with Dawn.

When they entered, Snowie looked like a deer in headlights. She heaved herself at Dawn, and embraced her. "Oh, my holy gracious me, I thought sure those crazy men were killin' you!" She kissed Dawn loudly and wetly all over her face. "I heard 'em all the way in here, laughin' and cacklin, like a pair'a devils!"

Dawn remained overwhelmed by her previous fright and the unpleasantness of what she'd been forced to swallowed just minutes ago. She tried to push Snowie away. "Honey, please. Now's not the time."

Snowie withdrew, pouting. "Well, dang it, I was just tryin' ta be infectionate!"

"That's *affectionate,* you cement-head. And I'm *not* in the mood right now."

But the Writer paid their banter little mind; his attentions, instead, were directed at the pallid, supine form of what was on the long metal table beneath the single yellow light bulb. *So there he is—he or IT. The Bighead.*

The bruised-banana pallor looked waxlike, and the curled fat tube of flesh that were its genitals seemed otherworldly. The overall image gave the impression of a field of static electricity, all maximized by the black plastic bag which concealed the mysterious lump that was its head. The Writer approached a step or two, asked himself, *Am I REALLY going to remove the bag and behold the legend's face?* then withdrew. The necessary testicular fortitude was not to be found.

But it was time for answers. "Girls, now that Paulie and Augie have left, you will both tell me *everything you know* about the Bighead. I need to know about its antecedents, its age, its history. Furthermore, I need to know why it's here—of all places–and why it has *remained* here for all these years," but when he returned his gaze to the girls—

No, no, no...

Dawn was spraddled out on the floor while Snowie was deftly sliding a long plastic specimen tube in and out of her vagina—her *pulsing* vagina, that is.

"Come on, girls! This is *my* time! I *paid* for it!" he yelled. "Do that later!"

167

They *weren't* going to do it later. Dawn's bare hips squirmed on the floor as Snowie hunched closer to offer an accommodating tongue-tip to ornament the insertion, extraction process. Dawn's unbra'd breasts had been pulled out (and formidable breasts they were); she tweezed each nipple hard betwixt index finger and thumb.

"Please, girls!" he bellowed. "The night is passing us by!" but the adjuration couldn't have been more baldly ignored.

Useless. The Writer resigned himself to walking around the dim room and its bare cinderblock walls. Deeper in shadows, he discovered some aluminum shelves upon which were stacked more bottles curiously marked JORE'S, coils of rubber tubes, and various apparatuses (*Shouldn't it be apparati?* he wondered) which obviously related to the mortuary profession, a topic he was not well-versed in.

An old Frigidaire refrigerator stood sentinel-like in the corner. A hand-written warning had been taped to the door: DO NOT OPEN. The Writer's *mores* made him typically one always to obey the law and never to break the rules. However, at just that moment he found himself in quite an indefensible state of curiosity, so...he opened the refrigerator door.

The interior light came on. On the top shelf lay several 2-liter bottles of Diet Coke and a foil-wrapped piece of candy: CHUNKY, with raisins. No other shelves existed in the compartment; instead, a large glass bottle—five gallons, by the looks of it—sat on the bottom. The material that nearly filled it looked nauseating, like swamp scum but tinted more yellow than green. Tiny brown flecks seemed suspended in it.

The sickly, barely describable color of the stuff was somehow giving him a headache and souring his stomach. He closed the refrigerator door—

—and rolled his eyes when he looked down. The shenanigans on the floor had not quite reached a terminus: Dawn, evidently, was experiencing throes of multiple orgasms care of Snowie and her plastic specimen tube. The vocalizations of her ecstasy were too ridiculous to bother describing.

Behold, he thought, rather depressed, *the human condition's most irrevocable force: the pursuit of orgasm.* If God existed as a sentient entity—and the Writer believed that He did—what must He have been thinking when he invented the human sex-drive? This drive, supposedly designed to propagate the species, caused participants to do the most *preposterous* things, and to assume the most *ludicrous* physical positions.

I wonder how hard God is laughing right now, looking down at this...

His attention had no choice but to wander further. Try as he might to keep his gaze averted from the thing's penis, he found himself staring at it nonetheless. Did the tiniest drop of some unknown fluid glimmer in the monstrous, slit-like "pee-hole?" Did any monster-urine remain in the bladder? And just how big did this creature's erection get back when it was alive? These and similar morbid questions popped up in his mind, as if just looking at the thing induced perverse query. Then—

The Writer leaned forward to inspect an incongruence...

Two half-inch-thick rubber tubes lay across the thing's massive right thigh, and they seemed to originate somewhere in the groin. These tubes extended about a foot, and were each capped by a small valve.

What on earth are these things?

At last, the lesbian bacchanal on the floor was wrapped up, and Dawn rose to a very wobbly standing position.

Snowie smacked her lips and winged the plastic tube quite accurately into a nearby sink.

"Well thank Keller and Oppenheimer you two girls are done," the Writer said, now rather irritated. "No more monkey business. Dawn, what is the purpose of these two tubes?"

A now very rosy-cheeked Dawn, looked listlessly at the Writer. "Huh? Oh, those? Those are the inlet and outlet ports. For embalming. The top one goes into the femoral artery; that's where you pump the embalming fluid in. The other one's connected to the femoral vein, where the excess comes out–a drain. Inflow, outflow."

The Writer nodded, thinking. "So...when was the Bighead embalmed? Recently?"

"No, twenty years ago. My boss, Mr. Winter-Damon did the job."

"I see..." The Writer stroked his shitty-looking beard. "Then these tubes have been implanted all that time?"

"No, no, only since—" but then Dawn exhibited a curious pause, as of one catching one's self just before revealing a secret.

The Writer stared at her. "Only since, *when,* Dawn?"

Instead of answering, Dawn's eyes darted to Snowie.

"What are you looking at her for, Dawn?" the Writer demanded. "Why don't you answer the question?"

Now she exchanged desperate glances between Snowie and the Writer, and said nothing.

Something is rotten in the state of Denmark, the Writer couldn't resist another Shakespeare quote. He sipped his beer, nodding. "You're lying, Dawn. Why is that? You've already shown me the Bighead's corpse, so why are you hemming and hawwing about those tubes?"

Now Snowie grinned crazily. "Tell him, Dawnie."

"No!"

"If you don't, I will."

"I'll beat your ass like a rented drum if you say one more word!" Dawn yelled.

Snowie leapt to the other side of the table, still grinning, and blurted, "Dawn uses them tubes to make the Bighead's dick hard!"

This information had been relayed just as the Writer had been taking another sip of his beer, and that sip was immediately spat out all over the floor.

Meanwhile, Dawn chased Snowie around the morgue table but her prosthesis forestalled any hope of success.

The Writer wiped beer off his face and shirt. "Snowie! Repeat what you just said. I couldn't possibly have heard you correctly. You didn't say—"

"You dumbass!" Dawn yelled at her friend. "Always running your mouth. Well, now that you spilled the beans, I guess we might as well show him."

"Yeah!" Snowie squealed. "Show him!"

The Writer stood inert as a disheveled mannequin as he watched what would come next.

Dawn resigned herself to the situation, and got busy at the counter, fiddling with more rubber tubes. "It's a trick I learned in the Army. I was what they called a 90M Combat Mortuary Specialist—the *worst* job in the world, but I took it 'cos the recruiter said the experience would set me up in a civilian career." She shook her head, frowning. "We'd dig graves with Army trenchers to bury enemy dead, and recover our own dead, get positive ID, then do prelim autopsies and embalmings and prepare the poor bastards to get shipped back home. My first field assignment was with an FET, that's Female Engagement Team, with the 1st AD Sustainment Brigade in Afghanistan. That was in 2015. But the shit was already flying in Syria with their bullshit psycho civil war and then these Islamic State assholes started moving in, cutting off baby heads and shit like that. So me and this other girl named Goodwin got TDY'd to Tal Afar, Iraq, which was very close to Syria..."

The Writer listened, intrigued. *A Combat Mortuary Specialist. Wow!* What an original kind of character to have in a novel!

Dawn continued to fiddle with things at the counter, and she still had yet to feel it necessary to put her pants back on. "So it was me and Goodwin. We were both Spec 4's, and when we got to Tal Afar, the Aid and Assistance Battalion set us up in a little field morgue, and it was our job to disinfect and embalm any enemy dead the grunts brought in. We had to do a three-day training block about new protocol first— for instance, we could not 'verbally abuse' dead enemy combatants, no 'ethnic slurs,' no 'defacement or desecration' of the corpus, shit like that. If we did, we could get court-martialed. It was a laugh riot. Can you believe it? Almost all the bodies the grunts brought to our station were ISIS, the psychos who burn babies alive because they had Shiite parents, for fuck's sake. They have a standing field order to rape all female captives before they kill them, including children. The scumbags cut off thousands of heads and won't even show their faces while they do it, fuckin' cowards. Well, lemme tell ya something," she said, and smiled at the Writer. "Payback's a bitch."

By now the Writer thought he had a fair idea of what this *payback* likely consisted of, but he did not consciously admit it to himself. Instead, he considered Dawn's diatribe, at the least, an interesting insider point of view.

"It's all about positive pressure," she said. "Embalming is no different from a radiator flush. You pump out the dead blood and pump in the Jore's. Out with the old, in with the new." From a one gallon jug, she poured a small amount of clearish fluid into a glass cannister which sat atop a machine. Then she took a long tube spouting from the bottom of the machine and connected it to upper tube on the Bighead's right thigh—what she'd previously designated at the inlet to the femoral artery–and she opened the tiny valve already in place. "All the mortuary textbooks say to set inflow pressure to 12 p.s.i's, that's the standard. But one time my partner Goodwin accidently set it to 15—this was in the 'Stan, before I met her—and anyway, she's pumping away and suddenly the dead guy on her slab pulls a fuckin' boner and a half. So she turned the machine off and didn't release the outflow valve yet. The dick stayed hard as a rock, and she fucked the radical Islam, baby-killing *shit* out of it. Said a dead 'Rab's cock was the best orgasm of her life." Dawn winked at the Writer. "Cool, huh?"

The Writer could not deduce a proper response, if, indeed, any response at all could be deemed proper.

He stared in mute paralysis as Dawn demonstrated the previously detailed process in real time.

She turned on the blender-looking machine. Snowie shouted "Let 'er rip, honey!" The machine buzzed and bubbled for a moment, then was turned off. In that moment— you will already have ascertained—the Bighead's massive limp penis had transformed into a massive *erect* penis.

"That's about as far as we go," Dawn said, but the Writer heard her words as if in an echo chamber. All his attentions were hijacked by the sick-yellow, worm-veined pillar of muscle sprouting from the Bighead's groin.

Snowie wasted no time disrobing and climbing on, nor did she waste time lowering her womanly parts onto the dead monster's erection. Of course, most would want to know some

precise *dimensions* of that erection, and the Writer guessed
ten-plus inches long with the girth of a tennis ball can, and
it was admirable how expertly, how *meticulously,* Snowie
engaged in the congress. Some element of care was obvious
(that was one big, gnarly pole of meat to be sitting on), but
just as admirably was the speed and forcefulness with which
she effected her copulation. The look on her face was that
of gleaming, rosy-cheeked, greed-incarnate ("chasing that
nut," the Writer reckoned in colloquialism, just as Corporal
Stephan chased Peace in Faulkner's A FABLE; and just as
the Prodigal had adventured himself into the Labyrinth in
James' "Mr. Humphreys and His Inheritance," to make off
with the Jewel which would enrich the finder thereof for his
life). Each time Snowie smacked her loins over the entirety
of the thing's penis, she grunted primitively, and restarted
the cycle.

By now the Writer's shock, outrage, disbelief, and
sheer stupefaction was growing less and less profound.
I'm watching a woman have sex with a monster cadaver,
he realized. *Oh, well.* Perhaps all that he'd witnessed since
arriving in Luntville was cauterizing him. What further
ministrations of outrage and bombast could *possibly* be left
to see?

"Hurry up, Snowie," Dawn complained. "We haven't got
all night. We gotta get to Backtown."

On and on, Snowie cycled her splayed hips up and down,
which made for interesting silhouette-shapes on the back
wall.

"So I presume you girls perform this spectacle for
Paulie's cameras as well?" inquired the Writer.

"Oh, hell, no! We'll *never* let that dago crackpot know
about the Bighead. He'd be bringing crackwhores in here three
at a time to fuck it. The Bighead is *our* private stock," Dawn

informed. "Me and Snowie, and that's it. *Fuck,* Paulie." She crossed her arms, tapping a foot as Snowie banged away. "But we fuck dead guys on camera all the time, in the main suite. Paulie *loves* that shit. Any time a man in town dies, he comes here, so during the embalming, we pump his dick up, fuck him, give the tape to Paulie, and he pays us a hundred each."

"Sounds like"—the Writer cleared his throat—"a profitable enterprise," but he was reflecting how a segment of her last verbiage had to be one of the most unique ever spoken in history: *...we fuck dead guys on camera all the time...Hmm.* "And you say you learned this very aesthetic process of erecting the dead...in the Army?"

Dawn's face beamed. "Sure did!"

Be, the Writer thought, *All That You Can Be...,* but then something kindled in his brain. "Tell me, what exactly did you mean a few minutes ago when you said 'That's about as far as we go'?"

"Huh? Oh, I meant that—"

Her answer was intervened by the vociferations of Snowie's orgasm, which were very loud indeed. Then the sweat-sheened albino laxed into silence and collapsed upon the creature's immense chest. It would be accurate to say that she was "sweetly exhausted."

Dawn chuckled. "Now you know why we don't need boyfriends. Who needs boyfriends when you've got *that?*"

The Writer nodded, impressed. "But, you were saying? 'That's about as far as we go'?"

"Yeah, I meant we don't inflate the thing's dick past about ten-inches."

The Writer stared. "You mean it gets *bigger?*"

Dawn laughed out loud. Even Snowie laughed out loud as she remained plopped over on the monster's chest, still drained in the "*la petite mort*" of her love-making.

"Eighteen, maybe twenty inches max," Dawn added, "and big around as the fat end of a wine bottle. Stands to reason. According to the legends whenever the Bighead raped a girl, his cock was *so big* it tore them up. Most of them bled to death."

Snowie was finally rousing herself off the slab and its grim tenant. "You wanna see? Dawnie, pump it up all the way for him—"

"No," the Writer blurted. "Uh, no thanks. I've beheld enough wonders for one night."

***

Dawn wasted no time in draining the Bighead's member back to its deflated state, putting her pants back on, and ushering them out, very mindful of locking the doors behind them. The Writer—always mindful of necessities—was sure to bring beer for the trip.

It was a warm, quiet walk out of the town limits. "We'll cut through these woods here'n git there faster," Snowie said, "just walk loud." "Walk *loud?*" the Writer posed interrogatively. "Yeah," Dawn said. "Footsteps scare the copperheads away."

Delightful, the Writer thought, stomping the underbrush.

A moment later, a foul redolence seemed to tinge the air, which Dawn recognized at once with a gag. "Fuck! Dead bodies buried shallow." "We'se smell that ever now'n then 'round here," Snowie added. "Local rummy named Stoodie once tolt me he seen the Larkins boys buryin' some of their kills here."

It's a wonderful life. Where's Jimmy Stewart when you need him? The Writer pointed to an old dilapidated shack just up ahead. "Let me guess," he jested. "I'll bet that old shack is reputed to be haunted."

Both girls came to abrupt halts and jerked their gazes at the Writer.

"What?"

"You psychic?" Dawn said.

"That ole place *is* haunted," Snowie said in a tone of hushed dread. "By the ghost of Jake Martin and his grandson Travis. They'se the scoundrels that brung headers back to these parts."

"Headers?" the Writer logically inquired. "What's that?"

"You don't want to know," Dawn said.

"Oh, but to the contrary, I very much *do* want to know. I thrive on local color. And I've heard that word elsewhere. What is it?"

"Just come on," Dawn insisted, "and don't ever look at that shack." She pulled the Writer away by the hand like a sack on a towline. Something told him to cast a glance behind him, and when he did...

He saw figures by the shack, not half-invisible specters, nor hazy outlines, but solid flesh and blood *people*. A ramshackle old man in a wheelchair, with legs that ended at mid-shin, then a tall brawny strapping young man who possessed the look in his eyes of someone who had copious violence and revenge on his mind. And then—

—then...

Two more figures stepped into view, and he knew who they were. *I'm pretty sure I'd met both of them when I was here in the past,* the Writer related to himself. *And I sure as SHIT saw them in my nightmares...*

These two new presences were, of course, Dicky Caudil and Balls Conner, both grinning, both aware of him. The latter stood hip-cocked in Levi's, stroked a goatee, and he mockingly tipped his John Deere hat to the Writer. The former had his jeans opened and his penis out, heartily masturbating. "I'se gonna cream all over that chubbie pegleg some day, Balls."

Don't let her hear you call her chubbie!

"Yes sir. Shine her up like a honey-dip," Balls contributed. "Me? I'll take care'a Snow White, turn that cheesecake pussy'a hers inside-out." Then the redneck thug looked pointedly at the Writer. "And you, Writer..." Balls winked. "We'se'll run inta you before long, up the house, likely as not, or maybe the abbey."

The Writer snapped from his trance. "Can you hear me?"

"Oh, yeah," Balls said but Dicky didn't say anything, too busy ejaculating on a fern.

"Can see ya too," Balls continued. "We got unfinished business from when you was last in town..."

Dawn yanked him harder. "I told you not to look at that place! Now come on!"

Dumbfounded (as he'd been for most of this trip thus far) he babbled, "Did you–did you hear him?"

"No! They're ghosts! Don't listen to them!"

The Writer snapped out of it, contemplating. *Up the house,* Ball's mirage has said. *Did he mean the Crafter house?* And...what else? What had he said?

Something about the abbey...

"Hey, Snowie, didn't you say something earlier about an *abbey?*"

"Why, yeah," the well-breasted albino confirmed. "It's where Dicky and Balls both got kilt...by the Bighead, they say."

"It's where the Bighead got killed too," Dawn added. "Shot in the head by a priest. How do you know about Wroxton Abbey?"

Interesting. A priest..."I just...heard about it somewhere," the Writer said.

178

They were tromping away from the haunted shack and its proximal stench. The Writer felt better presently. "So am I deducing this correctly? After the Bighead was shot, someone—your boss, evidently—brought the corpse to the funeral home?"

Dawn nodded. "You wanna hear the whole story?"

"I'd very much be prevaricating were I to issue anything less than and assenting response," the Writer said.

"I guess that means yes." Dawn's spectacular unbra'd breasts rode up and down beneath her blouse with each step. "No one knows where the Bighead came from, but some say Boone National Park, real deep dank forest."

"And no one knows what he really *is,*" Snowie added. Her breasts, too, just as spectacular, snagged the Writer's gaze without mercy, and at once, he was at odds with his perceptions and the manner by which his nature seemed to be changing since this adventure had begun. *What's with the sudden Tit Cognizance?* he wondered. *It's simply not like me to be distracted so indubitably by such trivial eroticisms.* Indeed, these girls were about to tell him something he really wanted to know, yet here he was, only half listening because, because—

Because I can't take my eyes off their TITS!

That being thought, Snowie continued, "Some say he's part human, part demon, on account many folks have it that when the swamp near the abbey drained, there was devil-worship relics and such found in the muck, and somethin' like a temple."

Dawn picked up, "And just as many others insist that he's a human-alien hybrid, when a spaceship crashed in the swamp, the operator survived long enough to fuck the daylights out of a local woman and knock her up. And what came out nine months later was the Bighead. It *ate* its way

179

out of her belly. Then some old hermit found the baby and took it far away and raised it in the woods."

"This certainly is diverse lore," the Writer managed to observe. "And I take it the Bighead, years later, came back to this area for some reason?"

Dawn nodded, finally leading them out of the forest and onto a dark paved road. "The Bighead was looking for something at that old abbey—"

"But no one knows what," Snowie said.

"And whatever it was he was looking for," the Writer postulated, "this priest managed to kill him in the process?"

"Shot the Bighead right in the eye, blowed his brains out," Snowie said. "The brains, they say, was yellow'n green, like custard."

They crossed the road, marked by a sign: TICK NECK ROAD. The Writer attempted some allegorical applications of the name but came up with nothing. "So let me get this straight. The priest kills the Bighead and then...Took the body to the funeral home?"

"No, no," Dawn elaborated. "He split as fast as he could. There was a lightning storm that night; in fact, it was one of the bolts of lightning that hit the plug and caused the lake to drain. The priest ran back to the abbey for cover, and some say he had a girl with him, a survivor. Inside, there were the dead bodies of Dicky and Balls, *all* fucked up."

Snowie: "'Twas the Bighead did away with 'em earlier. Yanked Dicky's spine straight out his asshole. And Balls... well, let's forget about what the Bighead did to him..."

Dawn: "But it was just about that same time that my boss, Mr. Winter-Damon, happened to be driving through the same area. First thing he noticed was the drained lake, second thing he noticed was the Bighead's body lying there. So, like any entrepreneur, he winced the body into the back of his truck, took it back to the parlor, prepped it, an embalmed it."

The writer winced. "Why on earth would he do that?"

Dawn shrugged. "He was always looking for extra ways to make money. That's why he let Paulie and his people film corpse-fucking in the work-up room. Anyway, Mr. Winter-Damon had this idea that he could use the Bighead's body as a freak show attraction, sell tickets and all but that never got off the ground. He had his first stroke and was immobilized, forgot all about it. His wife doesn't even know what's in that room, *nobody* does except me, Snowie, and now you. When I first started working here, I was gonna incinerate the damn thing but, well, that's when I started pumping its cock up and getting the best sex of my life."

"You're an industrious woman," the Writer said, shaking his head.

"Then I became friends with Snowie, so naturally I had to share the wealth with her."

Snowie grabbed Dawn's hand and kissed her. "She's so good to me, ain't she?"

"I'd say that observation in singularly undoubted." The Writer watched them pause in the road to noisily swap tongues. *What an intriguing world it is that we live in.* "So that's the story of the Bighead. I must say, it surpassed even *my* expectations." And, incredulous as the tale was, how could he disbelieve it? He'd *seen* the evidence.

Yet now there was more evidence to investigate—evidence of more of this town's legend-haunted mystery: the Crafter house.

My doppelganger—an entity of impossibility—told me to go there, he mused. *So there I shall go...*

***

Not a hundred yards up the road, a great blossom of white glare emerged, along with sounds of frolic. First the Writer spied a massive gravel-paved lot with haphazard old railroad ties lain down to designate parking spaces. Several high sodium lights accounted for the shifting white glare, and this illuminated an expanse of clunker cars and dented, lusterless pickup trucks–the redneck ride of choice. WELCOME TO BACKTOWN, a sign boasted. LUNTVILLE'S PREMIER MOBILE HOME COMMUNITY.

Ah, premier, the Writer reflected.

"Here we is," Snowie said with enthusiasm.

"No," Dawn said. "He we *are.* Did you learn *anything* in school?"

"Yeah, I learnt how to kick fat girls' asses."

Dawn pointed a foreboding finger. "Don't call me fat. I'm *not* fat."

Actually, the Writer observed. *You could both stand to lose a few, but who am I to talk?* "Neither of you is—not are—fat. You're both plush, curvaceous beautiful women, or, to use a more local parlance, drop-dead gorgeous brick fuckin' shit houses."

"Awww!" Snowie cooed.

"He's so sweet!" Dawn added.

Snowie slid up next to him and kissed his neck. "I could just eat you up! My millionaire boyfriend!"

"Boyfriend, my ass!" Dawn yelled.

"You mean your *fat* ass—"

"I swear, Snowie, you keep running that mouth of yours I'm gonna turn both of your pink bunny-rabbit eyes *black.*"

"That's enough!" the Writer yelled before Dawn could retort. "Honestly, you're like two pit bulls! If you don't stop this fighting and hostile talk, I'm never giving either of you money again."

Each girl fell gravely silent, to *grimace* at each other.

The Writer looked around in dismay. The entrance into this Backtown area was well-lit and sported many festive flashing lights, not to mention the sounds of much revelry, far more than one might expect even in the rowdiest trailer park at night. The main drag down which they proceeded was filled with partiers coming and going (a population much greater than the number of possible residents). In spite of this main passage being lined with trailers in various states of repair, it reminded the Writer more of the midway at a carnival.

"As if you couldn't guess," Dawn said, "this is where most Luntville folks come to party each night. It's quite a scene."

"Oh, yeah," Snowie added. "They got ever thing here: gamblin', cock-fights, dog-fights, moonshine—"

I'm sure the justice department, the ATF, the IRS, and the NSPCA would LOVE this place, the Writer mused.

"And that's just the conventional stuff," Dawn said. "Things heat up later."

"How so?"

"Well, spit-catching parties, snot parties, jizz-shooting parties..."

"What the *fuck?*" the Writer profaned.

Snowie chuckled, while Dawn seemed enthused to answer. "Spit-catching party's I guess self-explanatory. Two gals who hate each other stand out back and fellas all line up and pay five-dollar ante. Then they all hock loogies into the air, and the gal who catches and swallows the most wins."

The Writer stopped and stared.

"Snot party's no big deal but kind'a funny," Snowie said.

"Folks line up and see who can blow the longest line'a snot out their nose. And jizz-party's, well, sometimes they're a mite interestin' 'cos they get five fellas line up, each with a gal behind 'em, and then the gal's beat 'em off. Fella who shoots the farthest wins half the pot."

Now the Writer's mouth fell open.

"Oh, and they got ring toss, too," Dawn said.

"At least that doesn't sound quite as unconventional as the others," the Writer said, grateful for the break.

"The fellas with the biggest dicks get themselves hard and flip rubber rings back and forth," Dawn explained. "The pair of dudes who catch the most, win."

Snowie whispered in the Writer's ear, "It's more for the *homo* fellas, ya know?"

Actually, the Writer did *not* know. He had *no conception* of anything that he'd been told in the last few minutes.

"The later it gets, the gnarlier it gets," Dawn said, bumping hips with him. "There's strip shows in some of the trailers where girls do fisting shows, foot shows, zucchini shows, bullfrog shows, like that."

The Writer refused to picture those acts in his mind... especially the *bullfrog* show...

"And blossom shows!" Snowie stepped in, bumping his hip as well. "Gal puts her feet behind her neck, spreads her cheeks, and pulls her asshole inside out with her fingers."

Now the Writer was back to staring speechless.

Snowie, "And a'course, there's plenny of gals who lick their own pussies'n assholes."

"Plus that one tramp who got that whole rotisserie chicken up her snatch..."

Even the Writer had to raise a brow at that one. The feat was, at least, impressive.

"And, well," Dawn continued, "when it gets *really late*

there are worse things that go on—"

"Don't tell me!" the Writer pleaded. "I don't want to know!"

"—like, say, the cum-chugging parties. Lots of men in the park jerk off every day, drop their loads in a mason jar, and put it in the freezer so it doesn't spoil."

"Yeah," Snowie said, "*ever dang day* they do this. You get 30, 40 guys beatin' off every day in a jar, end'a the month they'se each gonna have a *rasher* of cum. Then they thaw their jars'n bring it here..."

The Writer's look of unheeding horror begged the wordless question.

"They all dump it in a single bucket," Dawn explained, "and the town girl who's the most desperate...well...you can guess. She drinks the whole bucket. And if she gets it all down, she gets money."

"I hope it's a lot!" the Writer blurted.

"Oh, yeah!" Snowie said. "Fifty bucks!"

The Writer was walking dizzy now.

"But we can't forget the piss-cannon," Dawn said. "I've only seen it once, and it was something. Back behind Belly Brandon's trailer, every couple of months I guess, they get at least 20 guys lined up in the backyard, and keep in mind, these guys have been drinking beer *all day,* and gotta piss like racehorses. Anyway, they bring in the dirtiest, straggliest, skinniest creeker girl they can find, then each one of those guys fucks her in the ass, cums, and then pisses. They empty their bladders in her, see? By the end of it, that poor tramp's got a couple gallons of redneck piss up her butt."

The Writer, now, was shivering in spite of his disgust.

"And...?"

"And then she gets on her hands and knees, tenses herself up, and blows it all out her ass like a piss cannon."

"If it goes at least ten feet," Snowie appended, "they give her ten bucks, and if it don't...well, then, better luck next time."

Snowie and Dawn both cackled laughter.

This is one high brow crew I'm being companioned by, the Writer thought, still dizzy. "Here's the new rule. No more telling me about the escapades of Backtown. We're simply going to this man's—this Grandpa Septimus—"

"Great uncle Septimus," Snowie corrected.

"—to find out where the Crafter house is, then we *go home.* Okay?"

"Shore, sweetie, whatever ya want," Snowie said. "But... don't you wanna hear about—"

"No!" the Writer yelled loud enough to turn the heads of passersby. "No more talking till we get to this man Septimus!"

The trek dragged on, down, down, down the rowdy and very macabre main drag. Every other trailer seemed to post a MOONSHINE, 5 BUCKS! sign. Other trailers were abandoned, some even half collapsed, and more than one puppy-sized rat was glimpsed milling about the rotten footings and tipped over garbage cans. Others signs indicated:

MAGIC CRYSTALS - 5 BUCKS!
NEWT SKIN POWDER - 5 BUCKS!
BAT BLOOD INK - 5 BUCKS!

It was no surprise that such occult superstitions should pervade an isolated place like this. But what came next was not so unsurprising. Three young topless women, all grievously pregnant, sat chatting on the front porch of a trailer. Each was teasing sprays of milk from distended nipples into small glass bottles. *Wouldn't you know it!* thought the Writer when he read the cardboard sign:

FRESH SQUEEZED MAMA'S MILK!
5 BUCKS HALF PINT!

His sigh followed him the rest of the way down the main drag. Here the "action" was thinning, and the flashing lights grew less numerous and intense. At last came the sign he most wanted to see:

PALMS READ - FORTUNES TOLT!
FROM SEPTIMUS THE SEER!

The Writer approved of the moniker, for he often regarded himself as a seer, though not in the same metaphysical way. *My life is a venture of SEEING, and this trip has afforded me MUCH to SEE.*

Creative pretensions aside, an ancient man in clearly handmade clothes rose behind a rickety table—*Very Rip Van Winklish,* the Writer mused (except the Rip Van Winkle of Irving's classic tale was *not* an albino). "Aye, thar she be, mine lovely kin Snowie!" the old man rejoiced with an tint of the Old Yankee in his voice. Perfect white hair hung nearly to his squirrel-tail belt, as did an equally white beard. Small, neon-red eyes seemed to blaze via their own light. He, as well, possessed the "Howard" trademark: a long narrow face and over-prominent chin.

Snowie embraced the old man as though he was a fragile object, kissed him on the cheek. "Hi, Great uncle Septimus! We brung someone for ya to meet," and then she introduced the Writer.

"It's an honor and pleasure to meet you, Mr. Howard, sir."

But Septimus Howard shook the Writer's hand in what could be interpreted as slow awe. "Naow it'all makes sense—" He looked the Writer right in the eye.

"You already know, don't you Uncle Septimus?" Dawn observed.

187

"Aye, Dawnie, and 'tis hard not to." The old man held his gaze.

"Why ya say that, great uncle?" Snowie asked.

"'Cos my hands was itchin'n arlier, just afore I found that box'a old Spanish coins whiles diggin' a new latrine, the same a-said ta been buried by Old Man Whateley back afore I was borned." The oldster nodded at the Writer. "'Tis always been tolt by the grandams that a aout-sider'd come and end the curse, bringin' good farchoon ta Luntville. You, son. The One. Bless my soul I'se lived long enough ta see it with mine own eyes..." And then the old man hitched and wiped a tear. "But hear me, son, and dun't ye scoff, fer yew're work's cut aout for ye. I see slivers'a the future, and I'se can warn ye, with all the good ye're naow a-bringing ta this town, yew got jest as much bad you'll be runnin' into shartly."

This comment steeled the Writer. He lowered his beer. "Buh-*bad?*"

"Bad, son. So bad ye'll think the gates'a Iblis done opened'n are a-dumpin' all the fiery sewage of Hades right smack dab on ye're head."

Now THAT'S bad, thought the Writer.

"'Tis already a-comin'. I'se can feel it in the air, suthin' black'n chock full'a horribleness jest chompin' at the bits ta start its evil workin's on this place again..."

The Writer leaned forward with urgency. "Sir, do the prophecies say whether this coming evil will be victorious?"

The old man raised a withered finger. "Oh, I'm shar they say, son, but they jest en't tellin'."

Terrific, thought the Writer. This was all very interesting but hardly pertinent. "And if I may ask something else, sir. We're trying to find a place in particular and perhaps you could be of assistance—"

"Yeah," Snowie said. "We'se got a fierce hankerin' ta git

to the house of a man named Crafter—"

The old man jerked his scarlet gaze in startlement. "That ole' crooked warlock? He's dead, *been* dead, I'd say, these ten, fifteen years, and folks was damn glad abaout that. 'Twas funny, like he *knowed in advance* when he was a'gonna die. Ah, and Dawnie—" the old man pointed at Dawn almost as if in accusation. "—'twas *your boss*, Winter-Damon, who done embalmed that ole' limb-a Satan."

"I remember hearing the name, and reading some old ledgers," Dawn said.

"Aye, and what happened was ole Crafter, he come daown to yer boss's office, bought hisself a plot, a sarvice, and the fanciest coffin your boss had to sell. And then—"

The pause left them all looking wide-eyed in anticipation.

"—he drop dead right then'n thar in the office. Ticker went out, s'what the fella from the county said. Winter-Damon said Crafter died with a smile on his face, if yew can believe *that*. I dew."

The Writer pinched his bearded chin. *Hmm. My doppelganger told me to bring a SHOVEL to Crafter's house...*"I see, sir. I guess I was misled. It was my inclination that Crafter's body was buried on his own property."

Another sharp-eyed glance, and Septimus Howard, too, pinched his bearded chin. "Haow'd yew know that, young man?"

It felt good being called "young," inaccurate as the appellation was. But the Writer couldn't tell this man about his double, could he? "I heard if from some unremembered source, sir. So you're saying Crafter *was* buried on his own land?"

"Ee-yuh, that he was. Dawn's boss took the paperwork to Beall's Cemetery but they up'n tolt him no way. Hell'd have ta freeze over afore they allaow it. See, thar were no way folks'd stand for that evil son'a'gun bein' buried next ta good Christian folks. The rellertives said they'd shar as tarnations dig the old coot up the next night'n dump him casket'n all in some ditch or what not. So Winter-Damon pocketed the money for the plot'n opening, droved the coffin up to the house'n paid Bud Tooler ta dig the hole. At *midnight,* which figgers, on accaount Crafter so instructed that his burial take place then." The old man smiled. "The Witchin' Hour."

"Indeed," said the Writer. "The Druidic Middle of the Night, it is said."

"Buried that wizard then'n thar, and never go back. Witches graveyard on his land as well. Crafter'd use the airth from 'em for his diabolic magic, 'ud even dig some of the witches up fer their bones, fer use in spells'n carses'n such. He'd take up old coffin planks'n build altars and special doors with 'em."

Special doors, the Writer mused. "Do you really believe he practiced the occult, sir?"

"Thet I dew, son. Dun't jest believe it, I know it. One time I see him'a comin' aout of Hull's store and some fat lady start yellin' at him and a cussin' him suthin' fierce, callin' him heretic'n Satan's acolyte'n baby-killer. So Crafter—he was much younger then, as were I, he jest point at that woman's face, say 'Never again will your lips part,' and, wal, they never did."

This is great background material for my book! the Writer reveled. He'd be up all night notating it all!

"'Twas seed once puttin' some powder'r some such in Cranston's well jest after Holly Cranston spit on him in taown. Wal, Holly Cranston were pregnant'n then some, belly stickin' aout like yew never seen. Couple days later, her baby was borned...borned, I should say, with no head."

The Writer, Dawn, and Snowie all stared at the old man in a hush.

"Dang l'il thing *lived,* too, lived far a *week.* 'Tis true, son, 'cos I saw it. Dumbest-ass thing I ever seen, Holly Cranston, with them big milkers on her, pushin' that stroller 'raound with a headless baby in it."

The girls seemed encased in an awed, even fascinated terror...

"Wust I ever saw was Truth Kenney's boy, Druck. One night Crafter catched him a'shittin' in his yard so Crafter say some wards in some other language, make a hand-sign over his crotch, then point to *Druck's* crotch. Druck screamed all the way back ta taown, he did. Got ta Crossroads with his pants opened, still screamin' till red in the face, and, see, he got his dick and balls aout but that's the thing. His balls was hangin' aout his dickhole by the veins'n what not. Couldn't no one think of a way to git 'em back in his sack! Took that useless punk-roysterer—what we used ta call 'em in the old days—took him ta harspital in Pulaski but there weren't *nuthin'* they could do. Had ta cut 'em off." Septimus chuckled. "Jest as well, though. Warld dun't need no kids that come from that boy's nuts, no sar." .

These were some tales, the sheer extremities of backwoods folklore, proof of a declining gradient of morality that heightens as the ages progress. *My book will be magnificent; it'll win the National Book Award!* But the Writer got back on track. "And if we can trouble you a little further, sir—where exactly *is* the Crafter house? Can you give us directions?"

Mr. Howard lost some of his verve. "Shar, I can, son, but I e'nt jumpin' fer joy ta dew so. That place is carsed. What'chew wanna go up there fer?"

"I have a keen interest in old rural architecture," the Writer fabricated.

"Ye're lyin', boy, kin see it in the way you look through

yer face...ah, but I too remember the rebelliousness of youth..."

I love this guy! the Writer thought. *He's implying that I'm a young rebel! I'm almost fucking SIXTY!*

"E'nt never been thar myself—in the haouse, that is, nor dun't want to—but I seen it from the road it settin' up thar on that hill full'a hangin' oaks. Make a good man sick ta his breadbasket jest lookin' at it. Ya go east daown the Tick Neck Road, abaout ten mile, then take a left on the old Governor's Bridge Road, mebbe another couple miles. Yew'll a'see it settin' up thar." Septimus shook his head woefully. "But dew yew're self a favor, son. *Don't* go to that blasted place. I heerd it ain't never been busted into, not a winder broke and not a stick of farniture stole—"

"So I take it even the local hooligans are afraid of the house's reputation?"

"Aye, they are, and with good reason. Couple'a the wilder young 'un's would go up at midnight on a dare, to neck in the graveyard'n such. Some was never seed again, and others come back all mazed, white-haired, couldn't tell what they saw and never got thereselves a fit night's sleep again." The old man paused through a chill. "But what folks remember most was the Cubbler Twins."

Snowie seemed alarmed by some sparked recollection. "I've heerd that story, grand uncle! That happened at the Crafter house?"

"The very same, young lady," and now the bent, tired man sat back down behind his table. "Not too very long after Crafter die, this par'a twin blondies, Ann and Nora Cubbler, see, they was interested in all this occult stuff. Prettiest things you ever see, thirteen, fourteen year old, I guess, but with racks'a boobs on 'em like they was both full-growed adults, and I kin tell ya sure as I is old, them two had tits that could stop a train.

But anyway, one Haller-ween night, these two idjits go up the witches cemetery in Crafter's yard'n and they take one'a them infernal *wee-jee* bards on account they's hoping ta talk with some'a the witches and mebbe even Crafter hisself, and, wal... Snowie, you tell him the rest. I jest en't got the nerve."

Snowie latched hold of the Writer's arm. She was visibly shivering. "Well, see, them twins, they never come home that night, so next mornin' some men was fixin' ta drive up there and look for 'em but jest about that same time, here they come, both of 'em, walkin' like zombies down Main Street with their mouths hangin' open'n eyes wide as saucers. Wouldn't tell no one what happened, or couldn't, and they both went through the wringer, they did, and I'se mean in a bad way. Both nekit as jay birds and, well, they was both *covered* in cum, 'twere *crusty* with it."

"How horrible," observed the Writer. "Sounds like they must've been raped by many men."

"Oh, they was raped, all right, son," interjected Mr. Howard, "but not by men. Tell him the rest, hon, the wust part."

Snowie had never looked more grave. "They was pregnant, both of 'em, and I mean pregnant as *fuck*. Like if a gal could ever be *fifteen months pregnant*, that's what these poor girls looked like, stomachs stickin' out like *double* that of a normal preggo. 'Twas a miracle they could walk at all, carryin' all that."

The Writer's face creased in confusion. "You mean they were impregnated the previous night, and had come to full term by morning? That's impossible!"

"Ee-yuh, imparsible," said the old man, "but true. Suthin' up that house fucked them girls like no girl's *ever* been fucked, and made thar bellies big araound as bushel baskets."'

What troubled the Writer wasn't the farfetchedness of the tale, but the *conviction* with which it was told. *I have a very disturbing feeling that Snowie and the oldster are telling the truth...*But the Writer could not help but ask the next logical question: "When...were the babies born? Were they—were they...all right?"

"Weren't nothin' all right abaout none of it, son, and what them gals both gave birth to weren't no *babies.* Right then'n thar, in the middle'a street they both dropped their loads, each of 'em at the same time—two piles'a this stinkin' blackish braownish slop like fifty pounds each'a riverbed clay. The Devil's *shit,* folks said it was."

Wow! The Devil's shit! Jack Kerouac WISHES he heard stories like this!

"Both them gals," Snowie added, "is still sittin' up at the Crownsville mental hospital, jest settin' and starin' out the winders, mumblin' to theirselfs..."

"So, son, like I done tolt ya, do ye're self a sarvice and *don't* go to that blasted house," adjured the old man. "Ye jest might come back full'a the Devil's shit yerself."

There's a thought! "I promise, sir, we'll just drive by and take a quick look tomorrow," the Writer answered. "And just one more question, and we shan't detain you any longer. I'm very curious about the progenitor of the Howard Clan. There are many sketches of him at the hotel and I must say, he looks maddeningly familiar. What do you know about him, this man *Howard.*"

Here, Septimus looked up abruptly, and nodded. "Aye, 'tis many questions ye got tonight. Back afore I were borned, guess it must'a been 1927 or 28 thereabouts, a man come to taown, a outsider, from up narth, they say. Jest passin' through," and here the old man plunged into a pleasant reminiscence. "Sharp, handsome, well-dressed they say, coat'n tie, like that. He stumble upon the taown by accident one night, an' what'cha gotta understand, son, back then? *Weren't* no real taown here, just a chicken-scratch dirty l'il village in the woods. These was *poor times,* boy, the poorest anyone remember. Woods was barren, carsed, they say. No food, everone twig-skinny, ettin' grubs'n roots'n tree-bark mold and such. No jobs, neither, no money'n no way ta git it. Folks was so miserable, lot of 'em jest said fuck it, and hanged thereselfs right here in these woods. Other men'd cut their throats jest so their kin could drink thar blood and have some meat ta eat. Awful times, Gard-awful..."

The Writer could not have listened more attentively, reveling in the nostalgia of the scene: the Town Elder discoursing to the younger folk, who circled round with wide eyes and clinging to every fascinating word of a time long ago—indeed, words of another world. Nor could the setting be more conducive to old-time story-telling: The ancient Wise Man holding court under crisp, multitudinous stars, his stark-white long hair and long beard nearly shining, the queer bluish tint of his albino complexion in the twilight, the small red eyes ablaze. And at this very terminus of the trailer park, the sounds of the populace were reduced to an extended hush, while the natural sounds of the woods (the cricket-throbs and the faint buzzings of cicadas) held dominion. The scenario could not have been more classic, and to the Writer, this was priceless.

"See, son, back then folks had nothin' ta live fer, carryin' on more like sad animals than human bein's. Kin mixin' with kin, folks starvin' and a-hatin' the warld, nuthin' ta do 'cept make liquor from crabapples'n acorns and spend all their time drunk. The village had no self-respect, nothin' ta believe in, no reason ta have hope. Meantime, crimes of all sarts was a-goin' on, turrible things. Evil people creepin' inta the village ta steal what little we had, ta rape our women'n diddle our kids. 'Twas Hell on airth, son, right here in this place ye're a-standin'. Yew tell me. Haow'd yew like ta live in a place like that, hey? Folks'a dyin' and a-killin' theirselfs, so piss-poor'n starvin' they gotta eat their own snot'n pick the corn out'a thar shit, and not even enough pride ta stand up ta the scum who come in'n fuck our children? Hmm? Haow'd yew like ta live in a place whar there ain't no hope fer nothin'? What would *yew* do, hey?"

The Writer considered the calamitous inquiry, paused, then answered honestly, "I suspect I'd commit suicide."

"Aye. 'Cos when thar be no hope a'tall, thar dun't be *nothin'*." The elder's eyes pierced the Writer's gaze, and then the sounds of the forest silenced at that moment, like a dramatic event...

And Septimus Howard very subtly smiled and nodded. "And then, son, *then*...the miracle happened," and here he embarked on a parable-like narrative. "Back then 'twas a big problem with these hobos—train-hoppers, they called 'em–and they weren't a bunch'a sad sacks who was down on their luck, they was thieves'n perverts. They'd jump a train to the next town, git off, steal, rape gals, even kill— jest fer fun. Then they'd hop the next train'n hitch to the next place fer more'a the same. Afore anyone knowed what happened, they was long gone'n no way ta catch 'em. Wal, one of these hobos jump off the old Gast Line'n git off right near here, and he had hisself quite a party, he did. Raped a couple'a girls, *young girls,* I'se mean—kids. Peed on 'em, shit on 'em when he was done. One of these little girls even died. But someone saw this devil leavin' his work and tried to rouse the men folk, but like I say, back then, the men folk weren't good fer much, jest a bunch'a drunks who lost all their fight, lost all hope fer anything good, give up on livin' altogether. Ah, but one of 'em, one'a the Martins, they say, he drag hisself up off his broken ass and start a'howlin', so mad was he! And he yell aout fer the other men in the village ta come try and catch this villain, and at fust no one do nothin', jest sayin' 'Aw, we'se a carsed bunch, ain't nothin' we can dew, we caint catch him,' but Martin won't hear of it, and he bellows back at these men, 'Are we jest gonna set here'n let our kids be fucked'n kilt by these scum? We just gonna all roll over'n look the other way? Are we cowards or men!" and he kicks some butts and slaps some araound, and about then some'a the other menfolk git a spark, and haul theirselfs up and foller Martin, and next thing he know, half the men and some women too are headin' out, all riled fer revenge. And they'se all got their torches'n pitchforks and all, and they run out the main road leadin' ta the village, and they *see* the evil bastard who done them turrible things ta them gals, but he's way up ahead and runnin' top'a his speed, and our menfolk? Dang, they's all skinny'n starvin' and sick and they jest cain't catch up. And it looked like this blammed hobo was gonna git clean away."

"But then!" the Writer guessed, locked on to the recital.

"But then a figger appear at that end'a the road, son, jest a tall shadder standin' thar in the dusk, and the hobo pulled a knife when he see that figger. The men call out, warnin' him but the figger didn't care that this hobo were a killer-rapist'n had a knife, and was racin' straight toward him. Folks thunk sure the fella were done for—but, no!—the figger duck and clothesline that hobo with his arm, hit him so hard he were out cold afore he even hit the graound, and that knife go a-flyin' off in the woods. The village men see this'n carn't believe it! And they finally catch up and they git that evil hobo tied so's he cain't do no more harm, and they surround the figger and hug him'n slap his back'n shake his hand, thankin' him fer doin' the justice they was too weak ta do theirselfs. And they ask him his name, and he say 'Howard.'"

Heavy silence rose in the wake of the old man's narrative, filled in with the faint sounds of the nighted wood around them. The Writer, Snowie, and Dawn all stood stooped over to hear, entranced as if the entirety of the Nabonidus Chronicle were being revealed to them...

"Howard," the Writer said. "His first name or last? Or does anyone even know?"

"'Twas his farst name, but as fer his last, he was never heerd a-sayin'. Here's the wee bit we know abaout the man who brung self-respect back to this dyin' taown. He was from up narth, Proverdince, Rhode Island, he say, and were travelin' by bus headin' saouth, ta the *New Ar-leans*. But, see, the bus break daown, so he an' hadda stay here till it git fixed next day, and since thar be a travelin' show set up near by, he go thar ta pass time, then later he start headin' back fer his bus but him bein' a aoutsider, he git hisself up'n lost, which is haow he come to be on that dirt road when he did. A'course, most folks say it were the Hand'a God pushin' him here'n I dun't know if ye hold ta that, but I shar dew. See, what Howard done jest by showin' no fear against that hobo'n riskin' his life—it show these village folks suthin' they ain't *never* seed: *courage,* ta stand up against evil when the odds are against ye, and stickin' yer neck aout fer what's right, stickin' it aout fer *others*. Ain't no one ever car abaout the folks here, our kind was all jest hill trash, they calt us, and we was thunk of a li'l mar than animals. Why help the likes'a *us,* huh? Not so fer Howard. Ta him, we was *all* people, desarvin' of hope'n justice'n decency jest like anyone. So he see his duty and, dag blammed, he *did* it!"

Mark Twain's The Man That Corrupted Hadleyburg in reverse! the Writer reflected. "And like so many humble heroes of legend, I suppose he simply smiled and disappeared back into the night whence he came..."

"Aw, fuck, no, son." The old man winced. "He accept the folks' skimpy offerin's of harspitality and come back the village with everone. A big feast was had, possum-roast, smoked muskrat, cattail cakes'n rhubarb pie, yes, sir. It were a celebration they throwed fer that man!"

"Fitting," said the Writer. "But...what happened to the hobo? I assume the police were called?"

"No, no, son. Weren't no police here back then. Shee-it, the state patrol didn't even start comin' through here till after the war. And that hobo?" The shaggy old man wheezed a chuckle. "I'se afraid I ain't got the stomach ta tell ye what happened ta *him.*"

I guess I better not press the issue, the Writer well considered. After hearing about the "long-necking" victim, and witnessing the drug addict blonde who's head had been torched, and her boyfriend tied to a dumpster and getting "dead-dicked," he was already aware of the tenor of southern vengeance against the perpetrators of criminality.

"Howard even honored us all the more by stayin' the night among us," Septimus said. But had he finished his tale?

Not quite, for, next, Septimus winked at Snowie. "And it's dang lucky fer me he did, because afore that day I wasn't borned nor even thought of. See, with a real life hero in our midst, the few purdy gals in the village couldn't help theirselfs. And *blest* if Howard didn't fuck ever last one of 'em. The poor man couldn't barely git no sleep they was pesterin' him so. Must've been ten, twelve gals he humped, and I mean he humped 'em ta High Heaven. See, the rumor has it that Howard was a-sportin' a dick bigger'n any of them gals ever seen, and they all had ta git theirselves the feel of it stuck up in their cooters all the way. And one sech gal, son, was my lovin' mother..."

Remarkable! The Writer hadn't figured it till just that moment, but the progenitor of the Howard Clan was Howard himself! "Ah, so you mean that Howard was an albino?"

"No, son, but my ma was. She were the only albina in these parts. Jest one'a them things that happened. Her name was Bleechy, on accaount she were white as bleach." The oldster chuckled again. "My ma were a wonderful, lovin' woman and aren't no one could ask fer a better mother, but before that time, see, well, she were a bit of a, well, yew know—a fuck-pot. Had a body on her that'd bdring daown a friggin' monastery, she did, and she made use of it ever chance she could. The type'a gal back then they'd call a Dumplin' Cart or a Sauce Box. Best-lookin' split-tail in the village and dag near every *pecker* in the village could speak ta that. Not the flatteriest way to talk'a one's ma, I know, but 'twas true afore that night, and things is what they is. But anyways, it must've been some a-paowerful high and might jism Howard socked up inta my ma's joy-trail, 'cos he knocked her right the fuck up, he did, and nine months later she have aout with *sextuplets,* yes sar! And I were one of 'em," and now the old man beamed a smile with what appeared to be wooden dentures.

At last, the genesis of the mystical Howard Clan! the Writer realized. "Absolutely intriguing, sir. Was *anybody* able to find out *anything* about this man besides the fact that he was a Rhode islander?"

"Dang little, son, dang little. 'Cept someone picked it up that he were writer..."

The Writer nearly spat out his most recent sip of Collier's Civil War Lager, staring at the oldster.

"How's that for a coincidence?" Dawn remarked.

"What *kind* of writer, Grand Uncle?" Snowie asked, her breasts swaying beneath her top as she leaned over the table.

"No doubt," the Writer offered, "Howard was most likely a newspaper writer. Is that correct, sir?"

"Naw, he weren't no news man. Howard, they say, was a *story* writer, like the kind'a stories what was in the old *pulp* magazines, they called 'em. The kind'a stories as was made up–dang, what's the ward? Ee-yuh. *Fiction* stories."

"Another coincidence!" Dawn delighted.

"And then some," Snowie added. "All them years ago, it were Howard who up'n saved the town, and now here *you* are. Savin' the town again!"

The malarkey scarcely registered with the Writer. Now his mind was pressuring the images of those sketches of "Howard" that he'd seen. *So he was a writer, too. And his face...Damn it! I know I've seen it before!* But considering the era, yet alone the fact that back then the village that became Luntville was an impoverished backwater, what were the chances that anyone had a camera? "I don't suppose there was ever a photograph taken of Howard," he said more than asked.

The old man looked up. "Funny ye should ask but, shar, there was some photos taken. See, someone in the Ketchum family had one's them what they called *box* cameras, and he even had film in the dang contraption. Taked hisself a couple'a pitchers with it, and then drove his horse all the way ta Christiansville ta git the photos made. Not many of 'em left, I don't expect, but—" Septimus held up a crooked finger, said "Lemme git my poke," and then after some effort, extracted a billfold of snakeskin, no doubt handmade. He opened it and fished around inside.

All the while the Writer's eyes were frozen open. *No way, no way in the world he's going to pull out a real photograph of Howard...*

"'Tis a rare item I got here, son," and he passed a small

format black and white photo, glossy but scuffed and cracked. It had a crinkle-edged white border that surrounded a foggy oblong field in which stood two figures: a man and a woman.

A busty, well-curved woman with crinkly hair stood on the photo's left, dressed in a skirt fashioned more or less from rags; her tos too, covering bountiful breasts, had been stitched together form random scraps of fabric. She looked ghostly with her over-white skin, and a bit devilish with the salacious grin. The Writer immediately guessed this to be "Bleechy," the mother of Septimus Howard, for her looks easily corresponded to the colloquialisms of "Sauce Box" and "Dumpling Cart."

Standing on the photo's right was Howard.

The actual photograph of the man gave the Writer chills, in spite of his seeing the likeness in sketch-form before. No doubt: this was the model for all those framed sketches. Howard stood thin and tall, in a thin-lapeled suit jacket and narrow tie as was the style of those bygone days. His eyes seemed staringly wide, as if wary, or as if insecure at being photographed. He was expressionless as he had his arm about Bleechy's bare albino shoulder. Was he uncomfortable? Flashpowder may have been used, for the background appeared depthless. Howard's most salient feature, aforementioned, was his long, narrow face and slightly protruding jaw.

Holy SHIT, the Writer profaned to himself. *He looks SO FAMILIAR! Where have I seen his picture before?*

"Yes, sir!" piped the old man. "Them thar's my ma and pa, and I'se dang proud my veins is full'a his hero's blood."

The Writer returned the photo, still waylaid by the familiarity of the face. "It's an astonishing glimpse into the past, sir. Thank you for sharing it with me."

Septimus rubbed his crabbed hands together. "Ee-yuh,

that's right, son'n not long after that pitcher be took, Howard was a-bangin' my sweet ma's pussy like no tomorrow—"

"Uh, yes, sir. So you've said."

"—filt her pussy *up*, he did, like it were a fuckin' cannoli! A man among men, Howard was. He plumb fucked *all* them girls and didn't stop till they all was crosseyed, so crazy they all went over that big ole hunk'a pipe he had fer a cock—"

Jeez. "That's, um, that's fascinating, sir. And now I'm afraid we have to be going, but thank you for you time and have a splendid night—"

"Aw, goin' so soon, are ye?"

Snowie gave him a quick hug. "Yeah, Uncle Septimus, 'tis gettin' late but we'se'll come back and see ya soon."

"Yew do that, honey," and then the ancient eyed the Writer intently. "And yew, son, mind what I tolt ya afore. Just as ye brung *good* back ta the taown, there be a butt-load of *bad* creepin' up right behind it—"

How could the Writer forget? *Like the gates of Iblis opening...*

Septimus Howard nodded with assurance. "And t'will be up ta yew, up ta *the One,* ta stop it in its tracks..."

The Writer gulped at the portent, silly as it seemed, and then they all finished bidding their farewells. But in all, this consult with the town's supreme elder had been fascinating and productive, and as they departed, he did indeed look forward to enjoying the oldster's conversation in the future.

Unfortunately, this would never come to be, and unbeknownst to them at that moment, they'd seen Septimus Howard for the last time because *he himself* would prove Luntville's first victim to the presaged *horribleness* that had already arrived.

He would, in fact, be torn apart once back at his lean-to in the woods, and his old flesh gobbled down with gusto...

***

Buzzed by beer and enthralled by new information, the Writer followed the girls the way they came, down the long main passage lined by ramshackle trailers and even more ramshackle human beings. *All in a night's work,* he thought. *The location of the Crafter House has been divulged, as has an encapsulation of the nature of Crafter himself, including suggestions of a SUPERNATURAL nature and—most intriguing—the legendry of the mythic figure known as Howard has been explained, not to mention the unexpected treat of an actual photograph of the man. Ah, and I see that Snowie and Dawn seem to be getting along now.*

The two girls dawdled ahead of him, arm in arm, akin to a couple deeply in love.

Then Snowie whispered to Dawn, "Honey, when we git back, I just *gotta* have my pussy et by you!"

Dawn shrugged. "Well, sure. Just make sure you wash it first. No offense, but your pussy tends to stink after you been walking around awhile."

Oh, no, speculated the Writer.

Snowie didn't process this information with much positivity. "The *fuck* did you say ta me!" And she stopped in her tracks and shoved Dawn.

"Watch that, honey, or I'll introduce your funny face to the dirt. I was only saying, you're a bit of a stinker sometimes, and if you wanna know the truth, there are times when your gash smells worse than roadkill on a hot summer day."

"It does *not!*" Snowie bellowed back, and with reflexes and agility that surprised the Writer, her open palm cracked across Dawn's face. "My pussy smells *good,* all the time!"

When Dawn recovered from the blow, one side of her face revealed a throbbing pink slap-mark. "You shouldn't have done that, 'cos now I'm gonna have teach you a lesson, and, Snowie? Hate to tell you this, but the county landfill smells better than *your* pussy."

"Shut up, gimp!"

"You can be five minutes out of the shower, and your pussy-stink could knock down a cinderblock wall. No wonder no guy wants to date you—half the time your pussy stinks so bad you can smell it through your fuckin' *pants.*"

And that was the end of the trash-talk. Both girls collided with fists a-flying.

The Writer groaned. "Seriously, girls? *Again?*"

Like a pro wrestler, Snowie raked her fingers across Dawn's eyes, then dropped the point of her elbow into her head. "I'm sick'a you always talkin' mean ta me! I'm gonna shove that fake leg right up your twat and churn me some butter!"

The Writer just sighed, sat down on a stump, and opened the last beer. *Fuck it...*

He was too tired to intervene now.

But someone else intervened instead. Just as Dawn was about to bite Snowie's face, and as Snowie's finger inched toward Dawn's eyeball—

"Hold up there, girls!"

A tall man who looked lust like Jed Clampett on the *Beverly Hillbillies*—right down to the wrinkled hat— appeared from nowhere, and had pulled both girls apart, shaking them both vigorously by their collars. "Ain't no street-fightin' in Backtown, and you two know better. You wanna *fight* in Backtown, you fight by Backtown *rules.*"

Snowie was practically foamin' at the mouth, and Dawn appeared so enraged as to be insane. They snarled at each other like animals.

"I'm talkin' a CKC, right now," said Jed Clampett. "Are

you girls sissies, or do you wanna settle this fair'n square?"

"Oh, let's do it!" Dawn seethed. "That bitch doesn't stand a chance in a CKC against me!"

The Writer squinted forward over his beer. *A "CKC?" What's that?*

"Bring it on, fat-stuff!" Snowie chuckled. "I'm SO gonna fuck you up!"

Jed Clampett guided both girls by their collars around the back of one of the lit trailers. A few moments passed, then a megaphone blared, "Gather round, folks! We got a CKC goin' on behind Cory Culp's poker house! Snowie'n Dawn is gonna have at each other! Come on down! Five dollars buys you a ticket!"

What ensued after this announcement was a mass migration of chattery rednecks from every point in the park to the indicated area.

I'm too old for this shit, the Writer thought, then groaned and heaved himself up. Beer in hand, he trudged toward the commotion. Whatever this was, he figured he needed to see it, for *seeing* was fuel for his creative fire...

Chaos and madness greeted him when he arrived. In the field behind the trailer, at least a hundred gap-toothed grinning hayseeds formed a great circle around the tract of land, shucking and jiving, crotch-rubbing, and beer-chugging. Men did not entirely comprise the spectatorship, for a fair share of ungainly women were present as well, one of them declaring, "I'se just *love* ta see me a good CKC. Gits my kitty a-purrin'!" Another remarked, "An' I just *love* the sound! Makes me have ta play with myself!"

Pole-mounted kerosene torches were being lit, as one man up front actually sold pre-made tickets. Jed Clampett continued to direct the event from his megaphone, "Come one, come all, folks! Step right up! Ain't no one wants ta miss a good CKC!"

The Writer finally huffed up, and at last the expected question was asked, "Sir? What's a CKC?"

Jed Clampett looked at him sharply, then nodded. "A cunt-kicking contest, mister. A cunt-kicking contest."

The Writer just stared at him.

In the center of the field stood Snowie and Dawn, both naked now, and standing fidgety in place. The torch-light gleamed on their skin, their ample breasts surging. They stood opposed like two boxers awaiting the bell.

Appalled as he was, the Writer had to ask, "How does this work?"

"Like the name say, they kick each other in the cunt, takin' turns, till one cain't take no more. Gal still standin' at the end is the winner, and the winner gits half the pot. Other half of the pot goes to the Backtown Chamber's Commerce, ta be distributed betwixt, uh, local charities."

The Writer frowned. "Well, does the loser get anything? A consolation prize or something."

"All the loser gits, sir, is one *hail* of a sore pussy."

That, it seemed, said it all.

The noise of this festivity rose to a din of madness. Snowie paced back and forth, leering at her foe, while Dawn bounced up and down on the balls of her feet (one ball, of course, made of stainless steel). The artificial leg itself gleamed like lightning.

All at once, the Writer cogitated the verisimilitude of his predicament: *I'm watching a one-legged woman in a cunt-kicking contest...*

Between the fluttering torchlight, the gibbous moon, the ancient forest barely visible in the background, and all those scruffy, ragtag rednecks leering wantonly at the pair of nude participants, the scene seemed truly medieval, like a rabble of peasants awaiting to see a witch burned at the stake.

Finally, Jed Clampett produced an old half-dollar coin, called out, "Snowie, you call it," and then he flipped the coin.

"Heads!" Snowie yelled.

The crowd hushed. Jed stooped to examine the coin. "Heads it is! Snowie, you git first kick!"

Dawn flapped a hand. "The bitch can have first kick. *I'll* have the last."

"Aw right!" Jed cracked into the megaphone. "Ya both know the rules. You *break* a rule, you gotta suck up a penalty kick. If'n ya move, or try ta cover your girly part with yer hand last second, you'll git *two* penalty kicks. Now, do you gals understand?"

"Fuck, yes!" Dawn said. "Let's get this show on the road. It won't take long."

"You're right, fattie," Snowie replied. "It won't take long afore someone's drivin' you to the harspital with a broken cooter!"

"Not *harspital,* you uneducated hill-trash tramp," Dawn corrected with grin. "It's *hospital.*"

Snowie ground her teeth. "Oh, I'm a-gonna kick your cunt so hard your fuckin' uterus'll be hangin' out'chore mouth like a big ole tongue."

"Aw right!" Jed barked. "Both of ya shake hands so we'se can git started."

Both girl approached each other, glaring, hesitant. Snowie, then, offered her hand, whereupon Dawn—

Kuur-HOCK!

—spat on it.

Snowie grinned and licked it off. "Your crunchy pussy's gonna look like a busted cherry pie by the time I'm done kickin' it!"

"Come on! Let's do this!"

Jed blew a referee's whistle, and the show began...

Dawn stood with her feet nearly a yard apart, her hands placed defiantly on her bare hips, and a brash grin on her face.

Snowie took three brisk lunging steps, and—

WHAM!

—catapulted the topside of her right foot hard into Dawn's bare crotch. The Writer winced at the impact's raw sound: like a pile of hamburger hitting a tile floor. The crowd "Ooooo"'d but Dawn barely reacted. "Is *that* all you got, squash-face? A two-year can kick harder than you!"

"Shut up, fattie! Take your turn!" Snowie bellowed, and assumed the spread-legged position.

A bit more awkwardly, of course, Dawn took several long strides and—

Ffff-WHUMP!

—launched her real foot up hard—punter-style, you might say–into the furred white triangle of flesh that was the headquarters of Snowie's womanhood. The sound, this time, was like a ball bat hitting a heavy-bag. However, and much to the credit of her resilience, Snowie showed no reaction to the vicious blow. "Was that supposed ta hurt?" she mocked. "Shit, I thought I was gonna *cum!*"

It would be an exploitation of the readership to relate any further details of the "CKC." The Writer thought, *I think I can safely say that the cup of my intellectual stimulus has been filled, and I, as a Harvard honors graduate, will NOT watch another solitary minute of my first and–I pray God—my LAST "Cunt-Kicking Contest,"* and then he turned blearily an began to walk back to town, and it seemed that that incontestably unique sound of impact, so much like a baseball bat smacking full-force into a heavy-bag, followed him all the way home like an invisible stalker.

***

It was one of those nights when one felt completely alone in the world. The feeling comforted the Writer. The trek back took him past dark, squat houses with little windows like staring eyes, white from reflected moonlight. Did he glimpse two shadow-figures standing in the space from which he'd removed the El Camino after being parked there some twenty years? Dicky Caudill and Balls Conner perhaps?

He was too tired to care.

DeHenzel's stood dark and locked up by this hour. And through the bay door's windows he could see the El Camino with the hood up and already gleaming black from it's new paint and lacquer job. *That's my baby now,* he thought. *Just what I need: a redneck hot rod...*

Was it really that late already? June's massage parlor was closed, and so was the strip joint and the Crossroads. *Time flies, evidently, when you're watching a cunt-kicking contest...*

The town's stillness and quietude might be described as profound. Finally arrived at the Due Drop Inn, the Writer stood a moment out front on the old-fashioned wrap-around porch and peered out into the plush night with its fireflies and choruses of crickets and cicadas. This sedate, natural beauty compelled him to stay awhile, to saturate himself the way Thoreau, Channing, and Alcott surely would. Swept away, then—however momentarily—were the awful images such as "dead-dicking," "long-necking," "cunt-kicking contests," as well as backwoods monsters in morgues, psychotic mafiosi, warlocks, and necrophilia for pornography's sake. A fragrant breeze eddied from the opposing woodland, which caused the Writer to breathe deep, to smile back into the wondrous evening and remember just what a beautiful place the world could be. Then...he shuddered.

A far-off sound ruined all the luxury of these meditations, and the Writer winced. The sound was a piercing human scream coming from the direction of Backtown, or perhaps even farther off than that, a sound so petrifying, so imbued with horror that he might've thought that something abominable had reached down a person's throat and yanked out not only his heart but his soul as well.

The Writer shuddered again in the silence which followed, then hurried inside.

The foyer, atrium, and library area, though gayly lit were vacant and eerily quiet. No sign of Mrs. Howard at her place behind the check-in counter, no sign of Portafoy. *Just as well...*He'd had sufficient conversation today and didn't need more. Tired as he was, though, he knew he'd not to able to fall asleep without first reading a few book pages, and none of the few books he'd brought with him would rise to the task. Naturally, then, he wandered into the library.

At once he was comfortably ensconced amid the shelves, his gaze taking survey of the inventory. A nice Kafka title would do nicely, or even Shakespeare, but, no, most of the library was full of a preponderance of paperback romances, westerns, cookbooks, as he'd noticed despairingly on his first visit to this repository. *Ah, here's a novel,* he saw. *House Dick* by convicted Watergate burglar E. Howard Hunt. And here was *Barbary Shore* by Norman Mailer, quite possibly the dullest book ever written. But...

What's this?

On the next shelf, a book spine protruded an inch. *Another cute note from my doppelganger?* he half suspected. But this book—a hardcover—wasn't blank, and its spine was easily read: *H.P. Lovecraft: A Life.*

Oh, Lovecraft! thought the Writer. *Now here's a surprise!* Though Lovecraft, a Rhode Island academic horror scribe of the '20s and '30s, wrote "pulp" horror fiction, since his death in 1937, he'd come to be critically lauded as the world's greatest artisan of the fantastic tale. Many of his stories transcended the "pulp" brand of writing and theme so prominent back in those days. Instead his most noted works served as portents of the future, allegories for major issues such as scientific research, totalitarianism, existential philosophy, and social dynamics. No mere haunted houses or bumps in the night, but fiction which incited intellectual postulation. The Writer had enjoyed many of Lovecraft's better known works—such as *The Dunwich Horror* and *Shadow over Innsmouth*–and recognized at once their uniqueness over standard escapist fiction. This book, in fact, would be perfect to take to his room tonight.

But then he slid the volume out of its place and looked at the cover—

To describe the impact of what he saw was like that of a stone quarry collapsing on his head would not be too much of an exaggeration. He staggered backward, nearly fell over, and brought a hand to his heart.

Why?

Because the face on the book cover—an old black and white photo of H.P. Lovecraft—was identical to the face on all the sketches in the hotel, and the face on the photograph Septimus Howard had shown him, and possessed of the same distinct features (the long narrow face and protruding jaw) as every member of the Howard Clan.

Holy Moly, came the revelation. *H.P. Lovecraft's first name was HOWARD! There can be absolutely no doubt! The original linear male forebearer of the local Howard Clan was Howard Philips Lovecraft himself!*

The Writer strode up to his room, energized by this revelation. Along the way he examined the framed sketches of "Howard" and compared them to the picture on the book; in the upstairs hallway too. It was indubitable, frankly undeniable: H.P. Lovecraft and the subject in the sketches were the same person...

With a smile, he eyed the sketch of Howard on his dresser. "Mr. Lovecraft, I presume. It's an honor to be acquainted with your son and your descendants." (It hardly needs to be mentioned that the Writer was now officially "buzzed.") He knew he would have to read everything Lovecraft had written, and every biography of the man, to discern if there existed any references or inferences to HPL's appearance in Luntville in the late '20s. An exciting surmise struck him: "What if there *are* no references? What if Lovecraft never had occasion to mention his visit in any way? Then that would mean I'm the only one in the world who knows!"

Of course, the Writer, in his beer-infused muse, was over-reacting. It wasn't like Leo Tolstoy or Herman Melville had come to town, but still...

It was cool...

He began to think in absurd connections (or as Lovecraft would say, *connexions)*. How may times had his own footsteps crossed over the footsteps of Lovecraft? If he went outside and leaned on a tree, might Lovecraft himself have leaned against it as well? And...

His brow popped up, and he may even have felt a surge in the loins...

If I banged Snowie without a condom and she got pregnant, then my child would possess some of my blood mixed with some of Lovecraft's!

These ruminations, however silly, made the Writer smile. He opened the window, anticipating some late-night fresh air, but was immediately reminded what this window faced: the town dump. A waft of foul air brushed his face, he was about to shut the window but...

He cupped an ear, listened.

He heard sirens in the deep distance; not the sirens of Greek mythology but sirens as of police cars or emergency vehicles. They seemed to be coming from the woodlands past Backtown, the same direction from which he'd heard—or *thought* he'd heard—the hideous scream just when entering the hotel...

Could the sirens and the scream be inter-related?

Oh, but why would he consider such a thing, (and why do I encumber the reader with such fragmentary observations?)

He closed the window, gagging. The dump odor tainted the room now so he stumbled to the door, opened it, and pumped it opened and closed to change the air. The hall lights seemed dimmer than usual, and just then the great long-case close in the stair panding tolled three. *Jeez. I sure hope Snowie and Dawn have finished their illustrious cunt-kicking contest by now. They'll be walking funny in the morning!* And here was someone walking funny as well. A male figure with longish swept-back hair, pressed blue jeans over cowboy boots, and a plaid sports jacket emerged from the stairwell. He appeared to have had a few drinks himself, for he was nearly stumbling, not to mention a sudden impediment to his gait: not so much a limp but a strained stride as if in considerable rear-quarter discomfort. It reminded the Writer of something, but he didn't know what...

Of course, the figure was none other than Pastor Tommy Ignatius, and when this illumined dignitary of faith noticed the Writer at his door, he made obvious effort to correct his afflicted gait. "Blessed evening to you, brother!" railed the pastor. "'And may your light shine before others and give glory to the Father who is in Heaven!'"

"Whereat, God be prais'd," replied the Writer, who very much hoped that the merciful Creator could forgive such transgressions as lusting after Snowie and Dawn's breasts, abandoning sobriety on a nightly basis, and being an unwilling participant in a creampie clip with a cadaver.

"God be with you, friend!"

"And also with you," replied the Writer, and then Pastor Tommy smiled, nodded, and proceeded to his own room down the hall, almost immediately resuming his pained stride. *That's* when it occurred to the Writer: *Now I know what it reminds me of! I walked the same way last year right after my colonoscopy!*

It appeared that the good pastor had gotten a bit more than the "corn finger" tonight at June's massage parlor–perhaps something more advanced, like maybe the "corn FIST." Also, a belated observation struck him: as Pastor Ignatius had walked by, the front of the Evangelist's jeans were printing an erection which could easily be described as formidable.

The Writer was so grateful, at least, that his life was certainly not commonplace, nor boring, and with that in mind, he went happily to bed.

***

His first spate of slumber was not one which he would ever recall with any positivity. Sleep began wholesomely enough, with no stresses to interrupt, and aided by the lulling effect of the beer. He began to sink calmly into visions of fuzzy tranquility, not unaccompanied by images of plump, high bare breasts and jutting gum-drop-sized nipples as he slipped into the embrace of Morpheus, child of Hypnos.

The sound of defecation cut rudely into his ears.

Sleep ruptured—or so he assumed—and he wakened at once and sat up in bed. *Did I REALLY hear that, or did I DREAM that?* If the latter, fine. If the former...not so fine because it would mean he was not the room's sole inhabitant. He snapped on the bedside lamp, then the other lights, wincing at how ridiculous he must look, in his Fruit of the Looms, a dress shirt pushed grievously out by a considerable beer belly, and holding the Lovecraft hardcover high, as if that would suffice as a weapon.

Fuck, he thought.

As menacingly as he could appear, he barged into the bathroom, snapped on lights, visually surveyed the small chamber, and hauled back the shower curtain. The room was empty, save for the ludicrous reflection of himself in the mirror. He was about to leave but...

A trace odor was present, unmistakably that of a recent bowel movement, and there, in the toilet, floated a single nearly foot-long piece of excreta. *Wow!* thought the Writer. *That's some bowel movement!* and indeed it was.

Moreover, he was *absolutely certain* that he had not put it there.

Immediately, he suspected, the Doppelganger. He flushed the toilet, but the barge-sized turd took two flushes to get down. When he turned, he saw something he hadn't noticed previously: words scrawled on the mirror in soap. The words were thus:

ANSWER THE PHONE

"But the phone's not ringing!" he complained to the air.

When he picked the phone up from the night stand, the device began ringing. UNKNOWN NUMBER the screen read, but he knew damn well who is was. He answered in Latin: "Qui est hic?"

The response came in German: "Ich bin dein Doppelganger, scheissekopf."

The Writer bristled. "Did you just take a giant shit in my toilet?"

"Of course," his own voice replied. "When you gotta go, you gotta go."

"And now that I think of it, there was no accommodating pieces of toilet paper in there with it. Which means you didn't even wipe your ass afterwards! You were raised better than that! What kind of shiftless vagabond doesn't wipe his ass?"

"I did wipe my ass, Marcel Proust. On your curtains. There was no toilet paper on the roll."

The Writer rushed in and frowned at the tacky curtains over the bathroom window; they were besmirched with brown streaks. *For fuck's sake!*

His evil twin went on, "I needed to touch base, wanted to let you know that I checked out our new car today at the shop—"

"*My* new car!" the Writer corrected.

"Whatever. I got the Hand of Glory. You'll need to remember that for a dire question in the very near future."

What? "Hand of Glory?" But the term rang a dim bell, then he recalled past studies in the history of occultism and witchcraft. A Hand of Glory was the severed hand of a convicted murderer, and said to have great use as an occult implement. "That's right. There was a severed hand underneath the passenger seat of the El Camino!"

"Um-hmm. And when utilized by a knowledgeable practitioner, it is said to open any lock."

The Writer ground his teeth. "Which you obviously used to get into my room so you could *take a shit and wipe your ass on my curtains!*"

"Yes, that and more. Remember that. But isn't it

217

interesting how you heard me taking a dump but then never saw me leave?"

The Writer pondered the information. "Why, yes...So, how *did* you leave?"

"Use your imagination. You've finally found out that H.P. Lovecraft was the male founder of the Howard Clan, you might want to go back and read his 1933 story 'Dreams in the Witch-House.'"

The Writer went to his laptop and immediately ordered the complete works of H.P. Lovecraft on Kindle. The wonders of technology! It took all of a minute.

Back on the phone, his doppelganger continued, "You took the Hand of Glory out of the Crafter house when you, Balls, and Dicky Caudill burglarized the place over twenty years ago."

The Writer stared at the arcane words. But it was now confirmed. He *had* known Dicky and Balls back then, and he *had* been to the Crafter house. It seemed that his eyes didn't close for several minutes.

"And don't lose that page from the Voynich Manuscript," his double instructed. "It'll come in handy tomorrow."

"Tomorrow?"

"Yeah, when you get our car out of the shop and go to the Crafter house with those two bimbos. And don't forget to bring a shovel."

The Writer tried to shake this madness out of his head. *This MUST be a dream, it MUST be!* On the nightstand sat the half consumed can of Diet Coke. He took a sip, not caring that it was warm.

"I'm not going anywhere tomorrow," he dared defy his twin. "I have to start my novel."

"Idiot."

"Pardon me?"

"The book is finished. *White Trash Gothic*. I wrote the whole thing for you over two decades ago."

This was ridiculous. "What are talk talking about?" the Writer said. "Only one page of the book was written. It was recovered from the typewriter way back when I lost my memory. My editor eventually sent it to me."

"You're not much of a capital thinker, are you?"

"I don't know why you say that."

"If there was one page written, did it ever occur to your peanut-sized brain that perhaps *more* pages exist?"

"Nuh-no, but I suppose that might be possible, though I have no way to know where those pages might be."

"Use your head for more than a hair-holder," said the double. "The porter found the old typewriter *where?*"

"Uh, in a storage room, I think he said."

"Yes! Now put on your Rhodes Scholar Thinking Cap. Might it be an efficacious quest to go see *what else* is in that closet?"

The Writer didn't like the insinuations that he was not deductive, even though he knew he wasn't. In moments he'd pulled on his jeans, stepped into his Walmart sneakers, and strode out into the hall. Was Portafoy working this late? *I doubt it.* But here was the closet, easily found at the hall's end, reading simply JANITORIAL. Would it be unlocked?

Yes!

But a moment of reflection seized him. What did he hope to find? A completed novel typescript written over twenty years ago, on the say-so of what had to be a vocal hallucination on the phone?

He opened the door, clicked on the light. Just stacks of supplies, cleaning fluid, a Kirby vacuum cleaner, towels. Immediately he pilfered a roll of toilet paper, much needed. Ah, but here was something odd: several boxes all of which read, "As Seen on TV! THERMO-FRESH FOOD SAVING SYSTEM!" *Those things for housewives to vacuum-seal leftovers...* What would a bunch of such devices, brand new, be doing in the janitor's closet of an old hotel?

Who gives a fuck? was the answer.

His vision riveted: on an 8.5x11 inch box of Eagle brand typing paper. This the Writer recognized as *the best* brand of typing paper. Now, he knew full well there was not a complete novel in it. It was just blank paper, which would certainly prove useful at any rate.

Nevertheless, for amusement, he opened the box, looked through the stack of papers, and expeditiously peed in his pants.

No blank pages rested within. Instead there sat at least 400 *typed, double-spaced* sheets.

Wet-spot notwithstanding, he hustled it and the toilet paper back to his room. .

The header on the first page read WHITE TRASH GOTHIC - p. 2. Then he thumbed through the entire stack to verify that every page was filled with typescript.

"You gotta be shitting me!" he bellowed into the phone.

"Don't bother reading it," the twin said. Was he, or *it,* eating something? "You're a lousy editor and proof reader. Just turn it in and get the rest of our three million."

"I don't believe you! I'm not gonna turn in something I didn't write! It probably sucks!"

"Okay. Read it then. But you'll be wasting time, and believe me, time will soon be of the essence."

I can't believe I'm having this ridiculous conversation, thought the Writer, exasperated. *But—* He read a few lines in the middle of the manuscript. *Man, this is pretty good...*

"Oh, and I meant to comment," the doppelganger said aside. "That was some classy move the other night at the mortuary. Bravo!"

"What move?"

His twin laughed. "When you 'cream-pied' that junkie cadaver. You're a piece of work."

"I was unconscious and subverted against my will!"

"Sure. Wow, mom and dad would be proud," then the specter laughed aloud.

This reference did not set well with the Writer. "I don't even remember my parents!"

"You will, give it time. They were great people. We couldn't have asked for better parents or a better upbringing."

Now the Writer felt cheated. He had almost no recollection of his upbringing. *Ripoff,* he thought. Everything his double told him seemed like privileged information which he, the Writer, was isolated from. "You know a lot. What else can you tell me?"

"Not much right now. But I can tell you this. I can tell you who won the Cunt Kicking Contest."

"I don't care who won the fucking Cunt Kicking Contest!"

"And I can tell you to remember well everything that old dead guy told you at Backtown."

The Writer's consciousness seemed adrift. "Septimus Howard? But he's not dead."

"He is now. Those sirens? Fuck. Well, anyway—there. I've told you something."

It's probably not bullshit, the Writer surmised. *Nothing has been thus far...* "The poor old guy. What a life he had. And to be the unknown son of H.P. Lovecraft. He must've been almost ninety. Was it his heart? A stroke?"

"His heart. He died of fright."

"Fright? What caused that?"

"Due time, brother. Due time. After that the poor guy was...never mind."

221

"Come on, what else can you tell me?"

"Sorry," said the twin. "That's it for now, I gotta go—"

"No! Wait!"

"And don't keep your guest waiting. It's rude."

The Writer frowned. "What guest? There's no *guest.*"

The line disconnected and immediately someone began knocking on the door. *Oh, in the name of—At THIS hour?* The Writer was not happy, regardless of becoming a millionaire today. His pants still damp, he opened the door: "Yes?"

A slightly overweight but uniquely attractive woman in her late-'20s stood opposite. Big bright brown eyes fluttered, and big robust breasts with dark coaster-sized nipples blared at him through a see-throughish nightgown. Tousles of brown-hair framed a cheerful, enticing face. "Hi, I'm Julie, and I'se terrible sorry ta bother ya but, see, I stay at this hotel ever now'n then for, well, for business, and last month I rented this room fer a week and I left sumpthin' terrible important in the closet. Would it be all right if'n I—"

"Please come in and have a look," he stepped back and said. He'd taken no mental inventory of the closet's contents (in fact, he'd scarcely unpacked); however, her request seemed harmless. He eyed her curvaceous figure ghosted by the nightgown as she traipsed to the open closet, rose on tiptoes, reached up, and squealed delightedly, "Oh, gracious me! Here it is just where I left it!" She took something off the top shelf. Of this, the Writer paid little mind, for his attentions were just then directed at a tiny tattoo on the back of her thigh, which read, THE BIGHEAD WILL GETCHA IF YA DON'T WATCH OUT.

"Miss, if I may, what is the significance of that tattoo?"

She turned at the waist, offering a delectable pose. "Huh? Oh, Jory? Just a ex-boyfriend. Scumbag, he turnt out ta be."

The Writer's vision shifted and he blinked. There was

no such tattoo as he'd believed but just the words, JULIE & JORY FOREVUR inside a crude heart-shape. He declined alerting her of the misspelling.

Weird, he thought, rubbing his eyes. Too much beer and too much commotion for one day was all. "Oh, I see," he bumbled, and felt a twinge of surprise when he noticed what she'd procured from the closet.

It was a box, as several he'd seen before, and it read: "As Seen on TV! THERM-O-FRESH FOOD SAVING SYSTEM!"

"I'se left this here last time. You's're a life-saver!" she said, and suddenly kissed his briefly on the lips. "Thank you so much!"

"My, uh, my pleasure..."

She headed back for the door but stopped, turned, then walked slowly to the window to peek through the curtains. "This is a nice room ta stay in, nice'n quiet and cozy but—"

"Indeed," he remarked. "The view leaves much to be desired."

"I swear, I seen lights out there at night. Don't you never see no lights?"

The Writer frowned at the question's grammatical catastrophe. "Lights? No, I'm afraid not. What li—"

"Only thing I don't like 'bout this room, this dang winder. Sometimes, I'd wake up late at night and look out, and I saw—"

"Yes?"

"Well, never mind what I saw," and then she rushed—as if suddenly distracted—to the front wall. "Aw, there's my sweeties!"

The strangeness of this most recent encounter didn't register with the Writer. Instead, his gaze was focused on Julie's body, whose silhouette was now crisply apparent by the way she stood between him and the night-stand lamp. Awesome breasts, awesome hips, and the abundant tuft of pubic hair thrust forward.

But...what was she doing?

She was leaning over now, looking at something on the wall, a blemish or water-stain or some such. Then, as if in slow-motion, she kissed her index finger and pressed it to the blemish.

This is fucked up, surmised the Writer. Before he could ask why she'd made so bizarre a gesture, "Thanks very much, sir!" she announced. "I'll leave ya be now. Oh, I just had me the wonderfulest day! First I find that envelope in the road with five hundred dollars in it, and now I git my Therm-O-Fresh back! Have a great night!"

"Yuh-yes. You as well," he stammered, and then she left.

Naturally, you will wonder what the "blemish" was, just as the Writer did. He examined it at once, stooped over. No, he hadn't noticed it before but why would he? A spot on the wall in a run-down old hotel? Intrigue, however, seized him now. He pressed his own finger to the mark, pushed a little, and found the surface "gave." Then—*Oops*—it cracked and fell off in minuscule pieces. Of course, it had been a thin layer of spackle painted over crudely to match the wall color. But what was beneath it?

The illustration of Lovecraft looked on from the night-stand, as the Writer pulled out some sort of stuffing that had been pressed into a hole in the wall. This hole bore the circumference of something just larger than a silver collar, while the "stuffing" proved to be nothing more than wadded up Kleenex. Human nature left him no choice but to delve deeper. *There's a hole in the wall and something in the hole,* he realized, now in quite a state of irrevocable curiosity. He'd significantly damaged the wall, but– *Big deal. I'll pay for the damage; I'm a millionaire!* Yet he wondered rather abstrusely if the existence of this hole had any relation to the bizarre event of the busty girl retrieving an absurd Therm-O-Fresh vacuum food-saving machine. But...

Why on earth would he wonder *that?*

Something else seemed to be ensiled deeper in the wall, and with some effort he managed to shimmy it out by using two Bic pens as chopsticks. As he did so, he found it impossible not to think of Roman Polanski's very Kafkaesque film *The Tenant,* based on the brilliant Roland Topor novel. The story includes an existential character named Trelkovsky who discovers a hole in his apartment wall, and hidden in the hole he discovers an archaeologist's tooth. Of course, the Writer hardly expected to find a tooth in his own wall, but here's what he *did* find...

Out came another wad of old Kleenex or paper towel, yet wrapped inside was one of those—you know, those plastic capsule things, like when you were a kid, they had gumball machines full of these things. You put your money in, twist the knob, and you got your prize. You opened this plastic capsule or bubble-thing, or whatever they're called, and there was a toy inside: a ring, a rubber bat, a kewpie doll, some little trinket. One such plastic bubble-thing was what the Writer now unwrapped, though its contents wasn't discernible because the bubble seemed to be filled with some murky fluid. Did a trinket await therein? *I'll have to open it to find out,* he concluded.

Given the unknown fluid, he elected to open the capsule in the bathroom sink, and this took some doing. Were the two hemispheres glued together? He twisted and twisted, huffed and puffed, muttered curses as he exerted himself, then—"Fuck!"—the capsule at last came apart, where after its contents spilled out. The fluid smelled like vinegar, but no vinegar he knew of was an opaque blackish-brown. And something else spilled out also (which the most astute of you will have already guessed), and it was *quite* a trinket.

It was a pair of mummified or otherwise "pickled" human fetuses the size of lima beans.

All right, that's it for today!

As best he could, he put the ghoulish prize back into the bubble thing, wrapped it back up, and jammed it back into the wall. Lovecraft's sketch seemed to supervise the task. *I just exhumed and re-interred two dead babies in my wall,* he clarified to himself, and then he thought, *To hell with it...*

But he grew agitated, which was reasonable. *Weird stuff's happening too fast and in too much profundity,* he thought. Her resolved to go to bed, but he knew he first must write down tomorrow's "To Do" list lest he forget it. *If I write it on the computer, I won't remember it's there, so...*

Wielding his black Bic pen, he wrote on the wall, TO DO LIST, TOMORROW. 1) Pick up my hot rod at garage. 2) Buy shovel at hardware store. 3) Bring Voynich page. 4) Pick up Snowie and Dawn. 5) Drive to Crafter House on Governor's Bridge Road. 6) Find grave and dig up Crafter's body.

There, much better, he thought. *Seems very simple—*

Oh, but he forgot something.

7) Buy beer.

His damp jeans reminded him that a shower would be wise before bed. Moments later, towel in hand, pale-buttocked, shrivel-penised, and beer-bellied, he thunked into the bathroom. At first he thought an old man with long hair and beard was looking in at him through a window—ah, but there was no bathroom window, was there? It was the mirror over the sink, and the old man was no one more than himself. *Great...*But something of a shock greeted him when he pulled back the Dollar Store shower curtain—not Anthony Perkins in a wig, but several red streaks wiped against the tile wall in distorted and seemingly geometric shapes.

His first concern, of course, was the composition of the streaks. *Please don't let it be blood...*

He moved a shaking fingertip to a streak, paused, then touched it. It was tacky and indeed red, but not quite the same hue of red we associate with blood. It came away sticky, even gelatinous, more akin to jelly or marmalade. So...it was *not* blood.

Then what the fuck is it? he wondered, more agitated now.

"Well, I'll tell you what it is," he affirmed to himself. It's *gone!*" and then he cranked on the shower, angled the showerhead upward, and washed it all away. Yet he had no choice but to think of Hitchcock's *Psycho* as he watched it swirl down the drain. *This is just too much fucked-uppedness for one day!*

To suffice as pajamas, he pulled on underwear and a plush robe that he'd evidently absconded with from the One UN Hotel in Midtown New York (the "evidently" a supposition because he did not remember ever staying at any such establishment). Then he got into the not-very-comfortable bed, leaving only the night-stand lamp on, but he'd brought with him his laptop, as was his habit, to read before he hoped to sleep. Yes, the doppelganger had suggested he read Lovecraft's story "Dreams in the Witch-House" as a clue to how he (his double) had left the room earlier.

Settled back now, he opened the just-purchased story on his Kindle program. The engaging first line was thus: "Whether the dreams brought on the fever or the fever brought on the dreams Walter Gilman did not know." *Interesting coincidence. Walter GILMAN had the same name*

227

as the hotel once had, the Gilman House.

The Writer need only read the first page before the answer he sought was reached.

The piece involved a 300-year-old New England boarding house that had long ago housed one haggish woman named Keziah Mason, a reputed witch, and it was in the attic of said dwelling that she hid from the King's Men. But her evasion was short-lived and she soon wound up in jail pending trial for witch-craft, idolatry, and various other wicked arts, crimes for which, in those dim times, she surely would've been found guilty and subsequently hanged.

Before justice could be administered, though, Keziah Mason disappeared from her locked cell.

Everyone from the Sheriff to the Witch Finder General to the Reverend Cotton Mather himself was certain that only occult sciences could explain the escape.

And in the witch's empty cell were found bizarre geometric shapes smeared on the walls in some reddish sticky fluid...

Hmmm, thought the Writer.

This story involves a math student's stumbling upon cosmologic secrets that offered methods of opening egression points to as many as 11 dimensions as well as the practitioner's ability to traverse time. The Writer was surprised by Lovecraft's astute references to real theories by actual mathematicians and physicists, including Einstein. Now, the Writer was fundamentally familiar with String Theories, M-Theories, non-Euclidian calculus, and pertubative "bosonic" free-space curvatation, and quantum mirror symmetry, but it all sounded a bit rich to him. How could he argue, however, with Einstein and Stephen Hawking?

At any long-winded rate, his doppelganger had clearly

implied that he had vacated the Writer's room the same way old Keziah had vacated her jail cell: by invoking the cosmic power harnessed by non-Euclidian geometric "devices" on the wall, summoning a portal, and walking through it.

The Writer sipped more hot Diet Coke, contemplating. *Maybe, just maybe, it's true...*

In which case he'd just washed the most important formula in all of human history off his shower wall forever!

Win some, lose some, he thought. He shut down the computer, turned off the light, and then took of his Timex Indiglo wristwatch and prepared to put it under the pillow, because it had long been his habit to do so every night. Why? If left on his wrist, its ticking, however minuscule, would keep him awake. If he needed to check the time in the middle of the night, all he need do was fetch the watch from under the pillow and look at it.

After he removed the watch, he began to slide it under the pillow—however, his hand did not proceed very far before it came into contact with something else...

It was another hand, a stiff, long-fingered hand...

Indeed, a *severed* hand.

Racked with horror, he jerked upright, switched on the light, and threw off the pillow, in seconds convinced that it had merely been some sort of fatigue-oriented tactile hallucination.

This conviction petered out a moment later, though, for... there was indeed a withered severed hand where his pillow hand been. It was hideous to look at, hardened veins sticking out, a sickish leaden color, stiff as wicker.

Ah, but then he remembered...

The Hand of Glory, of course! He'd found it yesterday under the seat of the Dicky Caudill's El Camino, along with the Voynich page, and he'd taken the page and left the ghastly

229

hand. His doppelganger had just told him that he'd stolen the hand from the car himself earlier and used it to enter his motel room, then, apparently, he'd left the room by means of the non-Euclidian devices he'd drawn on the shower wall.

The Writer gingerly picked up the hand and placed it on the night-stand. *Tomorrow,* he thought, *it might come in... handy,* and then he chuckled at the pun.

This day needed to end, and he resolved to end it right now. Lights back out, pillow back on the bed, he presumed at once to sleep.

And sleep he did, but not for long.

Dreams instantly marauded him, along with mental pictures more defined than those that we generally associate with dreams. First there came slices of wicked images that had recurred in his dreams for several years: some raging barely glimpsed monster thrashing in the woods, a great flaccid penis flapping back and forth, and a bloody human limb in each meat-hook hand. Next, a bodacious, curvaceous, absolutely drop-dead gorgeous nude woman standing in moonlit woods, perfect skin agleam with sweat, an impressive tuft of pubic hair just barely hiding the luscious cleft beneath. The only incongruence to the woman's overall sexual beauty was this: she possessed not the head of a human woman but the head of a horned bull. Next, a six-foot-tall erect penis scampering through the forest on, yes, human legs. Happy bunnies and chipmunks scampered after it, a Pied Piper for wildlife...only it was a six-foot penis. *Ridiculous,* thought the Writer, but then dreams were often just that; at least this one was funny. The next one, however, was not so funny. First, a curvy but very skinny blond woman staggered dizzily through what appeared to be the shopping aisles of a store. The whites of her eyes showed only blood-red, and blood ran from her ears and nose. No expression of horror appeared on her face but instead simply *no* expression of any kind. In moments, a very tall, very overweight man with a blond buzzcut caught up to her, grabbed her straggly hair, said, "Well, thar she is! Where yew goin', honeybunch? I reckon it's time for us ta make some beautiful music together!" and then he hauled her to the floor, pulled down his huge blue jeans, and proceeded to, in a very perfunctory fashion, rape her. Through the massive rigors of this, the woman's face remained entirely without expression. Meanwhile, elsewhere in this place, there came some hooting and hollering, soon replaced by a bizarre, forceful *humming* sound, as of a machine of some sort, and it was to this area that the eye of the dream roved next, and what that eye saw would, after some contemplation on the part of the Writer, explain much about the insensible condition of the aforementioned blonde. Two more men—both very tall and very overweight, with blond buzzcuts—had their arms around a man, holding him as though he were a rolled up carpet and, incidentally, these two captors looked *exactly* like the man raping the blonde. This is when the Writer realized he was in the midst of the infamous Larkins quadruplets. The victim—that is, the "carpet"—was a peculiar looking man in khaki shorts, rather fat-bodied but with skinny arms and legs, balding, and with a single braided ponytail hanging in back that more resembled a rat-tail. Another note: he looked a bit like a cross between Richard Simmons and comedian Paulie Shore. Odder still than "Paulie Shore" being held aloft like a carpet roll by two mammoth identical brothers was the undeniable observation that Mr. Shore's *head* had been clamped into a paint-shaker, as are often seen in places like the Sears paint department and Sherwin-Williams outlets. This was the source of the bizarre "humming" as the machine's clamp vised Mr. Shore's head and shook it in a combination of up-and-down movements, back-and-forth movements, and also orbitally, at a variable rate of up to 5000 cycles per minute. The real challenge in this procedure was the operator resisting the urge to turn the machine on HIGH and leaving the victim's head in it for an extended period, because, uh, it was fun to watch. But the efficacious Larkins brothers knew these intricacies, and didn't want their punishment of the victim (nor the quality of their own entertainment) to be cut short by the victim dying too soon. "Shut 'er down, Gut!" yelled Horace over the mechanical din. "We don't want him croakin' on us!" No, sir, they didn't, and that's why the machine was turned off after only thirty seconds of operating at three-quarters speed. This was just enough jazz to really put a good jiggling on the victim's brain, causing moderate cerebral hemorrhaging, and impairing sentience and motor skills. Clyde, the leader of our quartet, fished through the victim's wallet, discovering his expired West Virginia driver's license. Now, "Mr. Shore" had a name: "Ricky Smithson," Clyde announced. "Well, boys, I'd say we done just *changed* this fella's name—to Ricky Retardo!" and then he laughed heartily, along with Gut and Horace. (Tucker, the fourth brother, had not heard the joke because he was still busy trying to release his second orgasm into the stupefied vagina of the nearly brain-dead blonde who lay spread-legged beneath him.). Clyde clapped his hands once hard, as if to accent the situation: "Okay, boys, let him down. Let's see what kind'a job we done," and then Mr. Smithson's head was unclamped, and his two captors set him down on his feet. As might be expected, Smithson collapsed to the floor at once, quivering, making these extravagant and rather fascinating mewling-blabbering sounds. "Ya better git up, Ricky Retardo," Clyde advised. "Ain't no fun just watchin' you lay thar'n kick the bucket." Smithson began to convulse spectacularly, and foam at the mouth, and then, yes, "kicked" the "bucket" right there on the floor. "Aw- sheeee-it," Clyde grumbled. "Guess we left the shaker on a tad too long...No matter. We'se kin still make a 'zample of him." As an aside, perhaps it's proper to explain just what crime Mr. Shore—er, that is, Mr. Smithson and his meth-habituated blond girlfriend had perpetrated to warrant having their brains stewed by a paint-shaker. The answer: Mr. Smithson had very recently been released from prison, doing "a pound" for sexual assault of a minor. By the Law of the Land, then, his debt to society had been duly paid, but the *Law of the Larkins Brothers* saw it a different way. And the blonde? Smithson's squeeze before he went to the joint, a small time meth-whore and drug slinger. Therefore: guilty by association. Now came the rest of the judicial sentence...

Here, this segment of the dream ended, much to the Writer's relief. Needless to say, though, everything in it was true, but of course we already know that the Writer is sometimes prone to premonitory dreams. The short of it? By morning, the blonde will have been buried in the woods (yes, she'd been still vaguely alive when the last shovelful was dropped on her face), while a considerable volume of semen–the wares of multiple contributors–leaked from her sullied sex into the rich West Virginia soil. And our friend Mr. Smithson? A foot-long shepherd nail had been driven though his forehead, quite effectively pinning him to a tall, stately oak tree on Tick Neck Road. His shorts were gone, as were all vestiges of his genitals, which had been shorn out of the groin with Husky-brand shingle shears. A cardboard sign hung against Smithson's chest which read CHILD MELESTER! scrawled in "Cadet-blue" Crayola crayon. This was the Larkins' way of saying: Woe unto ye who wouldst defile a child. It proved an effective deterrent, and such sights were not infrequent within the gleeful, fun-filled boundaries of Luntville.

Now we have re-engaged our attentions to this tale's principle participant: the Writer, who was still asleep, still dreaming. There came the impression, first, of someone whispering, the speaker's lips close but not quite touching his ear. In an absurd rapidity, the emphatic declaration seemed to whisper in Latin "Venit deamonium," which the Writer knew meant "The demon cometh."

Here, then, an interval of silence followed.

Then the Writer awoke (or *seemed* to awaken) to the notion that a hand had weakly grasped his shoulder and shook him.

He sat, as the proverb goes, "bolt upright" in bed. Total blackness at first but then he remembered to open his eyes, an act that required some measure of courage because, well, he was, as the proverb goes, "scared shitless." Yet, open them he did, and though he expected to find the room very dim and only edged with moonlight from the window, this was not so. Instead, the room was tinged with low, grainy light that seemed to be possessed of a hue which he could only describe as *rotten,* a decayed and *sickish* color which chromatically corresponded to no component of the spectrum. It was a *ghostly* luminescence whose provenance could not be allied with any aspect of this normal world but instead a netherworld.

Enough about the light. What of the entity that had shaken the Writer's shoulder?

Standing over him, in an enfeebled fashion rather like a very old man, was, yes, an old man with long white hair and long white beard, and though half of this interloper's face was well obscured by the beard, it could still be identified as a narrow and over-long face and an over prominent jaw.

"Great Uncle Septimus!" exclaimed the Writer.

"Aye, son, 'tis me and none other."

"What a relief! I heard from an unreliable source that you had just died. I *knew* it was codswallop!"

The hybrid Yankee-Southern accent seemed to creak like timbers in an old house. "Nay, no codswallop, fella but only the bare truth. 'Tis why I've come, and I en't got much time. I'm only allowed to warn ye, nothing more."

"You mean like what you hinted at in Backtown?

The wraithlike figure did not directly answer. "You's a Seeker, fella, I'se kin tell by the look'a ye. I'se a Seeker too, so's I kin tell ya awl abaout it. One day it'll come ta yew, mebbe tomorrow, mebbe in twennie years, but, see, boy, someday it'll dawn on ye that what'cher seekin' is reely seekin' YOU."

The Writer thought hard about the statement, and its more symbolic insinuations, like how often in the past he'd referred to himself as a "seeker." *But I guess I never found anything I truly sought...*

The ancient specter went on in his creaking voice. "And jest as I said ye brung *good* back ta the taown, there's a butt-load of *bad* creepin' up right behind it—"

How could the Writer forget? *Like the gates of Iblis opening...*

Septimus Howard nodded with assurance. "And t'will be up ta yew, up ta *the One,* ta stop it in its tracks..."

The Writer stared helpless into the ill-tinged dark.

The old ghost winked with a smile. "Aye, I'se kin tell yew's damn sartain what I'se talkin' 'bout."

The words drifted off like a distant sound carried away by the wind. Septimus Howard was no longer in the room, but of course he'd probably never been there to begin with, right? It had indeed been a long tiring day filled with revelations, epiphanies, Secret Sharers and Steppenwolf-like Evil Twins, not to mention cunt-kicking contests. When he relaxed back in the bed he was happy to see that that "rotten" tinge to the moonlight was no longer evident. He closed his eyes, settled back to sleep, thinking *For to sleep is perchance to dream...,* and just as he would finally fall into a wholesome slumber...

His cellphone rang.

*Of all the...*He picked it up, without looking at the caller ID. "Hello?" hoping against all hope it wasn't the dopelganger.

No doppleganger replied; instead, he heard this:

Snowie's voice. "Mom! He's putting a gummy worm in his dick!"

The Writer dropped the phone, nearly gagging at the shock. Adrenalin dumped into his bloodstream. "Damn it, damn it to hell!" he yelled as he fumbled on the floor for the phone. He banged his ankle against the corner of the shitty night-stand. "MOTHER-fucker!" then found it.

"Mom! Come quick! You've got to see this!"

"Snowie!" the Writer growled. "This isn't your mother. You've dialed the wrong number, but I need you to tell me *exactly* what this gummy worm thing is all ab—"

"Sorry!" she blurted and hung up.

"Fuck, fuck! FUCK!" he yelled, and next he was up and plodding ineptly around like, well, like an old man, shucking off his robe and dragging his clothes and shoes on. *She must be in her room,* his thoughts scrambled, then, again, "FUCK!" for when he stood up he realized he'd put his jeans on backwards. Meanwhile, fast footprints were heard in the hall. "Fuck the pants!" he uttered and barged out of the room. Sure enough, there was just time for him to see Mrs. Howard, big breasts jogging magnificently, bound into her own room. The Writer—hair sticking up, jeans on backwards, and—yes!—even his shoes were on the wrong feet!—strode confidently into the hallway and proceeded to Mrs. Howard and Snowie's room right next door.

That sentence, that arcane verbal ejaculation: *Mom, he's putting a gummy worm in his dick!* was the key to the entire mystery, he felt. He'd heard it on the bus coming here, and since then, he formed the notion that it bespoke some nebulous *portent,* even some manner of *harbinger.* It was the weirdest thing he'd ever heard in his life, and since then, he'd been overwhelmed by the weirdest, nuttiest, and most inscrutable experiences of his life. *I must get to the bottom of it.*

The Writer, somehow, felt absolutely certain that if he was able to decipher the meaning of the sentence, then something indispensable in the future would be provided to him. He knew it the same way that Moses knew his summons to the top of Mount Sinai would lead him to God. He knew it the same way that Oppenheimer knew the world would be changed forever after he exploded the first atomic bomb in Alamogordo, New Mexico.

The Writer...just...simply...*knew it.*

Without even knocking (the height of ill manners) he barged into Mrs. Howard's room but neither she nor Snowie even took notice of him.

Instead they both sat at the edge of the bed, gazing in something like shock at a notebook computer in Snowie's lap. (Snowie, by the way, wore only a night shirt and panties, and at the crotch of the panties sat nestled a large bag of ice.)

"My good gracious, I don't believe what I'm a-seein'," remarked Mrs. Howard in a very low tone.

"Told ya, mom. It's a gummy worm all's right, and—aw, no! He's a putting another one in!"

Both women stared aghast, and so did the Writer, for over their shoulders he could see what *they* were seeing on the laptop screen: a naked man with a pot-belly, longish black hair (probably dyed) sitting widely spread-legged on an old couch, watching something on his own laptop screen. Hips twitching, he slowly masturbated an erection of considerable size, while he just as slowly inserted—

No, no, it can't be....

—a green Black Forest brand Gummy Worm into his (for lack of a better term) *pee-hole.*

The Writer thought, *I thought I'd seen everything with the Cunt Kicking Contest, the Therm-O-Fresh, and the pregnant woman being force-fed horse sperm.*

He stared.

I was wrong. NOW I've seen EVERYTHING.

And there could be no mistake; he was *really seeing* this: a grown man putting snack candy in his penis while watching pornography. More interesting than this, perhaps, was the identity of the man himself.

It was Pastor Tommy Ignatius.

Oh, dear, the Writer mused, and it was not just this outrageous spectacle but also the implication overall.

The Writer said, "Mrs. Howard? Snowie? You have cameras in the rooms, which is horrendously *illegal.* I need an explanation. Now."

Both women spun shocked gazes up at the Writer.

Snowie uttered, "Oh, um, uh, um—"

Mrs. Howard added, just as articulately, "Oh, my, my goodness, sir! It's-it's-it's not—"

"Not what I think?" the Writer finished with a smile. "Yes, I'm afraid it is. You have hidden cameras in your rooms. Why? Blackmail?"

Silence fell. Mrs. Howard got up, locked the door, and bade the Writer to sit. "Snowie, honey. Turn the screen off but keep the camera recording."

"Yes, mom."

The busty matron sat down and took the Writer's hand. "Yes, sir. You could say it's for blackmail. But what'cha gotta understand is we almost never do this except when it's to a bad person."

The Writer winced. "*What?*"

"See, what we got here is pretty much a nice little hotel fer folks passin' through, but ever now'n then, I'se afraid some *bad* folks stop by—you know, them drug dealer people, folks on the run from the law'n such..."

"Ah, so you *tape* them, and extort money from them. If they don't pay, you send the video to the police or their family, whatever."

Mrs. Howard nodded. "Most of 'em are just dirty-minded perverts, beatin' up whores or messin' with kids, stuff like that. See, Snowie, she got some friends who kind'a *specialize* in stuff like that. We give the tapes to them, and they take care'a the rest. But a'course, we get our cut."

What a racket, realized the Writer. *I guess the whole world's got some scam going.* And of course, these *friends* of Snowie's could only be Paulie Vinchetti and his bulldog Augie. "I've already had the pleasure of meeting your daughter's esteemed friends."

"What goes around, comes around, they say, and 'tis true," the older woman went on. "Figure, these bad people should *have* to pay some hush money fer their deeds. Makes 'em think twice afore tryin' it on again."

"That's the worst rationalization I've ever heard for blackmail." The Writer rubbed his eyes. Then Snowie pointed out, "Uh, yer pants is on backwards."

"I know!" the Writer blurted. "And what gives you the right to judge? You say you only blackmail *bad* people?" He pointed to the wall, in the direction of Pastor Tommy's room. "Sure, that guy's a fake, a charlatan, and a hypocrite, but he doesn't deserve to be blackmailed for jerking off with Gummy Worms in his dick!"

Mrs. Howard's brows rose. "Oh, yeah? Snowie, turn the screen back on please."

"Okay, mom."

"I don't wanna see anymore of that folly!" yelled the Writer.

Mrs. Howard squeezed his hand. "Hush, now. And look."

The computer screen glowed back to life, and there the scene continued. Pastor Tommy was really getting into it: he was inclining his hips, stroking his penis faster, and appeared to be inserting *another* Gummy Worm into his urethra. Was it the third, the fourth? The Writer shuddered. *Where do the fuckin' things go? Into his damn BLADDER?* Once more, he complained, "I don't need to see any more of this! A man can do what he wants in his room, even *that*. It doesn't make him a *bad* person worthy of having his life ruined!"

"You ain't lookin' hard enough," the matron insisted. "Look closer. Look at what *he's* lookin' at..."

What? The Writer leaned forward, squinting. As the good pastor went on masturbating, easing in the next Gummy Worm (this one was red, presumably cherry), the Writer peered at the smut the man was watching. He peered with an intent that quickly gave rise to revulsion and horror...

Yes, on Pastor Tommy's laptop screen there was indeed pornography, but now the Writer saw exactly what kind it was: *child* pornography.

He nearly threw up, turning away. And the scene on the other computer will not be described.

"So he ain't a bad man, huh?" Mrs. Howard jibed.

"Blackmail that scumbag to kingdom come, then ruin him," the Writer said.

"Oh, sure," Snowie chirped. "Paulie'll get as much

money as he can from the guy, then he'll post the clip on the ministry's website."

"It'll be wonderful!" Mrs. Howard celebrated.

Jeez. What next? The Writer stood stunned. At first he wanted to ask if they had a camera in his own room, but the consideration was moot. *What the hell would they film? My fat ass snoring?* "I'm going to bed now. It's been a trying day. And Snowie? Please be ready in the morning for our little venture."

"Sure will! Can't wait!" She patted the ice bag between her legs. "Don't you wanna know who won the Cunt Kicking Contest?"

"No!"

"I did," Snowie beamed. "Dawn kicked my cooter fierce, but it weren't long 'fore I got the best of her. Cryin' like a little kid, she was. Her pussy was *twice* as swole up as mine, and you know, she *shaves* hers, so's after I kicked the shit out of it, all swole up it got and *pink!* Looked like a baby's bare bottom!"

The Writer groaned, snapped "Good night," and left the room. Muffled laugher followed him through the door.

Back in his own room, he didn't even bother taking off his backwards jeans. *Some harbinger,* he thought, encased by disappointment. *Some epiphany...*He collapsed into bed, praying he would not dream of Gummy Worms. And, befitting for the sort of day he'd had, just as he drifted off to sleep—

His cellphone rang again.

*Maybe I've really died, and this is hell...*Appalled, he answered, and frowned deeply at the familiar voice on the other end.

"My God, you'll never guess what happened!" It was Dawn.

"No," the Writer groaned, "and I don't even want to

attempt it. I just want to GO TO SLEEP!"

"Listen! When I got back from Backtown, I came back to the funeral home to get some ice—long story—and, and, and—"

"And *what?*" the Writer fumed.

"The back door was open!"

The Writer's eyes narrowed in the dark. "You mean someone broke in?"

"They didn't *break* in, there's no sign of forced entry. The door was unlocked, standing open!"

"Terrific, Dawn. You forgot to lock the door when we left."

"No no no, I've *never* left that door unlocked! Are you kidding me? You know what's inside!"

Yet now that he gave it a thought, he did recall seeing Dawn lock the door when they commenced to Backtown.

"And that's not even the worst part," she went on. "Once I came inside, I found *another door* unlocked and standing open..."

The Writer's mind began to tick.

"The door to the auxiliary embalming suite! Get it?" Her voice grew hysterical. "The room the Bighead's body was in!"

Yes, I remember seeing her lock that too. The Writer stroked his beard, then— "Wait a minute. What do you mean, 'the room the Bighead's body was in'? You mean the room it *is* in, right? Present tense?"

"*Was* in," she seemed to choke. "The Bighead's body is gone."

"You mean somebody stole that damn thing?"

"Shit, I *wish* someone stole it. Whoever came in here pumped all its embalming fluid out, then pumped its blood supply back in. Back in the day, when Mr. Winter-Damon embalmed the Bighead, he *saved* all its blood. It's this yellow mucky-looking stuff, he kept it stored in a big five-gallon bottle in one of the refrigerators."

The Writer's eyes shot wide. *I saw that bottle, in the old fridge with the DO NOT OPEN sign on it.* "Dawn. Exactly what are you saying?"

Dawn gulped. "The Bighead walked out of here on its own. There are size-20 footprints in yellow blood leading out of this room and out the back door.".

A pause, then—*Impossible. She's drunk, or on drugs.* Beside, even if it were true, even if the Bighead's demonic or otherworldly blood somehow rejuvenated the creature, the Writer had seen Dawn lock the doors, and he'd seen the industrial-grade locks with their tubular keyways. They couldn't be picked, and even so, who else in this bohunk little shit town knew how to run an embalming machine?

At that moment, the Writer, holding the phone in his right hand, set his left hand down on to his side on the night-stand. And what did his hand land on?

Another hand. A *severed* hand, the one he'd seen in Dicky's car when he'd first looked in it and found the Voynich page.

The occult totem called the Hand of Glory, used by witches and sorcerers to open locks, and the same device his doppelganger had used to come into his room earlier.

"Dawn," he declared. "I believe you, and I think I know who's responsible, but...what are we going to do?"

"I don't know!" she sobbed over the line. "I don't even think we *can* do anything except get out of town as fast as we can. The Bighead's loose, it's out there now, and you can bet your dick it's gonna go on a rampage just like it did twenty years ago!"

***

Vile sweat seeped from its pores as it moved slowly but hugely through the humid night. Mosquitos landed on its ill-colored skin only to die before they could pilfer any blood. For there *was* no blood in it, not really.

There was something but it was far more than blood.

Brambles and thicket collapsed beneath its huge, cumbrous feet. It liked the crackling sound, which reminded it of another such sound, the cracking bones it remembered from a dim past or dim dream. It didn't know who it was—or *what* it was—but something in its head assured it that all its questions would be answered in time. The hole in its skull seemed to be refilling with something spongy, something growing and congealing, and soon, it knew, bone—or something *like* bone—would grow over and seal the hole. Soon, it would feel something very important beckoning him, the same something that has beckoned it in the past. Some paramount *purpose* lay in wait, it *knew* this, and once the matter in its head re-formed, all would be made known.

It felt...*excitement.*

Its heart *surged,* and so did the great thing that flapped between its oak-tree-sized thighs...

Its single large phlegm-colored eye peered out unblinking at the shivering, moon-tinsled woods. *The Outside World,* it thought. Where had it heard that before?

More ideas formed in its head. *The Lower Woods. Grandpappy. Pussy. Peckersnot.*

Then more...

Hungry. Need ta bust a nut. Need ta suck some shit out'a dead gal's butt...

Dead? Gal? It wasn't quite sure what any of this meant. Nut?

The massive flesh-covered hooks that were its hands reached down and squeezed the pair of fist-sized lumps in the big sack of skin under the thing between its legs.

Whatever all this stuff was between its legs, it sensed it would all become very important very soon.

Its malformed ear detected a sound, something rapid and steady. It stood at the edge of the woods and saw a long winding flat black surface which it would later remember was called a *road.* And on it, moving along on legs, was a... figure.

This figure had things it seemed to know, things that it liked. *Tits. Baby-hole. Ass. Mouth.*

Another word kindled: *Woman. Splittail...* Then the thing between its legs got longer, and firm.

Fuck! it thought in something like a jubilation.

More memories spilled into its head, and they were delicious memories, and it began to stride forward in the direction of the woman.

Gawd DANG it! its thoughts cracked and boomed. *I...I...I...I'se BACK!*

***

Indeed. The Bighead was back.

TO BE CONTINUED...

ABOUT THE AUTHOR

Edward Lee has authored close to 50 books in the field of horror; he specializes in hardcore fare. His most recent novels are THE DOLL HOUSE and WHITE TRASH GOTHIC. His movie HEADER was released on DVD by Synapse Film in June, 2009. Lee lives in Largo, Florida.

www.ingramcontent.com/pod-product-compliance
Lightning Source LLC
Chambersburg PA
CBHW070107030726
47506CB00002B/625

* 9 7 8 1 6 2 1 0 5 2 5 0 0 *